Gray Waters

Book 3 Secrets of the Blue and Gray

Vanessa Lind

Vanessa Lind Books

Gray Waters

Book Three in the Secrets of the Blue and Gray series

Featuring women spies in the American Civil War

**Inspired by the gripping
adventures of actual female Civil War spies, an irresistible tale of strength,
bravery, and love that will win over your heart.**

March 1864. During a perilous and uncertain time of war, a
dark secret pushes Union spy Hattie Logan deeper into her work. With her
feelings for Lieutenant John Elliott more confused than ever, she's determined
to prove herself on her own terms. Paired with former Confederate spy Mollie
Pitman, Hattie defies the men in charge, insisting they shouldn't trust Mollie.

But when Hattie dares to uncover a dangerous plot to hijack a ferry and raid a Lake
Erie island prison, she finds her own powerful loyalties put to the test. The
closer she gets to the truth, the murkier the waters. How far will she go to
keep a devoted friend's trust? Inspired by stunning history, this unrivaled historical
fiction novel of hope and resilience will tug at your heart.

Chapter One

MARCH 24, 1864

C louds hung low over New York Harbor, the waters mirroring the overcast sky. Hattie Logan huddled under the eaves of the ferry terminal, her damp hair curling around her face. There was a chill in the air, and she felt colder by the minute. March was a fickle month, even back in Indiana where she'd grown up. But she wasn't accustomed to this sort of dampness.

Despite the dismal weather, Hattie felt bright with anticipation. This was her first time in New York, and the city amazed her—more than 800,000 people on Manhattan Island alone, many of them immigrants crowded into the tenements of the Five Points district. And the Governor's Island ferry was due to dock any minute. Aboard was Kate Warne, the Pinkerton operative who'd overseen Hattie's spy work when she'd first come East.

She was ready for a change, and she hoped Miss Warne would provide the opportunity. In three years of spying for the Union, Hattie had traveled to Washington City, Richmond, and

Nashville. She'd decoded messages, posed as a courier's wife, and used her acting talents to endear herself to the enemy. She'd escaped prison and thwarted a Rebel attack. She'd found and lost love. This was far more adventure than she'd have known if not for the war, and while there were a few parts she could have done without, she was eager for more.

Having fallen in sheets only moments ago, the rain had become a steady drizzle. A bank of fog rolled in, obscuring Hattie's view of the boats plying the harbor's waters. All around, ships blew their horns, a cacophony of sounds emerging from the mist. As hard as the war had been on the nation these past three years, commerce appeared to be thriving.

Then the fog thinned a bit, and Hattie saw the ferry pulling up to the dock. With her chilled fingers, she clutched the edges of her cloak, keeping it warm about her shoulders as she scanned the faces of the disembarking passengers for Kate Warne. When at last Hattie spotted her, she had to look twice. Usually, Miss Warne dressed plainly. Today she looked as if she'd stepped from the pages of Godey's Lady's Book. Beneath her velvet cloak, she wore a black grenadine dress with a standing collar and a fashionable black silk bow at the neck, and the edges of a white braided sacque peeked out beneath her cloak.

Other than her manner of dress, Kate Warne looked much as Hattie remembered, her features becoming and yet unremarkable, her gaze soft and unassuming, inspiring trust. This served her well in her spy work, Hattie knew.

Spotting Hattie, Miss Warne's lips turned in a rare smile, and her pace quickened. Approaching, she held out her arms. "My dear," she said, pressing her cheek to Hattie's. "So good to see you."

From the generally reserved woman, the greeting was effusive. Hattie knew it was an act, a show of affection to suggest the two of them were longtime friends or family. Still, Hattie's heart warmed, Kate Warne being someone whose trust she coveted. "A delight to see you as well," she said. "You're looking well."

"As are you," Miss Warne said. "Though I fear you'll catch your death if you stand out in this chill a moment longer."

They linked arms, and Miss Warne set a brisk pace toward a waiting carriage. Acknowledging the operative with a nod, the driver helped them inside. To fend off the cold, they arranged a robe over their laps as the horses set off, hooves clomping toward Broadway, the main thoroughfare.

Miss Warne removed her hat and brushed raindrops from its brim. "I'm glad you could meet the ferry. There's a chance I'm being followed, and an encounter at the ferry terminal seemed less likely than other options to arouse suspicions. I wouldn't want you to be drawn unwittingly into my current operation."

"But I might want to be drawn in," Hattie said.

Miss Warne tilted her head, gazing at her. "After working with the Army Police, you want to return to Pinkerton's?"

"If I could be of use." Hattie shifted in her seat. "If you'd have me, that is."

Miss Warne looked away. Maybe this meeting had been a mistake. Maybe Hattie was being presumptuous. Miss Warne had enjoyed a long line of successes. While with the Pinkerton agency, she'd befriended bank robbers and nabbed Confederate spies. She'd feigned injury to gain access to a suspect's home, and she'd posed as a fortuneteller to extract information about a murder. She'd even helped thwart a plot to abduct President Lincoln.

By comparison, Hattie felt like a failure. In her first real assignment with Pinkerton's, she'd been arrested and imprisoned, as had her companion, Thom Welton, who she'd loved with all her heart. Unable to save Thom, she'd pursued Dr. Luke Blackstone, the man who'd betrayed them. But she'd ended up risking another man's life, and in the end, Blackstone had gotten away.

In light of these disappointments, Hattie had gladly stepped away from spying, accepting an offer to travel with her friend Pauline Carlton. But she'd grown restless. She knew she could do more. Not just for the Union cause, but for herself.

Miss Warne turned back to Hattie, her gaze softer now. "Of course we'd have you. Mr. Pinkerton feels terrible about what happened to you and Thom, you know. He tried everything to get you out of prison. Only..." Her voice trailed off.

"Only what?" Hattie couldn't hide the edge in her voice.

"Only he wonders why you didn't come to him when you first escaped instead of going to General Sharpe."

Hattie suppressed a sigh. Three agencies, with three men in charge, each claiming to be the nation's secret service director, adding a layer of confusion—and competition—to their work.

"I intended no slight," she said. "When I got back to Washington, I went to the house where you'd kept your office. But you were no longer there."

Miss Warne offered a rueful smile. "You're a spy, Hattie. If you'd truly wanted to, you could have found me."

Color rose in Hattie's cheeks. "I had something specific in mind, and I didn't think Mr. Pinkerton would go along with it. An assignment in Tennessee, where I'd been told I might find Luke Blackstone."

Miss Warne's lips turned in a slight frown. "You wanted revenge."

Hattie nodded slowly. Stated so bluntly, the error of her pursuit now seemed obvious, especially since she'd nearly gotten her Army Police supervisor killed in the process. "I wanted to stop Blackstone from harming anyone else. I discovered he was plotting to use a chemical gas to harm Union soldiers."

"So you had him arrested?"

Hattie jutted her chin. "I made sure the generals knew of his plans. That's the best I could do."

"I've always known you to do your best, Hattie. At times I've wondered what you're trying to prove."

That I'm competent, Hattie might have said. *That I'm worthy.* She sat up straighter. "So you'd give me another chance at Pinkerton's?"

"Of course. I take it you're no longer on assignment with General Sharpe?"

Hattie shook her head. "There were complications. I reported to the Army Police in Nashville. But the lieutenant there..." Her voice trailed off. How to explain John Elliott's troubled past, his desire to protect her, and the affections he'd shared, when she'd vowed to stay true to Thom Welton's memory?

Hattie cleared her throat. "The lieutenant is a good man. But I want to do more than what he'll allow."

Miss Warne nodded. "I see."

Hattie waited for her to say more, but she was close-lipped. *That's her nature,* Hattie told herself. *She's not passing judgment.*

"I thought I might be able to do something more meaningful at Pinkerton's," Hattie said at last, breaking the silence. "Something that would truly make a difference."

Miss Warne gave a half-smile. "Every case we pursue makes a difference. Currently, our focus is on exposing corruption and grift. The Army's quartermasters are uniquely positioned to profit from the war, and some are doing so quite handsomely. At Governor's Island today, I presented myself as the wife of a businessman proposing to sell camp stoves to the army at inflated prices. The quartermaster who approved the purchase would receive a share of the profits. Sadly, he readily agreed." Her gaze seemed to deepen. "Is that the sort of making a difference you have in mind?"

Hattie glanced out the window. To the east, she saw the tenements that housed some of New York's poorest working-class residents. They were the city's lifeblood, and yet she knew how they suffered as wartime prices rose and wages stagnated. For the wealthy to profit in such circumstances was egregious. Exposing their corruption would certainly be worthwhile. But it wasn't at all what she'd had in mind.

"It sounds like an important effort," she said guardedly.

"It's not glamorous. Nor is it especially exciting. " Miss Warne studied her. "I suspect you're looking for more."

Hattie felt the relief that comes with being found out. "Your powers of observation are as acute as ever."

"An occupational hazard." Kate nodded at the window. "There's your hotel,"

The carriage slowed, the driver steering deftly through traffic to the curb. A pang of sadness struck Hattie. For as much as she'd anticipated this reunion, it was ending all too soon, and she'd gained no real clarity about her future.

"It's been good to see you, Miss Warne. You've always..." Her voice caught in her throat. "Always believed in me. I appreciate that."

Miss Warne straightened, seeming uncomfortable at the emotion of this. "I have every confidence you'll find your way, Hattie."

"I appreciate that." She wished she shared Kate Warne's belief in her. "If I may, there's another matter that's been weighing on me heavily. She blinked back tears. "It's about Thom Welton. I've been wondering...wondering what became of him after his death. Where he's buried, I mean."

"I'm told the Confederates interred him in a pauper's grave outside of Richmond. An inglorious end, I'm afraid."

"I'd like to see him properly buried on northern soil," Hattie said, overcoming the wave of emotion. "It would take some effort, I know, but I could travel to Washington and make some inquiries. General Sharpe might be of assistance. Perhaps I could even get Mr. Lincoln's attention."

Miss Warne clasped Hattie's hand, another unexpected gesture. "That's kind of you, Hattie. I know Thom would have appreciated your concern. But there's something you should know." She paused a moment, studying Hattie's face. "The decision about Thom's final resting place lies with his family. With his wife."

His wife. That couldn't be. Hattie was Thom's wife, in all but the ceremony. She'd repeated his words over and over in her head, more times than she could count. *No matter what anyone says, you are my one true wife.*

She felt the weight of Kate Warne's gaze, assessing her reaction, and so she took care to keep her voice measured. "Yes, of course. His wife. I'd enlist her help. Only I'm not...not sure where to find her."

Another long moment passed. "Mr. Pinkerton reached out to her some time ago, offering his assistance. But she's understandably upset knowing Thom was killed in his service with Pinkerton's, and she rejected his overtures. Perhaps you'll have better luck." From the carriage box, she took a pen and paper. She jotted a note, then handed it to Hattie. "It's a small town, I'm told. You shouldn't have much trouble finding her."

The coachman opened the carriage door, letting in a blast of damp cold. "Ready, miss?" he asked.

Numbly, Hattie stood and gathered her skirts. She mumbled her thanks to Miss Warne, then took the coachman's hand and descended the steps, the street a blur of horses and carriages and pedestrians intent on their destinations. She felt as if her world had been stripped away, the planet off-kilter.

A wife. Thom had a wife.

Chapter Two

Hattie couldn't fathom it. Thom had loved her, and she had loved him. There had to be some sort of misunderstanding. Something she couldn't process in her current state of shock and confusion.

One thing she knew for certain—she couldn't bear the thought of telling anyone what she'd learned about Thom. So when she returned to her hotel room and Pauline asked how her reunion with Kate Warne had gone, Hattie only smiled and said it had been good to reconnect with an old friend.

She'd promised Pauline she'd go with her to tonight's event at Barnum's Museum, but now she was having second thoughts. She could say she wasn't feeling well, which wasn't far from the truth. But Pauline would only fuss over her, and that would make matters worse.

Better to carry on as if nothing was amiss, Hattie decided. The Barnum's lecture might be a good diversion from her reeling thoughts. Pauline was certainly excited about it. As Hattie helped her into one of her finest gowns, she jabbered on and on about how the showman P.T. Barnum was interested in her own story and how that could open doors to all sorts of opportunities to enhance her fame.

Fastening the last of Pauline's stays, Hattie realized she'd tuned out much of what her friend was saying as she'd turned the news about Thom's wife over and over in her mind. She shook her head, refocusing her attention.

"I hope he introduces his wife," Pauline said.

"Who?" Hattie asked, shocked that Pauline seemed to have somehow read her thoughts.

"Why, Tom Thumb, of course." Pauline tilted her head, her dark eyes quizzical. "Surely you haven't forgotten he's giving tonight's lecture."

"Of course not." Thanks to Barnum, the dwarf was the subject of much fascination throughout the country. "I just hadn't realized about his wife."

Pauline looked stunned. "Really? She's the talk of the town."

Hattie fumbled with the button at the base of Pauline's neck. "I suppose she is," Hattie said. "But you know what they say—someone's always the last to know."

~ ~ ~

After dinner, Hattie walked with Pauline from their hotel to Barnum's Museum at the corner of Broadway and Ann. Plastered to an outside wall were posters advertising Three Giants, Two Dwarfs, Indian Warriors, and French Automatons, plus Dramatic Entertainments Morning, Afternoon, and Evening.

This wasn't Hattie's first visit. Pauline thought Barnum's American Museum was one of the city's top attractions, and she'd insisted they go there on their first full day in New York to view its curiosities. It made sense since on the lecture circuit, Pauline was promoting herself as something of a curiosity, too—the actress turned spy turned Rebel prisoner. Following a harrowing escape from her Confederate captors, her health had suffered, which was why she'd asked Hattie to go along on her tour, assisting with logistics that were too taxing for her to take on herself.

At the museum's entrance, Hattie and Pauline paid twenty-five cents each for admission. Inside, they passed spectators gathered around the Feejee Mermaid, a dried-up creature with a fish's tail and a monkey-like head, its mouth frozen in what seemed like horror. Pauline said she could've gawked at the mermaid all day.

Hattie preferred the more substantive exhibits, such as those featuring stuffed pelicans and egrets. The birds reminded her of her brother, George. He'd always loved nature. Early in the war, Hattie had lost track of him. All she'd heard was that he was somewhere in Canada. If he was, she hoped it was in a place where wild birds soared and sang.

They proceeded past the Giant's Chair, where people were taking turns sitting, and then past Tom Thumb's miniature carriage. Making their way to the museum's center, they passed wax miniatures of generals and statesmen and a gigantic aquarium where a beluga whale swam.

Finally, they descended into the lecture hall. "Palatial, isn't it?" Pauline said.

Hattie agreed that it was. Grander by far than any of the lecture halls on Pauline's tour, the room was large and airy, with ample windows and doors. Corinthian pilasters separated the private boxes, and the seats were upholstered in velvet that shared its crimson shade with the damask that papered the walls. Craning her neck, Hattie recognized several familiar faces featured in painted medallions that radiated from the ceiling's center, including President Andrew Jackson and author Washington Irving.

Hattie and Pauline found their seats, halfway up in the center section. As they settled into them, Pauline chattered about what a clever man Phineas Barnum was. "He's traveled all over the world, sparing no expense in his quest to inform and entertain," she said.

Hattie nodded along as Pauline rattled off more of Barnum's accomplishments, but her mind kept slipping back to Miss Warne's revelation. She had to get her mind off it, she told herself. Had to focus her attention on something else.

Within moments, the gilt chandelier's brilliant gas light dimmed. From the orchestra section, a man began plunking a lively march on the pianoforte. Then the curtain rose, revealing a man whose dark hair curled over his high forehead in a rather disheveled way. He had a wide, prominent nose, a bemused smile, and bright, inquisitive eyes. Beside him were a tall stool and a round table covered with a cloth that matched the room's wallpaper.

"Ladies and gentlemen," he said in a booming voice. "Welcome to tonight's instructive entertainment. Prepare to be delighted and amazed. I am your host, Phineas T. Barnum, the sun of the amusement world from which all lesser luminaries borrow light."

Applause erupted from the audience. Hattie joined in, though without Pauline's robust enthusiasm. Barnum had confidence, she'd give him that.

"Tonight, you'll enjoy one of this venue's star attractions," Barnum said when the applause died down. "Throngs besieged London's Piccadilly to see him. It was the same in Paris. A stranger might ask what had attracted the long lines of splendid carriages, what had drawn such crowds that extra policemen had to be brought on duty. The answer was always the same. Ladies and gentlemen, General Tom Thumb!"

The spotlight shifted to the right, dropping to floor level to illuminate a small man as he strutted on stage. Grinning and waving at the thunderous applause, he sidestepped toward Barnum.

"I had no idea he was so small," Pauline whispered in Hattie's ear. "They say he started touring with Barnum when he was four years old. Now he's making money hand over fist."

Since quitting the life of a spy to give lectures and work on a book, Pauline had become obsessed with money. She only wanted to support herself, she'd told Hattie, and to be beholden to no one. But it seemed more than that. Hattie thought of the profiteers Miss Warne was investigating. In some ways, she supposed Pauline wasn't so different, turning a profit from her wartime exploits. But while Pauline might tell some tall tales, at least she wasn't cheating the government.

The applause receded, all eyes focusing on the stage as Barnum bent down and scooped Tom Thumb up under the arms as if he were a child. He set the tiny man on the tabletop, then sat on the stool next to him.

"General Thumb, you are ever the sensation," Barnum said. "Thirty-two years old, and you're how tall?"

"Thirty-eight inches," the little man said proudly. "And weighing only a trifle over fifteen pounds."

"Ah, but nature has accommodated an abundance of gifts in your small body." Winking, Barnum poked Tom Thumb's belly as if he were a loaf of bread fresh from the oven. "And there's now a lucky little woman with whom you share them."

"My lovely wife, Lavinia." Tom Thumb bowed, then gestured toward the wings. Only inches taller than Tom, an attractive woman sauntered toward him, elegant and poised in a gray taffeta skirt trimmed in blue velvet.

"Mr. Barnum arranged their wedding," Pauline whispered to Hattie. "And they honeymooned in Washington. Mary Lincoln invited them to the White House."

Mr. Barnum set General Thumb down to join his wife. The orchestra struck up a tune, and the happy couple paraded about the stage, Tom singing a lively tune to his bride.

Hattie shifted uncomfortably in her seat. Far from taking her mind off the crushing news about Thom Welton's marriage, this display of love and marital bliss only inflamed her pain. Surrendering to her thoughts, she indulged her memories. Thom Welton's smile, his laugh, his charm. The twinkle in his eyes, the warmth of his hand, the magic of his lips on hers.

They'd fallen deeply, blissfully in love. Hattie knew that with all her heart. And yet there had been much they hadn't known about one another, much they were still exploring when fate cruelly separated them. But a wife? She simply couldn't fathom it.

The tiny couple was presenting their final song-and-dance number when an explanation came to her. Thom was the consummate spy, adept at inventing identities. He must have fooled even Mr. Pinkerton and Miss Warne, telling him he was married. He would have had his reasons. Maybe he'd invented the story to assure them he could be trusted with Hattie playing his wife.

That had to be it, she decided. Thom had invented a marriage, and everyone had believed his story. No need to breathe a word about it to anyone, or to dwell on it any more than she already had.

The Thumbs took their bows. Returning to the stage, Barnum paraded out more of what he called his "human curiosities," among them a bearded lady and a pair of giants who, like General Thumb and Lavinia, were joined in wedlock. With that, the spectacle ended.

Hattie rose to her feet with the rest of the audience, sending Barnum and his curiosities off with yet another round of applause. As people around them began to leave, Pauline clasped Hattie's hand. "Come with me," she said gleefully. "There's someone I want you to meet."

She led Hattie to the front of the auditorium, then ushered her backstage. To one side, the giant husband was laughing with his wife. To the other, General Thumb and his bride were squabbling over something. Pauline craned her neck, perusing the scene, then tugged Hattie toward Phineas Barnum, who was talking with the bearded lady.

Approaching them, Hattie shuddered. She understood that a war-weary nation needed distractions. But Barnum's "curiosities" were people who loved and laughed and fought. She hated the idea of the showman exploiting them simply because they were different, all with the aim of lining his own pockets.

As Hattie and Pauline approached, the bearded lady nodded briefly at Barnum, then scurried off into the darkness. The showman turned to face them. "Well, well, well." Voice booming, he thumped Pauline's back. "This must be the friend you mentioned.

The little lady who nursed you back to health. Poisoned, wasn't that it?"

Pauline nodded vigorously. "That's right. A veiled lady brought me a basket of cakes, and not knowing they were poisoned, I foolishly ate them all." She laughed, a little too loudly, Hattie thought. "I've always had a weakness for cakes." Pauline nudged Hattie forward. "Hattie Logan, meet Mr. Barnum."

Hattie shot Pauline a look. She knew full well that as part of Hattie's cover as a spy, she went by the surname Thomas now. Hoping the slip-up hadn't registered with Barnum, she offered her hand. "A pleasure to meet you. You put on quite a show."

His smile broadened. "And it's about to get even better with the addition of Pauline."

Hattie drew a sharp breath, then turned to Pauline. "You've signed on with...this?" she asked, waving her hand vaguely at the backstage scene.

"That's right," Pauline said excitedly. "Starting next week, I'll be giving lectures right here in this hall."

"Pauline's tale is remarkable," Barnum said. "A female spy prowling about behind enemy lines. Of course, we'll need to fine-tune the content, embellish a bit."

"Flourishes," Pauline said with a grand sweep of her hand, citing her preferred term for the titillating details that crept into her accounts of her exploits. Accompanying her on the lecture circuit, Hattie had never quite gotten used to Pauline's story changing each time she told it, making herself ever more the hero.

"So you're done with the circuit?" Hattie asked. "You're staying here in New York."

"That's right. And Mr. Barnum has generously agreed to provide accommodations. No more hotels."

Barnum set his hand on her shoulder. "Pauline will have her own room right here at the museum. Only the best for my human curiosities." He cocked his head toward the corner, where the spat between the little couple was escalating. "Speaking of which, I sense a lovers' quarrel brewing. If you'll excuse me, ladies." He nodded at Pauline and Hattie, then turned and went briskly toward the Thumbs.

Leaving the museum, Hattie felt almost too stunned to speak. Outside, she took a deep breath of night air and turned to Pauline. "Are you sure this is what you want? To become a human curiosity?"

Pauline jutted her chin. "You don't think we're curiosities already? We're female spies, for God's sake."

"Not anymore," Hattie said as they started down the street. "You gave that up to do your lectures. And I..." Her voice trailed off. She wasn't going back to the Pinkerton Agency, not to investigate quartermasters skimming off the top, and not after Miss Warne's revelation about Thom.

"Don't get me wrong," Pauline said. "I've appreciated your help. Truly."

"And I've been glad to help. But I don't know that I want to settle into a room at Barnum's Museum."

Pauline laughed. "Don't be silly. Mr. Barnum hasn't invited you to stay at the museum. He invited me." In the glow of the gaslights, her expression turned serious. "You don't have to worry about me. Mr. Barnum will take care of me now. And you're lucky, you know. You can go back to working for that lieutenant in Nashville who's so fond of you. Me, I'll never spy again. I'm too well known." The pride in her voice was unmistakable.

It would be nice to be known, Hattie thought. Nice to feel as if she'd accomplished something truly noteworthy, not to mention a welcome distraction from the secret she hoped to bury.

Chapter Three

MARCH 26, 1864

Under other circumstances, Hattie wouldn't have spent her last night in New York taking in another show at Barnum's Museum. Though it wasn't a show, Pauline was quick to remind her. It was an educational lecture featuring female scout and spy Pauline Carlton, though as Hattie sat listening, she had her doubts about the educational value. Under Barnum's tutelage, Pauline had embellished her story considerably, adding several new flourishes.

Barnum had opened the show with his usual self-promoting flair, introducing tonight's featured speaker as Major Pauline Cushman of the Cumberland Army. Hattie had to wonder how this rise through the ranks would sit with Lieutenant Elliott and Colonel Truesdail of the Cumberland Army's police, who'd supervised her and Pauline's spying back in Nashville. Perhaps they'd take it in stride, for as P.T. Barnum noted, Pauline's tale was bound to inspire the northern public and Union soldiers alike in what everyone hoped would soon be the waning months of the war.

Barnum had also outfitted Pauline for the part. She wore an approximation of a Union officer's uniform, from the kepi hat to the brass-buttoned coat to the trousers. Hattie's friend Dr. Edith Greenfield would have approved of the trousers, which the doctor herself wore, not to simulate a military appointment but as a protest against women's fashions which she blamed for restricting their freedom of movement.

Brandishing a sword, Pauline was an imposing figure, her dark hair curled beneath her hat, her expression solemn as she conveyed her story with more drama than Hattie had heard before—and with regard to Pauline, that was saying a lot.

Around the auditorium, patrons listened with rapt attention to Pauline's telling of how she'd grown up at her father's trading post in Northern Michigan, an account Hattie had heard many times and only half-believed. Then she launched into telling how she'd come to spy for the Army of the Cumberland, giving the impression that she'd reported not to Truesdail or Elliott but directly to General Rosecrans.

She spoke of how her landlady had been a Rebel sympathizer. "You'll guess what I caught her doing," Pauline said, stepping to the edge of the stage. She swiped the air with her sword. "Attempting to poison a Union soldier."

Hattie sat up straight. That had happened, all right. But it was Hattie who'd caught Mrs. Fletcher in the act, not Pauline.

"I noticed a light on late one night," Pauline said in a conspiratorial stage whisper. "So I crept downstairs." She demonstrated, padding the stage with the lightest of footfalls. "There she was in the kitchen, mixing a white powder into ground coffee. Real coffee, mind you. Not the chicory stuff. I startled her, but she relaxed once I assured her I'd only come down for some cologne, as I was feeling ill. Believing I shared her Confederate sympathies, she told me her plan."

Pauline switched to what Hattie had to admit was a fair imitation of Mrs. Fletcher's voice. "Them tarnal Yanks are fixing to quarter wounded soldiers here. I aim for them to go out in coffins."

The woman next to Hattie gasped.

"She showed me the packet that the white powder came from," Pauline said. "Sure enough, it said POISON. The next day, I fairly flew to the provost marshal's office to turn that evil woman in."

Hanging on Pauline's every word, the audience exhaled a collective sigh of relief. Hattie shifted in her seat. She supposed she should be angry at Pauline's claiming the tale as her own. But it wasn't as if Pauline had taken a true feather from Hattie's cap. It hadn't taken any special skill to deduce what the landlady was up to, and Hattie had never expected any credit for reporting the incident to Lieutenant Elliott. He hadn't even bothered to arrest Mrs. Fletcher, arranging instead for Union soldiers to be quartered elsewhere.

Likewise, Hattie didn't much mind when, later in her performance, Pauline claimed to have made a public toast to Jefferson Davis and the Confederacy. In fact, it was Hattie who'd made the toast, though to be fair, it had been Pauline's idea. It had earned Hattie the trust of Nashville's Secesh sympathizers, but in the end, what good had she made of that trust? Precious little.

As Pauline launched into an embellished account of her mission behind enemy lines, Hattie considered her options for the future now that her friend no longer needed her. Not that there were many. Hattie had vowed never to go back to her home in Indiana, where her parents were the town pariahs and had in any case disowned her. Nor could she return to Pinkerton's under the present circumstances.

Maybe she could go back to Washington City, where she and her good friend Anne Duncan had once worked in Pinkerton's mail room. Last year, when Hattie was newly escaped from prison, she'd returned to Washington. There, she'd gone to General Sharpe, head of the army's secret service. He'd agreed to send her to Nashville, where she wanted to track down the man who'd had her and Thom arrested.

Perhaps Sharpe would see fit to dispatch Hattie on another assignment. But with so little to show from her last pursuit—in the end, Luke Blackstone had gotten away—she felt uncertain about the prospect. Besides, there were too many memories in Washington, memories of her and Thom in happier times.

But Hattie had to do something. On the lecture tour, Pauline had been covering her expenses. Now she would be on her own, with barely enough cash to cover the cost of a train ticket and a few weeks' lodging. In the end, she'd decided her only viable option was to return to Nashville.

She knew Lieutenant John Elliott would help her out. He'd made known his feelings for her. But she wasn't sure what she felt for him, and in any case, he had always been inclined to protect her. That didn't square well with her wanting to achieve something noteworthy. Not that she wanted a stint at Barnum's. She just wanted to know she'd made a real difference.

If she went back to Nashville, she'd be better off connecting with Edith Greenfield, who was both doctor and spy. Steadfast, determined, and forthright, Edith was a woman Hattie looked up to despite her unconventional views and manner of dress. And Edith had said that as long as she was in charge at Nashville's Hospital No. 11, Hattie would have a place running the hospital's dispensary as she had last year. That would ease Hattie's concerns about money. And with her connections in Washington, Edith might be able to get Hattie situated in a spy operation.

In the meantime, Hattie would at least have a way to support herself. Before the war, women rarely had to worry about such things, relying on their husbands and fathers for support. Hattie's parents would have tried to marry her off to some old codger whose wealth would have enhanced the family's fortune. But the war had upended all of that. All over the North—and the South, too, Hattie suspected—women were fending for themselves, some with much aplomb.

Which was why, when all was said and done, Hattie couldn't fault Pauline for her flourishes and embellishments. It was true what she'd said—she was too well-known to return to spying. Not Hattie. She wasn't even sure she wanted to be well-known, not really. She just wanted to matter.

~ ~ ~

Backstage after the show, Pauline looked both exhilarated and exhausted, her cheeks flushed and her eyes feverish. Removing her hat, she patted her curls. "I did well, didn't I? The audience seemed attentive."

"You were magnificent," Hattie assured her. "They were hanging on every word."

Pauline tipped her head as if Hattie were a mirror in which she might admire herself. "I thought so. You don't mind me claiming credit, do you? For the poison and the toast to Jeff Davis?"

"Well, my doing the toast was your idea, even if you intended it as a way to get rid of me."

Pauline's eyes flashed. "That was in no way my intent."

Hattie raised an eyebrow. "You weren't a tad resentful of Lieutenant Elliott's forcing his new recruit on you?"

Pauline shrugged. "Maybe a little. And the poison—well, either of us could have caught Mrs. Fletcher in the act. It just happened it was you. Mr. Barnum said it was exactly the sort of flourish to get the audience in the palm of my hand."

"My ears are burning." Coming around from behind them, Barnum looked from Pauline to Hattie, his eyes twinkling. "And you must admit, those flourishes got exactly the response we wanted." He set a hand on Pauline's shoulder. "I predict a long run of Barnum's lectures for Major Pauline Carlton."

"I hope so." Pauline smiled, but in her smart uniform, her shoulders slumped.

"I'd best be going," Hattie said, feeling every bit the third wheel now that Barnum had inserted himself. "I'm catching an early train in the morning."

Pauline reached for her hand. "I'll miss you, you know."

Hattie swallowed back an unexpected swell of emotion. "Take care of yourself." She thought of the three empty laudanum bottles she'd found while packing this afternoon. But she could hardly say anything about that with Mr. Barnum looking on. Besides, doctors prescribed laudanum all the time for pain, and she knew Pauline suffered more from her afflictions than she let on.

"I'll send a card now and then," Pauline said. "Let you know how famous I've become."

Blinking back tears, Hattie squeezed Pauline's hand. For all her brashness and flamboyance, she'd become a true friend. "The uniform becomes you," she said, hoping to lighten the moment before she broke down entirely. "You may have missed your calling."

"Any day now, the war will be over," Mr. Barnum boomed. "Soldiers will be a dime a dozen."

Hattie hoped so. But ever since the Rebel attack on Fort Sumter three years ago, people had been saying the war would end soon. Somehow, it never seemed to happen.

~ ~ ~

Three days after leaving New York, Hattie was in Indianapolis, having dinner with her friend Anne Duncan at the home of Anne's parents, enjoying a spread so sumptuous she could almost forget there was a war going on. After feasting on beet pickles, boiled ham, and turnips, she hardly had room for dessert. But the custard was too tempting to refuse.

To no one's surprise, little Jo, Anne's four-month-old, loved custard too. Jo was a big part of why Hattie had decided to stop over in Indianapolis on her way to Nashville. She hadn't seen the child since her birth in November.

Propped on her mother's lap, Jo gummed her spoon greedily, holding out her hands and cooing for more as it emptied.

"It's gone, you greedy little piggy," Anne said at last, pushing aside her empty dish.

"She can have mine," Hattie said. "I've eaten a longshoreman's share of the food here already."

She started to pass her custard dish to Anne, but instead, Anne plopped the baby on her lap.

"I've no experience with babies, you know," Hattie protested.

"Jo doesn't care. She adores you. Look how she's ogling you."

"She's ogling my dessert," Hattie said, and everyone laughed. But in truth, Anne was right. Jo's blue eyes were fixed on Hattie. Reaching a chubby hand to touch her cheek, the child offered a toothless grin. Hattie's heart swelled. Even if no one else appreciated her, Josephine did.

"You're a natural," Anne's mother said, beaming as her grandchild gobbled the spoon full of custard Hattie offered.

"And you look quite fetching with a child on your knee," Anne said. "It's too bad Lieutenant Elliott isn't here to see."

"Have a beau, do you, Hattie?" Setting aside his empty dish, Anne's father leaned back in his chair. "An army man?"

If she didn't have a baby on her lap, Hattie might have throttled her friend. "Lieutenant Elliott is my supervisor in Nashville," she said. "Was my supervisor, I mean. Our relationship is strictly professional."

Anne smiled knowingly. "If you say so. All I'm saying is that if you open your eyes, you might find an opportunity for marriage and motherhood yourself."

Motherhood felt like the last thing Hattie was ready for at this point in her life. But she understood Anne wanting her to have what she did. A husband, a home, a family.

"Speaking of marriage," Hattie said, eager to shift the focus of the conversation. "How has Lavina handled Richard's return to battle?" Richard was Anne's older brother, who'd helped Hattie escape from a Richmond prison last year. He'd made his way home but then had returned to his regiment only weeks later.

"She's a bundle of nerves, the same as I am," Mrs. Duncan said. "If you ask me, Indiana's 19th could have gotten on just fine without him."

"Richard's not one to sit on his heels and let others do the fighting," Mr. Duncan said.

"I'd have thought he'd gotten his fill of fighting at Gettysburg." Mrs. Duncan shook her head. "So many of his friends lost."

Mr. Duncan wagged his finger at her. "You know what Mr. Lincoln said, dear. 'These dead shall not have died in vain, that this nation, under God, shall have a new birth of freedom.'"

Mrs. Duncan sat up straighter. "I should like to have my freedom and my sons too."

Finished with her second round of her custard, little Jo sighed. Curling into the crook of Hattie's arm, she batted her long lashes sleepily, gazing up at her. What bliss, Hattie thought, to know nothing of the world's troubles.

"At least Henry's safe in Washington," Hattie said.

"Safe but distracted," Anne said. "His letters are full of nothing but talk of him courting cousin Julia."

"Second cousin," Mrs. Duncan said, correcting her.

"They must be incredibly happy," Hattie said. At one time, Anne's earnest younger brother had been head over heels for Hattie. She'd been thrilled when his cousin Julia Trent had taken an interest in him, nursing him back from his injuries at Antietam.

Mr. Duncan harumphed. "Henry's too young to settle down."

This was the sort of thing people said about men but not women, Hattie thought. At twenty-three, Mr. Duncan must think her an old maid.

"And what of your plans, Hattie?" Mrs. Duncan asked. "You haven't said what you'll be doing in Nashville."

"I hope to take up a position at the hospital where I volunteered last year," she said. "And perhaps also make myself useful again as an operative."

"I'm sure Allen Pinkerton would take you on," Mr. Duncan said. It was through his friendship with Allen Pinkerton that Hattie and Anne had first gotten on with the agency. "I understand Pinkerton's in New Orleans at present. I could send a telegram."

"That's kind of you, Mr. Duncan," Hattie said. "But Mr. Pinkerton's associate Kate Warne has already assured me of a position with the agency should I want it. For the time being, though, I intend to pursue other options."

"Just don't go taking any unnecessary risks," Mrs. Duncan fretted.

"I'll be careful." Looking down, Hattie saw that little Jo had nodded off.

Anne pressed her hand to her mouth, covering a yawn. "Jo was up at the crack of dawn. I'd best get her home before I fall asleep right here at the table."

"You and Jo can stay the night here," Mrs. Duncan said. "If Hattie doesn't mind sharing the guest room, that is."

"Not in the least," Hattie said.

"Thanks, Mother. But Franklin would fret if he came home and found us gone."

As Anne pushed back from the table, Mr. Duncan shook his head slightly. Hattie wondered if, given the choice, he'd have selected someone other than Franklin Stone as his son-in-law.

Anne reached for the baby. "It's been so good to see you, Hattie, even if it's just for one evening."

Hattie started to hand Jo over to her mother, but the child stirred. "I'll settle her in the perambulator," she said. "Then I'll walk you home."

Anne smiled. "I rest my case about you and motherhood."

~ ~ ~

If not for Jo in the perambulator, it felt almost like the old days, walking beside Anne along an Indianapolis street. The orange sun was sinking low in the west, and there was a whiff of spring in the air.

"I'm glad you got to see Miss Warne," Anne said. "How is she?"

"The same as ever," Hattie said. "Calm. Precise. Mr. Pinkerton has her hunting down profiteers. She assures me it's important work, but—"

"Not exciting enough for you," Anne said, finishing her sentence. "You've always been one for adventure. I figured you'd end up in the arms of some handsome stranger while you were on the road with Pauline."

"I enjoyed seeing places I'd never been. Detroit, Pittsburgh, Philadelphia, New York."

"But you didn't want to stay on with her in New York?"

"She doesn't need me now that she's with Barnum's. Although I do worry over her health," Hattie said, thinking again of the laudanum bottles.

"She won't find a friend there as true as you, I'll wager. You're one of a kind, Hattie."

Hattie raised an eyebrow. "I should take that as a compliment?"

Anne's lips turned in a smile. "Of course."

It was now or never, Hattie thought, to broach the subject that had been on her mind since her arrival in Indianapolis. On her last visit, Anne had insisted Hattie stay with her and Franklin. This time, Anne had met her at the station, but then she'd said her mother had prepared the guest room for Hattie in the Duncans' spacious house. Hattie was fairly certain she knew the reason, and she knew no was to broach the subject other than directly.

"Franklin doesn't think much of me, does he?" Hattie said.

Anne's bright expression crumpled. "You shouldn't assume that. It's just that he's been so...busy."

"Too busy to allow his wife's best friend to spend a single night under his roof?"

"He's a private person, Hattie. Having people in the house makes him uncomfortable."

Truth be told, Franklin Stone made Hattie uncomfortable. "Because of his involvement with the Copperheads?"

"No. Why would you think that?"

"You told me once they had big plans," Hattie said, recalling what Anne had written in a letter last year. "You said no good would come of them."

Anne's laughter seemed strained. "Oh, but that was back when I was expecting. I worried over the littlest things."

"So you're fine with Franklin's associating with the Copperheads?"

"I wish you wouldn't call them that. They're Peace Democrats. All they want is an end to the war."

"An end that allows Southerners to keep people enslaved. I can't imagine you think that's the direction the country should take. Your family risked a lot, helping Negroes escape." As Hattie had inadvertently discovered, the Duncans' house had been a stop on the Underground Railroad.

"Franklin and I don't see eye to eye on everything. But you have to understand, Hattie. He's my husband, and I need to stick by him. And you should see him with little Jo. He simply adores her."

"I'm glad he's a good father." Hattie hesitated. She wanted Anne to understand the reason for her concerns, but she didn't want to drive a wedge between them. "Still, there's something I've been wanting to tell you. Last November, right after Jo was born, I found some tickets in Franklin's desk drawer. They came from the Knights of the Golden Circle. That's a vigilante group, Anne. Radicals who'll use any means to achieve their ends."

Anne shook her head forcefully. "That's exactly what Franklin was afraid of, that you'd go snooping around in his things."

"I wasn't snooping," Hattie said. "I was looking for a pen."

For a moment, there was only the clicking of the perambulator's wheels and the trilling of a nightingale in a treetop as they passed.

Anne gripped Hattie's arm. "Hattie, I love you like a sister. But this war is going to be over one of these days, and we'll all have to pick up the pieces of our lives. I want to keep you as a friend, and I want Jo to have her father. So I need you to promise that whatever else you do with your spying, you keep Franklin and me out of it."

"Why would I involve you?" Hattie said. "I'm leaving here to-morrow."

"Don't be cross." Anne linked arms with her. "My being married to Franklin doesn't change anything. You're still my best friend in all the world. I know I can count on you."

"And I you." Hattie's irritation melted away. She and Anne had always looked out for each other. If Anne was willing to overlook Franklin's political associations, Hattie should be able to do the same. That's what friends did. They stayed true to each other, no matter what.

Chapter Four

APRIL 1, 1864

In some ways, Nashville seemed unchanged in the months since Hattie left. The Union Army still had a strong presence there, with many of the townspeople open in their disdain for the occupying forces. As she passed through the market, Hattie heard women muttering as always about the inflated prices and shortages.

Buildings like the Nashville Female Academy, the First Presbyterian Church, and the Western Military Institute were also still housing makeshift hospitals to care for what seemed an endless parade of soldiers wounded in battle. There were casualties of a different sort, too, Hattie knew—soldiers who'd been forced from the battlefield because they'd contracted venereal diseases. They were treated at Hospital No. 15, a space converted from Nashville's newest high school.

Then there was Hospital No. 11, otherwise known as the Pest House, housed in what had once been a mansion at the corner of Broad and Vine. As Hattie approached, she noticed how the building was showing its age, as if wearied by the many transformations it had seen over the years, from private residence to Federal building to medical school to hospital. With Nashville's infamous Smokey Row only blocks away, it made sense that prostitutes would be treated here.

The familiar smells of camphor and ether greeted Hattie as she entered the hospital. Thanks to Edith Greenfield, this was the closest she had to a place where she felt like she belonged. When Hattie had announced last winter that she'd be touring with Pauline, she'd seen a fleeting expression of disappointment cross Edith's face. But Edith was a no-nonsense sort of person, so Hattie wasn't sure whether this meant Edith would miss her or simply that she disapproved of Pauline's venture.

Either way, it felt good to be back, Hattie thought as she followed a quiet hallway toward Edith's office. For a time, at least, she would be glad to get back in the dispensary, its rows of vials and beakers and formulas providing a sense of order and calm amid the chaos of the war. And with any luck, Edith would also have spy work that Hattie could assist with.

To Hattie's surprise, some of the rooms she passed were empty. She hoped that didn't mean the army had made another attempt to solve Nashville's prostitution problem by rounding up the women and forcing them out of town on a steamship. When they'd tried that last summer, none of the towns along the river had allowed the women off the boat, and the steamer had returned with its passengers hungry, disgruntled, and angry.

Marked with the brass number 13, the office door was open. At the polished desk, a figure bent over some papers. "Doctor

Greenfield," Hattie began. Then she stopped short. The person who looked up from the desk was not Edith Greenfield but a man. Like Edith, he was slight in build and had brown hair, but there the resemblance ended.

"Exams are next door, room 15," he said in a tired voice. "You'll have to wait your turn. Show your paperwork and pay your fee there."

Paperwork? Fee? She had no idea what he was talking about. "I'm not here for treatment."

"No exam, no license." He waved his hand in the air as if to shoo her off.

It dawned on her then. Edith had been advocating for the town to legalize prostitution. Licensing that required exams, she'd argued, was the best way to prevent the spread of disease. She must have finally gotten the authorities to see reason.

"I haven't come from Smokey Row," she told the man at the desk. "I'm here to see Dr. Greenfield."

"Gone," he said curtly. "To Chattanooga. Working at the measles hospital."

"Oh," Hattie said. The thought of Edith's no longer being here had never occurred to her. After years of fighting to convince officials that her medical training was as good as any man's, she'd been so pleased to finally be given charge of a hospital.

The man at the desk went back to his work. Hattie backed from the doorway and started down the hall. As she passed a door numbered nine, a woman emerged. She held her head high, her blonde hair neatly coiffed and curled and her complexion fair and dewy. If not for her red silk frock, too fancy by far for daytime, Hattie might have mistaken her for a nurse.

Smiling, the woman flashed a paper at Hattie. "Good for another week."

"You like the new system, then," Hattie said, falling in step with her as they headed toward the exit.

"Who don't?" the woman said. "They treat us like real professionals. And if we come down with the pox, why they take care of it right away."

"Did you ever see Dr. Greenfield when she was here?" Hattie asked.

"Sure did. A good one, that doctor, even if she dresses a mite peculiar. They say us getting licensed was her idea."

"It was," Hattie said. "She spoke of it often when I ran the dispensary here."

The woman tilted her head, looking quizzically at Hattie. "I never heard of a woman running the dispensary. Dr. Burle wouldn't have stood for it."

"Dr. Burle," Hattie said. Assigned to work under Edith's supervision, he'd done everything he could to run her off. "Is he in charge here now?"

The woman shook her head vigorously. "Got Dr. Greenfield run off, but then he got the boot too. Serves him right, that's what I say."

They reached the exit door. Hattie held it open, and the woman went through ahead of her like a proper lady. Outside, she turned, flashing a smile. "Nice talking with you, Miss."

"Likewise," Hattie said, nodding her goodbye.

Hattie stood watching as the woman set off in the direction of Smokey Row. Then, remembering someone she should've asked, Hattie called after her. "Ma'am?"

She hoped that was the proper way to address a public woman. That wasn't a topic Miss Whitcomb had covered at the Ladygrace School for Girls.

The woman turned. "Yes?"

"I was wondering...are you acquainted with a woman of your..." Hattie paused, searching for the right word. "A woman of your profession named Marlena."

"Sure," the woman said. "Only we ain't seen her in weeks. Kept some bad company, that one did."

Hattie's heart sank. The last time she'd spoken with Marlena, the prostitute who'd tipped Hattie off to Luke Blackstone's devious plot, she'd sworn off contact with Champ Farmington, the ruthless Tennessee guerrilla who'd joined forces with Blackstone. If Marlena had fallen back in with Farmington, there was no telling what might have become of her.

"I'm sorry to hear that. If she comes back, tell her Hattie from the dispensary was asking after her."

"All right. But I won't be holding my breath."

Hattie stood in the building's shadow, watching as the woman continued on her way. A cool wind blew from the west, gray clouds tumbling over the low sun. Without Edith, there was nothing to do but return to the City Hotel, where Hattie had dropped her bags earlier in the day. She had the funds to stay a week. After that, she'd been counting on the salary Edith would have arranged, a salary that she'd hoped would carry her over until Edith's connections led her to the sort of spy work in which she might truly make a difference.

She pulled the edges of her cape tighter, fending off the chill of a winter that seemed not quite ready to loosen its hold. Then she started toward the center of town. Without Edith, what was the point of staying in Nashville? A year after her onstage toast to Jefferson Davis, people on the streets no longer seemed to recognize Hattie, especially since she'd quit darkening her hair and growing it out. But at the theater where she'd made the toast, the manager would remember, so there was no hope of a position there.

That left the Army Police. When Hattie left the city, her relationship with Lieutenant John Elliott, her supervisor there, had been awkward, to say the least. Together, they'd survived an ordeal in the woods of East Tennessee, and Elliott proposed the two of them working side by side. But Elliott's interest was more than professional, and Hattie had vowed to stay true to Thom's memory.

But what did that vow mean if the man she'd loved had kept secret his marriage to another? Hattie pushed the thought from her mind. It was all a mistake, a misunderstanding of one of the many tales Thom had told in his line of work. If she'd felt uncomfortable around John Elliott last fall, there was no reason to think she'd feel different about him now.

Hattie sighed. She supposed she could track down Edith in Chattanooga. But then what? The man had said Edith was working at the measle hospital. She wasn't in charge, so there would be no position for Hattie. The idea that Edith could point her toward some meaningful spy work was beginning to seem farfetched too. Hattie should have swallowed her pride and joined Miss Warne in tracking down grifters.

Ahead, Nashville's Public Square came into view. She turned toward the City Hotel, a Southern-style establishment with long porticos extending along its entire length. A ship's whistle blew, carried on the wind from the Cumberland River below. Weary and disappointed, Hattie thought she might just skip dinner and go straight to bed.

But as she neared the hotel's entrance, she felt a hand on her elbow. She whirled around, her first thought being that some untoward fellow had made a wrong assumption about a woman walking the streets alone.

Instead, she found herself looking directly into John Elliott's warm gaze.

"You're a hard one to catch up with, Hattie Logan," he said.

"Thomas," she corrected. He knew full well her assumed name, she thought crossly. "You've been following me?"

"Under other circumstances, I'd say that I'd follow you anywhere. But given our history, let's just say it's all in my line of work."

Blushing, Hattie swept an errant curl from her cheek. "It seems I've gotten rusty. There was a time when I'd have been more alert to someone trailing me."

As always, his smile seemed both gentle and knowing. "You've proven yourself more than alert."

"I don't feel as if I've proven anything," she said before she could stop herself.

He raised a questioning eyebrow. But to her relief, he only said, "I hope you haven't stayed away on purpose."

"I thought Colonel Truesdail would have told you—I've been touring with Pauline."

"He did tell me. Is she speaking in Nashville?"

Hattie shook her head. "She's staying in New York." She paused, not wanting to mention Barnum. "An extended engagement, and she no longer needed my assistance."

"Her health has improved?"

"I hope so," Hattie said.

"Look at me, asking after Pauline's health while making you stand in the wind and converse with me."

"You of all people should know I've more stamina than that." She sounded crosser than she'd meant to.

He dipped his head. "Point taken. That was my clumsy way of proposing you join me in the hotel dining room. I was on my way to dinner when I spotted you on the street. The waiters here are quite attentive, and the tables are supplied with the best the market affords, such as that is these days."

Hattie hesitated. It would be easy enough to demur with an excuse about being tired from her travels. But she hadn't eaten since breakfast, and hunger gnawed at her stomach.

"I must admit, I'm overdue for a meal," she said.

"Very good." Reaching around her, he opened the door, holding it as she went inside. The hotel lobby was warm and quiet, a relief from the chill air outside. Side by side, the two of them crossed the lobby, then entered the hotel's restaurant. Smells of fresh-baked bread and roasting meats assailed them as a waiter escorted them to a table. Whatever the complaints about Union occupation, there was food in Nashville for those with the means to pay for it, Hattie noted, which was more than could be said for many parts of the South.

Stopping at a table near the front of the dining room, the waiter reached to pull out a chair.

"Something more private, perhaps?" Elliott said, his tone pleasant but firm.

With what seemed a derisive nod, the waiter pushed the chair back to the table. Seeming determined to make a point, he led them to the farthest and darkest corner of the dining room. It was out of earshot of the other patrons, to be certain, but it brought to mind the dark saloon table she'd shared with a very inebriated John Elliott on Independence Day last summer. He glanced at her uneasily, and she thought he might be remembering that day too.

Wordlessly, the waiter seated them. He lit the single globed candle at the table's center and left menus for them to peruse.

"Attentive," Hattie said when he was gone. "Though not especially pleased to see us, it seems."

"It's the uniform," Elliott said. "Since the Federals aren't exactly welcome in most parts of town, I usually change before venturing out."

Hattie raised an eyebrow. "You followed me all the way from headquarters?"

He held up both hands, palms out. "Guilty as charged. I thought my eyes must be deceiving me. When I was well enough to return to work after our..." He hesitated, clearly searching for words. "After our expedition, and Colonel Truesdail said you'd left town, I was worried I'd run you off."

She shifted in her seat. She'd hoped they could have simply shared a meal, conversing in general terms about the Army Police and the war. But here he was, veering quickly into intimate territory.

"I thought we'd parted on clear terms," she said. This was perhaps an overstatement. The terms included love, his for his wife, killed by Rebel guerrilla Champ Farmington, and hers for Thom Welton, dead because of Luke Blackstone. But Hattie had had her fill of seeking revenge while he'd thought they should pursue Blackstone and Farmington together.

"Clear as mud," Elliott muttered.

Returning, the waiter spared her an immediate response. Unsmilingly, he took their order, then left them to their dark corner.

"Has Champ Farmington been apprehended?" she asked.

Grimly, Elliott shook his head. "He's dropped back under Morgan's protection," he said, referring to the Confederate general who encouraged bushwhackers like Champ Farmington. "But every now and then, a story surfaces with Farmington's mark on it. An elderly Union supporter shot in the back. Negro prisoners of war with their throats slashed."

Hattie shuddered, remembering the evil she'd seen in Champ Farmington's eyes. "I don't blame you for wanting to catch him."

To her surprise, Elliott shrugged. Despite the dark, she thought she saw his gaze soften. "You were right, you know, about the dangers of an obsession," he said. "Much as I'd like to, there's little chance I could hunt Farmington down singlehandedly."

She nodded. It was a lesson she'd learned the hard way. Still, she'd be happy to see Farmington and his associate Luke Blackstone one day brought to justice for the harm they'd done.

"Do you think General Morgan is protecting Luke Blackstone too?"

Elliott rubbed his beard. "As a doctor, Blackstone likely doesn't need Morgan's protection. He can move about freely."

"I hope no one on the Union side trusts him to spy for them," Hattie said bitterly.

"Between Blackstone's plot to infect Northerners with yellow fever and the cyanide scheme you uncovered, he's made a reputation for himself. And a tip came through our office recently, someone saying he'd crossed over into Canada."

Canada. If Hattie had the money, she'd like to go there and try to find her brother, George. But between having no husband and with father's disowning her, her means of supporting herself were limited. She was beginning to understand why women like Marlena were forced into selling their bodies.

"I hear there's quite a beehive of activity among the Confederates in Canada," she said. "I hope the Federals are keeping an eye on them. They could be plotting trouble."

Elliott's lopsided grin was endearing. "Ever the spy, aren't you? But you haven't told me what brought you back to Nashville."

"When Pauline asked me to go with her on her lecture tour, I thought it would be exciting to visit so many places I'd never been. And it was, for a time. But I found myself growing restless. I kept thinking how I could have done more when I was with Pinkerton's, more when I was here in Tennessee."

In the flickering candlelight, his eyes looked bemused. "You saved my life. That wasn't enough?"

She felt her face flush. "I only did what anyone would have done under the circumstances. It was the least I could do, seeing how it was my fault you'd been shot in the first place."

"I went with you willingly," he said. "In fact, I believe I insisted on it."

"You kept tabs on me, that's for certain. I took it as a lack of confidence."

"Far from it. You know now what Champ Farmington did to my wife. I just didn't want him harming anyone else I cared about."

She glanced down at the table, feigning sudden interest in her place setting. This was the reason she hadn't wanted to see John Elliott. He cared about her in ways she'd rather not deal with, especially not in her current confusion over Thom.

Elliott's hand, reaching across the table, came into her field of vision. His fingers brushed against hers. Looking up, she saw that his expression was at once tender and pained.

Pulling his hand away, he shook his head. "I promised myself that if I saw you again, I wouldn't do or say anything to push you away. Please tell me I haven't."

"You haven't." She felt herself blushing like a schoolgirl.

"I know you're still grieving Thom Welton's death," he said. "Lord knows I understand that. But it will get better, I promise. One day you'll wake up and realize it's time to move on."

"I've moved on," she said, defensiveness creeping into her voice. She knew he meant well, but he had no idea how complicated her love for Thom had become.

He leaned back in his chair. "Fair enough. You said you came back here because you want to do more. What did you have in mind?"

Another topic she'd rather not pursue, considering what little idea she had herself. "I thought I'd check with Edith Greenfield about a salaried position at the dispensary," she said.

He looked puzzled. "That's doing more?"

The waiter brought their food then, sparing Hattie an immediate response. Breathing in the delightful mix of smells from her bowl of lamb stew, she admitted, "Before I can do much of anything, I need a salary," she admitted. "But I found out this afternoon that Edith is in Chattanooga."

"Not anymore." Elliott carved off a bite of his chicken fricassee. "She's been arrested."

Hattie's first bite of warm stew went cold in her mouth. She swallowed hard. "But I was told she's doctoring at a measles hospital. I don't see how anything she'd do there would get her arrested."

"She left the measles hospital," Elliott said. "Assigned for duty with the 52nd Ohio, serving as a contract surgeon of some sort."

"I know how much she wanted an army appointment. What went wrong?"

Elliott mopped up a bit of gravy with his roll. "The 52nd has been holding Confederate territory in northern Georgia. From what we're told, Dr. Greenfield aroused suspicions while crossing back and forth over the line to tend to patients. In short order, the Rebels had her arrested."

Crossing enemy lines. Edith had been spying, most likely, while also tending to patients. "Where is she being held?"

"Last I heard, Richmond."

Imprisoned in Richmond. Knowing what those prisons were like, Hattie shuddered to think of it. But if anyone could survive a Confederate prison, it was Edith Greenfield.

"If you hear any news of her, anything at all, will you let me know?"

Elliott held his fork mid-air, gravy dripping to his plate. "For that, I'd need to know where to find you. And I'll confess, I've got a proposition to facilitate that." He gave another crooked grin. "Though I suppose leading with the telling of another spy's arrest isn't exactly the best way to recruit you."

She found herself returning the smile. "Please tell me your recruitment effort has nothing to do with Felicia Ford and her wretched Soldiers Aid Society." That had been the only assignment John Elliott had ever allowed her. Little of value had come from it.

He laughed. "No. You've done your time with Felicia and her ladies."

"Thank heavens. I couldn't bear another recitation of her bad poetry, not to mention that legbone," To open their meetings, Felicia's traitorous group gathered around a legbone that had once belonged to a Union soldier.

"None of that." Elliott dabbed his mouth with a napkin, then pushed aside his empty plate. "You've heard of Bedford Forrest?"

She nodded "One of Felicia's Society ladies was quite enamored of him. Some sort of family connection, apparently. She kept us apprised of his exploits. Passed around a photo as well." Even in the photograph, Hattie had sensed malice in Forrest's gaze.

"She's not alone," Elliott said. "Forrest is admired throughout the South. He raised up his regiment with the slogan *Let's have some fun and kill some Yankees.*"

"That alone would be enough to endear him to Felicia's ladies," Hattie said darkly.

"General Grant dreads Forrest more than any other Confederate cavalryman. Of late he's been up to his old trick of conducting sporadic raids in West Tennessee, trying to weaken Union defenses there."

"He's had success?"

Elliott's expression turned grim. "Far too much of it. Everywhere he goes, I'm told, he rounds up deserters and adds fresh recruits. We fear he's gearing up for a big attack, one that might allow the Rebels to retake control of Tennessee. If that happens, other border states would be vulnerable. That's why President Lincoln had placed so much emphasis on us holding the line here."

Hattie straightened. "How can Forrest be stopped?"

Fingering his napkin, Elliott gazed at her intently. "Word has reached us of a female spy who has been gathering information for the Rebels in West Tennessee. Claims to be a niece to Bedford Forrest. Goes by Mollie Pitman, which may or may not be her real name. We believe she's currently staying near Fort Pillow."

"And that's where?" Hattie asked.

"On the Mississippi. Initially, it was a Rebel fort, but we captured it. Now Forrest wants it back, and we believe Mollie Pitman is supplying all the information he needs to succeed."

Hattie turned this over in her mind, considering the possibilities. "If Fort Pillow is under Federal control, why not have our men there arrest her?"

"Colonel Truesdail and I are concerned that the officials there will underestimate her because she's a woman. The last thing we want is them hauling her into the fort for questioning and then letting her go, equipped with all the intelligence Forrest could ever want about our defense capacities there. The colonel and I think we'd do better with a female spy who could befriend this Pitman woman and learn her secrets." He leaned forward, folding his hands on the table. "So you see why I made a point to come after you when I saw you on the street today."

Hattie felt a twinge of disappointment. His dinner invitation had been strictly professional after all. Her fingers brushed the slender gold chain at her neck, holding the watch Thom Welton had given her. She should be glad for Elliott's forbearance, she told herself.

She squared her shoulders. "If you're proposing an assignment involving Mollie Pitman, Lieutenant Elliott, I should be happy to accept."

For a moment, worry clouded his face. He was thinking of the risk, she thought. If her purpose became known, there was no telling how General Forrest would retaliate. Then his expression cleared, and he was all business again.

"Very good. Come by in the morning, and we'll equip you with everything you'll need."

Chapter Five

APRIL 3, 1864

Two days after meeting with John Elliott, Hattie got off the train in Bolivar, a small Tennessee town northeast of Memphis. Now on the Army Police payroll, she had funds sufficient to cover three weeks' expenses, with orders that permitted her to draw more if her assignment went longer. And if apprehending Mollie Pitman was the key to securing Tennessee from Forrest's plans to retake it, she also had a chance at something big.

Bolivar had once been a pretty little community, Hattie surmised, with home after home built in the Southern style she recognized from visiting her grandfather's Louisiana plantation. But the Union's occupation hadn't been kind to the town. Fences had been torn down and trees felled for wood for the Federal encampment, to which she was now headed. Having dropped her satchel at her hotel, her first order of business was to present herself to Union General Benjamin Grierson.

Twilight gave cover as she approached the encampment. But the streets were eerily quiet, and as she made her way there, Hattie had to shake off the feeling she was being watched. It was only nerves, after having been away from spying these past few months. The only ones watching her were the Union soldiers posted on every street corner, and they seemed more curious than threatening. Probably not many women left here, she thought. In this corner of Tennessee, most people had supported the Confederacy. When the Union took control, those who had the means fled to the South.

At the entrance to the Union encampment, she presented her pass from Lieutenant Elliott and asked for a word with General Grierson. At first, the picket refused, owing to the late hour. But when she said she was on urgent business regarding a Rebel advance, he relented, escorting her to the commander's tent.

Though it was evening, General Grierson was still at his field desk. Tall and lanky, with a thick shock of dark hair topping his high forehead, he looked up from his work.

"A Miss Thomas to see you, sir," the picket said. "Her pass is from the Army Police in Nashville. Says she has information about the Rebels' advance."

With weary eyes, the general looked Hattie up and down. "If only I had a nickel for everyone who claims to know Forrest's next move." Sighing, he gestured for Hattie to come forward, and the picket backed out of the tent.

Hattie stood before him, hands clasped at her waist. "I've been sent to befriend Confederate spy Mollie Pitman. I'm told she was last seen here in Bolivar. And I'm to be given a horse." From her shirt pocket, she took the slip of paper on which Lieutenant Elliott had scribbled his instructions and handed it to the general.

The general glanced at the paper, then returned it to her. "We aren't in the habit of reuniting friends and family here. Rather the opposite, I'm afraid."

"You mistake my purpose, sir. I've been assigned to befriend Miss Pitman for the purpose of gaining sufficient information for her to be arrested and tried as a spy."

Grierson pressed his palms flat on his desktop. "My picket said you have information on the Rebels' advance. If that's the case, you may share it, though I have to tell you I've found the testimony of women mostly unreliable on such matters. If you have no such information, I must ask you to take your leave. I've got work to do here, and at some point tonight, I'd like to get some sleep."

Drawing herself up taller, Hattie held his gaze. "Mollie Pitman is passing secrets to General Forrest. That will directly affect the Rebels' advance, don't you think?"

He leaned back, clasping his hands behind his head. "So I've been told. All nonsense as far as I'm concerned. A woman can't keep a secret, let alone pass one along."

Hattie's jaw tightened. "The Army Police wouldn't have dispatched me if they didn't have reason to think Miss Pitman is a threat."

"One or two silly women get caught spying, and all of a sudden everyone in a skirt is suspect. I'll be straightforward, Miss Thomas. I don't believe women have the capacity to spy. And I've got enough problems as it is dealing with camp followers without having to worry about some woman thrust upon me by the Army Police in Nashville."

Her ire rising, Hattie spoke as evenly as she could. "I assure you I'm not a camp follower, General Grierson. My only business here is to alert you to my presence and to learn whether you have any suggestions as to where I might find Miss Pitman, as well as a horse, per Lieutenant Elliott's instructions. I've accomplished my part of this purpose, and seeing as how you're reluctant to do yours, I'll leave you to your work."

She stepped back, and the general's gaze sharpened. Now she'd done it, she thought. Only hours into this assignment, and she'd made an enemy of a powerful man who had the authority to set her back on her heels. Plus she had no clue as to where to begin looking for Mollie Pitman, and without a horse, no way to travel the back roads looking for her.

She reached for the tent flap.

"The Pillars," Grierson said.

She turned to face him. "Sir?"

He held a paper in his hand. "This report from one of my sentries indicates that Miss Pitman arrived in Bolivar a few days ago. She is staying at the Pillars." He squinted at the paper. "Or rather, in a cottage on the grounds there."

"Thank you," Hattie said.

"Proceed to the stables," he said resignedly. "I'll send word that you're to be outfitted with a horse, plus an escort to the Pillars. A lady shouldn't be about the streets here after dark sets in."

~ ~ ~

Hattie was grateful for the horse, a gentle-eyed Chestnut mare called Bess. She could have done without the escort, but she accepted the help in part to placate the general and in part because she had no idea where she might find the Pillars.

More people were milling about Bolivar's streets when she left the encampment than when she'd arrived. She sensed a general feeling of hostility in the air, no doubt associated with the Union presence there, and wished she didn't have a soldier trotting along beside her. She'd have to devise some explanation so the townspeople—and Mollie Pitman—didn't look askance at her. In the meantime, she might as well try to learn from the soldier, who didn't look a day over fifteen, how much he knew of the town.

As it turned out, he knew a fair amount. Hailing from a farm some twenty miles to the east, he was among the few Union supporters in Western Tennessee. She supposed that made him valuable as a sentry since he knew firsthand the few townspeople who could be trusted.

"I seen how bad colored folks get treated," the lad said as they turned onto Bolivar's main thoroughfare. "Wouldn't give my life to defend that. No way, no how. Got plenty of family that think otherwise, though. The Union loses this war, I'll have to hightail it outta here."

"The Union won't lose," Hattie said, as much to reassure herself as him.

He offered a lopsided grin. "Not if I've got any say in it."

"What do you know about the Pillars?" she asked.

More spirited than Bess, his horse flung its head, and the soldier pulled back on the reins. "One of the nicest houses in town," he said. "John Bills, he's the owner. Cotton man, and you can bet he's got the money to prove it. Bought his furnishings from all around the country, that's what folks say. Never been inside the place myself, but there's talk Andrew Jackson spent the night there. Sam Houston, too, and Davey Crockett. Plus Jefferson Davis, Bills being a cotton man and all."

"Is that why there's a cottage on the property—for the guests?"

"No, ma'am. That cottage Mr. Bills put up for his daughter, Mrs. Evalina Polk, when her husband went off to fight with the Rebels. Couldn't stay in the main house on account of it being used for a hospital, first for the Rebs and then for the Yanks."

"And a guest arrived there recently?"

He pulled again on the reins, getting his horse focused forward. "You could say that. Missus Polk, she left town last week. Visiting relations, folks say. Then this other lady, she rides in from who knows where, and now she's at the cottage. There's some say she's a spy." He shook his head. "A female spy, if there even is such a thing."

"The general doesn't seem to think so."

In the slanted light of the setting sun, a massive house loomed. Hattie counted eight columns along a veranda that ran the full length of it.

"There it is," the soldier said. "The Pillars."

Hattie slowed her horse. "I'll go on alone from here," she said. "They might not appreciate a Union soldier at their doorstep."

"You can bet on that." With some effort, he turned his horse, which seemed to have only going forward in mind. "Good evening, ma'am," the soldier called over his shoulder.

Her horse at a slow trot, Hattie circled the property, keeping to the road so as not to attract attention. Lamplight shone from a few of the windows in the main house. Servants, probably, since the mistress was out of town. On the back side of the property, she spotted several outbuildings. One looked like a kitchen, another an icehouse. Beyond the stables, tucked in a far corner, sat a little cottage. Smoke curled from the chimney, but the windows were dark. Hattie kept going, circling around to the front of the property. Now that she knew where the cottage was, she would return tomorrow.

As she started back toward the hotel, a dark-haired woman approached from the opposite direction. Under the darkening skies, it was hard to make out her features, but she looked not much older than Hattie, small-framed and plainly dressed.

"Have you seen a horse, ma'am?" the woman called out. Though her voice was firm and measured, Hattie detected a hint of urgency. "It seems my Flora has wandered off from the stables. Or was stolen. There's no telling these days."

Tugging the reins, Hattie shook her head. "But I've only just arrived in Bolivar, so I haven't seen much."

Gazing up at Hattie, the woman had the look of an earnest child trying rather unsuccessfully to conceal her distress. "Just passing through myself," the woman said. "Though without my horse, I suppose I'm stuck here."

Hattie looked down the street toward the hotel. Another half hour, and it would be fully dark. "If you're comfortable riding behind me, we could have a quick look around."

Though pressed firm, the woman's lips turned, hinting at a smile. "That would be a great kindness. It's hard to cover much ground on foot, and night's fast approaching."

Hattie steered Bess toward a park bench, and the stranger followed. Lifting her skirts, she climbed on the bench more easily than Hattie would have imagined. Hattie offered her hand. The woman took it, her grip strong, and slipped easily onto Bess's back.

As they continued down the street, Hattie could tell her passenger was an adept rider, not just from her ease in mounting the horse but from how she shifted her weight, such as it was, adjusting to the horse's gait. Coming to the town's center, Hattie saw that aside from the hotel and two taverns, most of the businesses around the square were shuttered.

Her rider leaned forward, scanning the horses tied to hitching posts outside the tavern. "She's not here," the woman said. "I'm told there's a tavern out on Water Street, on the hill above the spring. If you'd take me there, I'd be much obliged."

Hattie hesitated. Two women crossing town on a horse were bound to attract attention. But she supposed one more stop before dark wouldn't hurt.

Steering Bess onto Water Street, she eased her into a quicker gait. The houses on either side of the street thinned out as they approached the hill on the edge of town. As the stranger had indicated, a small, well-lit tavern sat atop the hill. Bess trotted up the road toward it, seeming not to mind the bit of extra weight.

As they drew near, Hattie saw there were a good number of horses hitched outside. This must be where locals came to get out from under the scrutiny of the Union soldiers patrolling Bolivar.

"There she is!" the woman behind Hattie said, pointing toward a dappled horse near the end of the row. "My Flora. Some lout stole her, all right."

Hattie steered Bess alongside a mounting block, and the stranger slid from her back. Without a word to Hattie, she went directly to the horse. Unhitching the beast, she gazed affectionately at it. "Who made off with you?" She patted the horse's neck. "Not that you'd tell."

Hattie felt as if she was interrupting a reunion between two old friends. "I'll be off to the hotel now," she said.

"I don't know how I can ever repay your kindness," the woman said. "And I don't even know your name."

"Hattie Renfrew," she said, giving the name she'd picked for herself.

"Mollie Pitman," the stranger said.

Hattie smiled gently, covering her surprise. "Pleased to make your acquaintance. I've been riding a good while among strangers, hoping to catch up with General Forrest. My brother Charlie's one of his recruits. He's only just turned eighteen, and we need him back on the farm."

"I should think General Forrest needs him too," Mollie said.

"That's what Pa said, that without recruits, the Confederacy's sunk. But Charlie hadn't been gone a week before the apoplexy struck Pa. Now there's only womenfolk left to do the spring planting, so Ma sent me to bring him home."

Mollie tipped her chin as if she was inwardly dissecting point by point what Hattie had said. From the woods below the hill, a chorus of croaking bullfrogs rose up, the sound of them filling the evening air. "I've had some dealings with General Forrest," she said quietly. "He won't be passing through any time soon. But there's trouble ahead for this town, so I suggest you move on as soon as you can."

"I'll do that," Hattie said. "I just wish I knew where to find General Forrest."

Mollie hesitated. Then she said, "I'm staying over at the Pillars, not far from where I met up with you. In the morning, come around to the back and look for the little cottage. I'll see if I can help you locate this brother of yours."

~ ~ ~

Hattie rose the next morning to bright sunshine and a sense of optimism. What good fortune, to have come upon Mollie Pitman so readily, and in a way that had left her somewhat in Hattie's debt. Lieutenant Elliott would be pleased. Now Hattie just needed to find a way to get Mollie to divulge what she'd been up to.

She unloaded the contents of her satchel into the saddlebags she'd procured at the encampment, then rolled up the satchel and stuffed it in too. One benefit of having nowhere to call home was that she'd pared back her wardrobe, getting by with only the bare minimum of clothes. In the guise of a farm girl, she'd brought only the calico work dress she was wearing now plus the slightly fancier one she'd worn yesterday. The rest she'd left for safekeeping at the Army Police Headquarters in Nashville.

She fastened the saddlebags and was about to pick them up when, touching her fingers to her neck, she realized something was missing. Every morning since leaving Thom Welton, she'd fastened the gold watch he'd given her around her neck. Today, she'd forgotten.

She started to undo the saddlebags so she could retrieve the watch from the silk purse where she'd stashed it. Her feelings about Thom were so confused now. With so much of what she wanted tied to her success with Mollie Pitman, she didn't need any reminder of her doubts. She'd put the watch on again when her way forward felt clearer, when she had a plan in place for proving she'd been right about Thom all along.

She shouldered her saddlebags and left the hotel. At the stable in the back, she retrieved Bess and headed for the Pillars. Though the day was young, the sun's long rays promised warmth. She passed yellow forsythias and pink magnolias in bloom. Even in the yards where Union soldiers had torn up fences for firewood, daffodils and tulips still made a colorful display, oblivious to the ravages of war.

The Pillars looked even more stately in the morning light. Hattie proceeded around to the stables, where the stableboy assured her he'd keep a close eye on Bess while she paid a visit to Mrs. Polk's guest. No doubt Mollie had warned him of the scare the horse thief had given her.

Hattie followed the path from the stables to the cottage, a quaint little affair built in the Gothic style with a steeply pitched roof and fancy scrollwork. The sweet smell of hyacinths wafted up as she neared. Hoping she hadn't arrived too early, she rapped on the door.

Almost immediately, Mollie opened it. "There you are," she said as if she'd been waiting hours for Hattie's arrival. "The housemaid just brought over tea and scones. Fancier place than where I've spent some nights, and I admit I enjoy it."

"I know what you mean," Hattie said as she followed Mollie across the small but beautifully appointed room. "It's wretched trying to find a bite to eat and a place to lay your head when you're a woman alone. Every time I'd get close to some troops, someone would take me for a camp follower and shoo me off, saying they had too many mouths to feed as it was. And then of course it never was the soldiers I was looking for."

"More Rebel soldiers than you can shake a stick at hanging around this part of Tennessee." Mollie motioned for Hattie to sit at the table for two set in front of a bay of three tall windows. As Hattie settled in the chair, she poured the tea, holding the teapot awkwardly and spilling a bit as she handed Hattie her cup. Her hand wasn't shaking, and she didn't seem nervous, just unaccustomed to such niceties.

Hattie forked a corner from the scone on the plate in front of her, then lifted it to her mouth. She felt as if Mollie were watching her every move.

"Delicious," she said. "Ginger?" Savoring the sweet warmth in her mouth, Hattie became aware of her hand, softer and more supple than a farm girl's should be. She hoped Mollie didn't notice.

"So I'm told." Not bothering with a fork, Mollie bit directly into her scone. "No idea how they come by butter and sugar these days. I suppose the family has connections."

Illegal connections, Hattie thought. A cotton trader's options were limited these days. But like Hattie's own father, the owner of this property might be trading in all sorts of contraband. "How is it you know the family?" she asked, hoping to divert Mollie's intense gaze as she forked off another bit of scone.

"I don't," Mollie said bluntly. "It was Uncle Bedford who suggested I come here." She offered her version of a smile. "General Forrest, I mean."

"General Forrest is your uncle?" Hattie said, sounding surprised.

"That's right."

Though not prone to elaborating, Molly Pitman was certainly forthcoming. But why wouldn't she be, with Hattie presenting herself as a woman whose brother had answered Forrest's call for recruits?

"How fortunate of me to have met just the person to help me find Charlie," Hattie said.

"Happy to reward your kindness," Mollie said. "But I'll be leaving Bolivar tomorrow. If you like, you can ride along with me, and I'll take you to where General Forrest is headed."

Reaching across the table, Hattie took Mollie's hand, which felt limp. "Thank you. Thank you so much. You have no idea what it will mean to be able to bring Charlie home."

Mollie pulled her hand away. "Just don't make a nuisance of yourself."

"Oh, I won't." Hattie dabbed her mouth with a napkin.

What a strange woman, she thought. But as long as Hattie got enough information to expose her as a spy, what did that matter?

Chapter Six

APRIL 4, 1864

Hattie left Bolivar the next morning, riding beside Mollie. Before the war, two women riding alone would have been a rare sight, but many uncommon sights had now become common, and travelers they met along the road paid them little mind.

The day was warm for springtime, but a brisk breeze cooled Hattie's skin, the sun peeking out only now and then from beneath billowing clouds. As they rode alongside the Hatchie River, Hattie learned that Mollie was a farmer's daughter from northern Tennessee, or at least so she claimed. If this were true, Hattie worried that Mollie might eventually see through her ruse of being from a farming family herself.

But Hattie had grown up in a farm town, and while she had never milked a cow or butchered a chicken, she figured she could talk her way around such details if the occasion arose. And at any rate, Mollie asked little about Hattie's background. A bit odd for a woman said to be a spy, Hattie thought. But Mollie did listen intently whenever Hattie spoke, and judging from her furrowed brow, Hattie suspected she was assessing and remembering every detail.

Mollie was also surprisingly forthcoming about how she'd come to assist the Confederates. "When the war broke out, I had no family left alive, only aunts and uncles," she said. "It was only natural that I would seek out Uncle Bedford. Like my folks, he'd started out poor, but he got in the business of trading slaves and bought up cotton plantations all around West Tennessee."

Hattie smiled noncommittedly, concealing her abhorrence for everything connected with the enslavement of Negroes. "I expect he's well-off."

"To say the least," Mollie said. "He claims to be worth well over a million dollars. Not that he's shared any of that with me. But I had few other prospects." She gazed off at the rolling hills, and for a moment the only sounds were the spirited hoofbeats of the horses and a mockingbird's song from a nearby treetop.

"I'll have few prospects myself if Pa passes without Charlie around to see to the farm," Hattie said, breaking the silence.

Turning her face, Mollie offered a wry smile. "Still, I doubt you'll be forced to do as I did. To get Uncle Bedford's attention, I enlisted, dressed as a man."

Hattie's eyes widened. "I've heard talk of women soldiers, but I never did believe it." This wasn't entirely true. In Richmond, one of Hattie's fellow prisoners had been a woman named Loreta Velasquez who had dressed as a soldier to fight for the South.

"You may believe it or not," Mollie said. "I wanted real action, and I got it, teaming up with another soldier and raising a company. I led it too. Lieutenant Thomas Rawley, I called myself."

"You saw battle?"

Mollie nodded curtly. "We were a roving band at first, skirmishing with the Federals where they least expected it."

"You were bushwhackers?" Hattie had a hard time imagining a woman being as ruthless as Champ Farmington. But then Mollie might be making all of this up. She was a spy, after all, skilled in deception.

Mollie shrugged. "That's what they call us. A rough life, but an interesting one. I saw a few things a woman should never see, did a few things a woman should never do. No need to shock you with the details. The important point is that we were able eventually to attach ourselves to Uncle Bedford's troops. By that point, he'd made quite a name for himself."

"We need more like him," Hattie said, filling her voice with fervor. "To drive the Yanks back where they came from."

"So much bloodshed," Mollie muttered. "So much brutality." She shook her head as if in doing so she could shake off the memories. "Uncle Bedford took a bullet at Shiloh, but he recovered swiftly. I was with him there and at Murfreesboro and Chickamauga."

"Was he shocked to learn your true identity?" Hattie asked.

"I suppose he was. I'd kept my secret well. It wasn't until he called me up for secret service duty that I revealed myself."

Exactly the information Hattie was seeking. Nonchalantly, she shooed off a fly buzzing near Bess's mane. "Secret service duty? What's that?"

"I'm a spy," Mollie said simply. "Punishable by death if I'm caught."

This Hattie knew all too well. "Your uncle allows you to put yourself in such danger?"

Mollie laughed. "You don't know Uncle Bedford. He's a big man, but no one would ever accuse him of being bighearted. He gets angry, you'd best get out of his way."

Hattie shook her head. "I can scarcely believe it. Me, riding alongside a spy."

Mollie glanced toward the hills in the distance, then looked back at Hattie. "That's why I was in Bolivar, scouting in advance of the troops that will be coming through any day now."

"Confederate troops?" Hattie said. "You know that because you're a spy?"

"I don't spy on my own side," Mollie said.

"How silly of me," Hattie said. "But what does a spy do, exactly?"

Mollie shrugged. "It depends. Mostly I assess Union positions and estimate how many soldiers they have, though getting any sort of accurate count is tricky. I also determine whether they're preparing for battle."

"Are they?" Hattie asked. "At Bolivar, I mean."

"They haven't a clue," Mollie said. "I expect the Union encampment there will be forced to surrender. But the real prize will be at Fort Pillow. Uncle Bedford is headed that way, and so are we."

Hattie's skin prickled. It was too late to warn General Grierson about the Confederates descending on Bolivar. But if she played her cards right, she'd have time to warn the officials at Fort Pillow while also seeing to Mollie's arrest.

"Fort Pillow," Hattie said vaguely. "Isn't that somewhere along the Mississippi?"

"That's right," Mollie said. "We'll be there by nightfall."

"And you'll do the same there?" Hattie asked. "Find out about the troops and such?"

Mollie nodded. "And convey that to General Forrest. Only..." Her voice trailed off, and a clouded look passed over her eyes. Then she waved her hand in the air as if to dismiss whatever had come over her. "When the troops arrive, you should be able to locate your brother."

In a show of emotion, Hattie pressed her hand to her chest. "You're an angel, Mollie."

She shook her head. "Not an angel. Not at all."

~ ~ ~

Hattie had been anxious to get to Fort Pillow and share what she'd learned from Mollie. But night was falling fast as they'd neared the Mississippi River, and she could hardly have ridden off in the dark without arousing Mollie's suspicions.

Instead, she'd accepted Mollie's offer of a bed at a nearby farmhouse belonging to a dour-faced Confederate sympathizer. Hattie would go to Fort Pillow at daybreak, she decided. In the meantime, Mollie might let slip more evidence that could be used against her in an arrest.

But Mollie had clammed up, falling asleep early, while Hattie had lain awake half the night repeating to herself all she'd learned, information that would bring deserved recognition when Fort Pillow was saved and a Confederate spy apprehended. She only had to figure out how to break away and get herself to Fort Pillow without drawing Mollie's attention.

Hattie woke just after daybreak. Across the room, Mollie was dressed and sitting on her bed.

"You're leaving?" Hattie said groggily.

Mollie stared, an unnerving gaze that Hattie had yet to get used to. "I've got surveilling to do."

"At Fort Pillow?"

"Where else?"

In the fog of waking up, an idea came to Hattie. "I could come along."

Mollie tilted her head quizzically. "Why would I bring you?"

Inspired, Hattie sat up in bed. This was her chance to find where the fort was and observe Mollie's spying so there would be no question of her being what she said she was.

"I could help with the counting," Hattie said. "I've nothing else to do until General Forrest arrives, and I'd like to be useful. You said it's not so easy making the estimates on your own."

"Very well," Mollie said crisply.

Hattie got up and dressed as quickly as she could, Mollie waiting impatiently. They descended the stairs, and after a breakfast of thinly buttered bread and chicory coffee, retrieved their horses from the barn. Since yesterday, the wind had stilled, and the smell of manure filled the air as they rode from the farmhouse.

As they rode, Hattie tried to draw Mollie into conversation, but she had little to say until Hattie mentioned Lincoln's freeing the slaves, a topic guaranteed to get a rise out of anyone supporting the South.

But Mollie's reaction was not at all what Hattie expected. "And why shouldn't they be freed?"

Genuinely surprised, Hattie gasped. "All your fighting and spying, all the horrors you've seen. Isn't that to ensure nothing changes concerning the Negroes?"

"If I've learned anything in this war, it's that everything changes, no matter how much you might wish otherwise," Mollie said. "As for the horrors...well, you don't want to know."

"I'm sure I don't," Hattie said. "I prefer to stay as far from the war as possible."

Mollie gave her a sharp look. "Then I don't see how you expect to find your brother."

Too late, Hattie realized she'd misspoken. Rather than dig her hole deeper, she rode along in silence, occupying herself by shooing off flies until the fort came into view.

"There it is," Mollie said, drawing her horse to a stop.

Bringing Bess alongside, Hattie surveyed the scene before her. Scrabbled together at the start of the war, the fort had little to recommend it. For its defense, there were only three lines of earthworks arcing toward the east from a Mississippi River bluff. Scattered between the earthworks were several tents and some hastily erected cabins.

From below the bluff, a steamboat's whistle blew. "I know nothing of a fort's defenses," Hattie said. "But I see little here to stop General Forrest."

"Nothing much does." Mollie turned to face her. "Start your counting. I'll ride the perimeter."

As Mollie rode off, Hattie did her best to count the men. By her estimate, about half of them were Negro soldiers. From what she could see, all the soldiers, both black and white, seemed to mill about rather aimlessly in the areas between the earthworks. With little to occupy them day to day, soldiers could easily be lulled into complacency. That was what made surprise attacks so successful.

Not here, Hattie thought as she counted the distant figures. *Not on my watch.*

Mollie rode back around. "Several batteries," she announced. "But otherwise woefully prepared. How many men?"

"Seven hundred," Hattie said. "Give or take." A high estimate, but in case Mollie managed to convey it before Hattie had her arrested, she hoped it might deter Forrest's advance. "I wonder how soon they'll be called to arms," she added, hoping this came across as mere idle musing.

"A few days at most," Mollie said. "Uncle Bedford has come by this way once already, rounding up irregulars. I doubt anyone down there noticed. Men can be so blind to what's happening right in front of their noses.

Hattie nodded her agreement. A few days—plenty of time to warn the commander and see to Mollie's arrest. Hattie had all the information she needed. Now she just needed an excuse to get away.

Chapter Seven

APRIL 6, 1864

Eager as Hattie was to get away, Mollie had other ideas. "If you want to intercept Forrest's troops, this farmhouse is your best chance," she said. "You might as well stay till they arrive."

Not wanting to weaken her cover, Hattie agreed. She spent the next day, and the next, watching and waiting for a chance to return to Fort Pillow on her own. But Mollie kept a watchful eye on her, so much so that Hattie began to feel as if the tables had turned and she was the one slated for arrest. But that was nonsense. This part of Tennessee was under Union control, and Hattie intended to help keep it that way.

At least Hattie wasn't called on to demonstrate her non-existent skills in milking or slaughtering chickens. Those chores Mollie gladly took on, assisting the old widower who spent his waking hours grumbling about the Yankee occupation. Conveniently, this also meant she could position herself to keep an eye on the horses, preventing Hattie from riding off.

Hattie passed the time mending and washing for the old man. She even made some fair attempts at cooking for the old farmer, who mostly relied on women from neighboring farms to cook for him now and again. And if frustrated by waiting for an opportunity to sneak off, Hattie was at least rewarded by Mollie's revealing even more about the work she'd done as a Confederate spy.

Besides scouting for General Forrest, Mollie revealed that she sometimes smuggled supplies across enemy lines, traveling south from St. Louis by steamship. Musket and pistol caps, cartridges, and pistols were among the items she named. Not in small quantities, either, but by the tens of thousands, she said. She'd even procured personal items for General Forrest—leggings, a gun cloak, an officer's belt.

All this information Hattie tucked away as evidence for when Mollie was arrested. In return, she invented a few dark secrets which she shared with Mollie. Hattie's made-up father had been a drunkard, she confided, a condition that the doctor said had made him prone to apoplexy. Her mother suffered from bouts of hysteria, demanding her daughters' care. All the women in the family idolized Charlie, Hattie said, underscoring the importance of her search.

In her strange, detached way, Mollie shared that she, too, had been close to her brother, who'd died of typhus only months before the war broke out. She was a tough woman, Hattie had to admit. Under other circumstances—and if she knew for certain that the things Mollie said were true—she might have felt some genuine sympathy for her.

On her third night at the farmhouse, Hattie finally got the opportunity she'd been waiting for. The old man had gone up to bed, and the women were in the kitchen, Mollie plucking a chicken and Hattie churning butter from the morning's milk.

"I'll be away tomorrow," Mollie announced in her usual plain manner.

"Where?" Hattie asked casually.

"North of here, a town called Ripley. One of Uncle Bedford's advance scouts is to meet me there. You can ride along with me."

Observing an exchange between Mollie and Forrest's soldier would be useful, but even better would be the chance to get out from under Mollie's watchful eye so she could warn officials at Fort Pillow about the pending attack.

Pumping hard at the churn, Hattie said nonchalantly, "I suppose he'll tell you when the troops are coming."

Mollie shrugged. "Probably. At any rate, it won't be long now. I do fear for those soldiers."

Hattie paused, her arms aching. "But surely General Forrest wouldn't attack unless he thought he could win."

"I don't mean the Confederate soldiers," Mollie said. "I mean the ones at Fort Pillow. The Negroes."

"The Negroes? Why would you fear for them?"

Mollie wriggled a pin feather from the nearly naked chicken. "If there's anything a Confederate soldier despises more than a Yank, it's a Negro who fights with the Yanks. The irregulars who've joined up with Forrest, they're the worst. You should hear them talk of what they'd do if they ever got their hands on a Negro soldier."

Of all Mollie had told her, this was sadly among the easiest facts to believe. But why would Mollie, a Confederate spy, concern herself with the fate of Negro soldiers?

Hattie pushed the thought aside. Mollie had her quirks, that was for certain. And quirky or not, she would soon get her due.

~ ~ ~

Hattie woke the next morning with a plan. Holding her hand to her abdomen, she winced as if in pain.

From across the room, Mollie gave her a sharp look. "What's wrong?"

Hattie sighed. "Monthlies."

Mollie offered one of her sly smiles. "You think they're troublesome here, you should try hiding them from a whole regiment of men."

"I can't begin to imagine." Hattie rolled to her side, hugging her abdomen. "I'm sorry I can't go with you today."

"Don't be. I'm used to it. Not that I haven't enjoyed having a bit of company. There was a time..." She shook her head. "Never mind. Water under the bridge."

"Will you ask after Charlie for me?" Hattie said.

"I'll ask, but don't get your hopes up. Scouts know a lot more about the enemy's troops than they do their own."

Hattie sighed. "I suppose I'll just have to bide my time till Forrest gets here."

"It won't take long for the dust to settle," Mollie said. "Unprepared as they are at Fort Pillow."

"We can only hope," Hattie said, leaving unspoken where her true hopes lay.

~ ~ ~

After Mollie went downstairs, Hattie lay in bed another hour, feigning sleep until she was certain Mollie was gone. Then she got up, dressed, and left the house. Outside, the sun blazed from a cloudless sky, the air already warm. Shielding her eyes from the sun, Hattie saw the farmer was out sowing seeds in his field. She slipped into the barn and saddled Bess, the horse looking eager for an outing. She doubted the farmer saw her ride off, but even if he did, she could say she'd decided a bit of fresh air would ease her aches and pains.

The road was even less traveled than it had been when she and Mollie had surveilled Fort Pillow. Hattie brought Bess to a brisk trot and kept her there much of the way. Nearing the fort, she proceeded past their lookout point to the fort's entrance.

"Lieutenant Elliott of Nashville's Army Police dispatched me," she told the guards, presenting her pass. "I need to speak with the commander. The matter is urgent."

One guard, a skinny white man with a stubbled beard, chuckled. "An urgent matter, is it? Cow's giving sour milk, or maybe it's that the hens won't lay?"

The other guard, a square-shouldered man with coffee-colored skin and a closely cropped beard, took her pass and studied it. "If Nashville's sent you, it must be important."

"There's a threat to this fort," Hattie said. "And a Confederate spy who should be detained."

Concern registering on his face, the black man looked at the other guard, who lifted his hands in a gesture of mock surrender. "Go ahead, Samuel. And when Major Booth reams you up and down for bothering him for no good reason, you just be sure he knows I've got nothing to do with it."

Samuel acknowledged this with a nod, then gestured for Hattie to enter the fort. She came alongside, and they walked briskly toward a patch of high ground where a lone uniformed man stood observing a group of soldiers doing drills.

"Is Major Booth as unreasonable as that man let on?" she asked.

"Not at all," said the guard. "The major's a good man. Has to be, the abuse he gets for leading a colored regiment. He'll hear you out."

The uniformed man turned as they drew near. Tall and slender, he had reddish hair and sideburns that merged with his mustache. Hattie saw by his epaulets that he was the major in charge of the fort.

Samuel saluted. "Sorry to bother you, Major Booth, but this woman's got something I think you'll want to hear." He handed the commander her pass, then stepped back several paces, allowing them to speak in private.

Booth studied her pass, then looked up at her. "So Elliott's still got women in his employ even after that debacle last summer."

He must mean Pauline's capture and escape, Hattie thought. "That situation ended well enough," she said, trying not to sound defensive. "Now it's a Confederate woman spy the lieutenant has sent me after. I tracked her down in Bolivar."

Major Booth rubbed his chin. "Bolivar. A scout just brought word that a skirmish there between the Union cavalry and a contingent of Forrest's men has ended badly for us. Twenty men dead, and more than that taken prisoner, including two captains. Our forces have abandoned the encampment and are headed for Memphis. The Rebels are now in possession of their remaining wagons and teams, plus their ambulances and ammunition."

"The Rebel spy, Mollie Pitman, hinted that Forrest would stage an attack in Bolivar. But by then we'd left the area, and I had no way of getting word back there."

Major Booth shook his head. "Grierson's men should have been able to hold them off." His blue-eyed gaze fell again on his troops as he returned her pass, which she slipped into her skirt pocket. "So what is it you want of me?"

Hattie straightened. "I've come to warn you of an imminent attack on this fort."

Turned to her, his brow furrowed. "This Pittman woman thinks Forrest will attack here?"

She nodded. "Any day now."

"And you believe her credible?"

"She proved credible concerning the attack on Bolivar. But I've managed to befriend her, and she has been rather forthcoming. Earlier this week, she brought me to a lookout point not far from here to assess your fortifications and troop numbers. Today she's gone to Ripley to make her report to one of Forrest's scouts."

"I see." The major squinted into the sun. "Well, we shall be ready for them. In the meantime, if you'll let me know where we can find Miss Pitman, I'll send some of my men to arrest her before she passes any more information to Forrest."

Hattie gave him directions to the old farmer's place. Confirming that Mollie was expected home by evening, the major promised to dispatch a contingent to see to her arrest.

Leaving the fort, Hattie could not suppress a swell of pride. She'd seen to the arrest of a Confederate spy, and she'd warned Fort Pillow's commander of an imminent attack. She could hardly wait to get back to Nashville and report her success.

~ ~ ~

When Hattie brought Bess back to the barn, the old man was there. His disgruntled expression softened only slightly when she explained that while she hadn't been feeling well that morning, a leisurely ride had done her good, and she was ready to resume her chores. Washing and hanging out clothes proved a welcome distraction as she waited for Mollie's return.

As expected, Mollie was back in time for supper. Hattie told her what she'd told the old man, that a ride in the spring air had done wonders for her health, and Mollie didn't question this. Throughout a supper of chicken stew and biscuits, Hattie was on pins and needles, expecting Major Booth's men to pound on the door any minute. But the evening proceeded like any other, the old man retiring early while Hattie and Mollie did up the dishes.

Ever unsuspected, Mollie relayed to Hattie what she'd learned from the scout. Having raided a Union encampment in Kentucky, General Forrest was indeed headed south to attack Fort Pillow. In the meantime, the scout wanted Mollie to stay alert to any sign that the fort's officers were preparing for an attack.

"I suppose they want the advantage of surprise," Hattie said, wiping a soup bowl.

Mollie tilted her chin, studying Hattie in her off-kilter manner. "That's generally the idea," she said.

Her scrutiny unnerved Hattie, as if Mollie somehow suspected the surprise of Booth's men swooping in to arrest her. But that was impossible, Hattie told herself. If Mollie had any idea that Hattie had exposed her, she wouldn't continue to chat with her about Forrest's plans.

As the evening wore on, it became clear that Major Booth's men weren't coming. Perhaps Hattie had been wrong to assume they'd make the arrest that evening. After all, she hadn't known exactly when Mollie would return, and if they'd come in advance of her, the old farmer would've become suspicious.

But the men didn't come in the morning either, nor did they show up that afternoon. Frustrated, Hattie replayed over and over her discussion with Major Booth. What if he'd decided not to believe her after all? She could try to get word to the Army Police in Nashville, but what good would that do when they were so far away?

Caught up in her thoughts, she knocked a plate from the table as she was setting it for supper. As she was sweeping up the pieces, Mollie came in.

"So careless of me," Hattie said, brushing the remaining shards into the dustbin.

"Jittery," Mollie observed.

"I suppose you're right," Hattie said. "It's hard, knowing Forrest will arrive any day, and I'll finally have a chance to find Charlie."

"You wouldn't make much of a soldier," Mollie said.

"I suppose not." Hattie hung the broom on its nail. As she bent to pick up the dustpan, there was a loud banging at the front door.

"Army," a man called out loudly. "Open up."

Mollie eyed her. "Now what could they want?"

"I surely don't know," Hattie said. After the arrest, Mollie might question this. But what would it matter? Hattie would never see her again.

The old farmer came from the back of the house, his overalls streaked with dirt from the fields. "What's all the ruckus?"

"Open up!" the man called out again. "Army."

Eyes narrowing, the farmer limped to the door and unlatched it. Sneering, he stepped back as three blue-uniformed men entered. One of them was Samuel, the black soldier who had brought Hattie to Major Booth.

A barrel-chested white soldier stepped forward, his glance shifting between the women. "Miss Mollie Pitman," he said, clearly unsure of which one he was addressing. "You're under arrest, suspected of espionage."

The old farmer shook his head. "Damned women. Shoulda known you'd be trouble."

Samuel edged toward Hattie. "You're to come along, too, miss," he said in a low voice. "Major says he needs your testimony."

Mollie tipped her head toward Hattie, looking more bemused than angry. "I can tell you a lot more than she can."

It was all Hattie could do to keep her mouth from falling open. No spy willingly gave up her secrets.

Adding to her shock, Mollie held out her hands to the third soldier as he advanced toward her with handcuffs.

"I'm glad to see you boys," Mollie said. "You see, I've decided to switch sides."

Chapter Eight

No matter what Mollie said about switching sides, Hattie didn't believe it for a moment. Certainly, both sides had their deserters. Men who were homesick, men for whom the brutalities of war became too much, men who had reassessed how much they were willing to risk their lives for. Once they decided to lay down their arms, they might even provide valuable information to the enemy.

But spies were cut from a different cloth. Their service was voluntary, and they could quit at any time. Some might work both sides, like Luke Blackstone, the doctor-spy who'd betrayed Hattie and Thom. But like Blackstone, whose true loyalties lay with the South, they always favored one side or the other. They didn't just switch.

This was only Mollie's way of wriggling out of a tight spot. After all, Union officials had executed Confederate spies. Maybe not women—not yet, anyhow—but it was entirely possible they'd decide to make an example of her. If it meant saving her skin, of course she'd claim to come over to the Union's side.

Surely Major Booth would recognize that. But to make sure, Hattie was more than happy to follow after the soldiers as they hauled Mollie off. In any event, she couldn't remain at the farmer's house, not after Mollie had all but accused her of spying for the Federals. She'd spend the night at the fort, give her statement against Mollie in Major Booth's inquiry, and get back to Nashville.

At first, the soldier in charge of billeting had proposed the women share a tent. Hattie balked at the idea, pointing out that a tent was far from secure. Samuel agreed, and after some back-and-forth with the billeting officer, Hattie had gotten her own tent, and Mollie slept alone in a cabin.

The next morning, Major Booth conducted only a cursory interview with Mollie, then warned Hattie it might be a day or two before he could let her leave.

"But General Forrest is planning an attack," Hattie said. "If he arrives while Miss Pitman is here, he'll see to her release."

"He won't get that far," Major Booth said. "Besides, my scouts tell me he's been delayed. Some sort of trouble with his troops. To be expected, I suppose, when he's marching with a bunch of irregulars."

She left Booth's tent shaking her head. "If he doesn't act soon, she's going to get away," she muttered to Samuel, who was waiting outside the tent to escort her back to her quarters.

"Major's got a lot on his mind," Samuel said as they started from the tent. His voice, soft and melodious, had a soothing effect.

"I'm sure he does," Hattie fumed. "But he needs to make Mollie Pitman a priority."

Samuel shrugged. "Hasn't caused much trouble so far."

"Maybe not here, but she's done plenty to aid General Forrest. If he attacks this fort, it's her information that helped in his planning."

Samuel rubbed his chin. "Not to be contrary, Miss Hattie, but ain't she come around to the Union's side?"

"So she says," Hattie said. "I don't believe it."

"Folks can surprise you," he said.

"That's my fear," Hattie said. "Mollie will get Major Booth eating out of her hand, and before you know it, she'll be passing secrets to the Rebels from inside Union ranks. She's already turned the tables on me after I saw to her arrest. And now I'm stuck here trying to convince the major not to believe her."

"I know how you feel, Miss Hattie. There's a lot of us that feel like we're just passing time when we'd rather be fighting. Especially us colored soldiers."

Hattie felt a twinge of embarrassment. Frustrated as she was at having to prove herself at every turn, she knew colored soldiers like Samuel faced far greater challenges. "How did you come to enlist?" she asked.

"Came up from Louisiana. Word went round the plantation, how Uncle Abe set us free. 'Course that meant nothing to the white folks down there, seeing as how they'd left the Union with hatred in their hearts. But I saw that if we could manage an escape, me and my wife and our baby girl, and get north to a Union state, we'd have our chance at freedom."

A shout went out from the fort's inner embankment, an officer walking his orders through drills. "It must have been a harrowing journey," Hattie said.

Samuel gazed off toward the bluff that looked out over the Mississippi. "It was. Snuck off in the dead of night, then hopped a riverboat headed north. Hid under a tarp. It weren't easy keeping the baby quiet, let me tell you."

"I can imagine," Hattie said, knowing how impossible it would be to keep little Jo silent under those circumstances. "But you made it."

Samuel looked back at her, and in his dark eyes, she sensed both suffering and relief. "Just barely. The riverboat captain, he was known to transport folks like us, escaping the South."

"Like the Underground Railroad," Hattie said, thinking of the enslaved woman she'd helped back in Indiana. "Except on the water."

"That's right," Samuel said. "But downriver of Memphis, a slave catcher came aboard. Captain had to sneak us off the boat. We walked from there. Never was so glad to see a place as we were to see Memphis." Smiling, he shook his head. "Ragged and tired and hungry. We was like folks that crawled from a grave. But we made it."

They passed a group of Negro soldiers gathered in front of the infirmary tent. "And yet after all that, you enlisted. Why? It must have been hard, leaving your wife and daughter."

He turned, looking her square in the eyes. "We been trampled under the white man's heel our whole lives, Miss Hattie. Now we got a chance to elevate ourselves and our race. What little I can do toward it, I'll do most willingly."

Never had she heard a soldier speak so earnestly of his commitment to the cause. "But there's a chance...a chance you might never return to them."

He straightened, standing taller still. "If necessary, I'll give up my life willingly to benefit my race. And if I should die before I see those benefits, I'll at least have the consolation of knowing that generations to come will receive the blessing of it."

As they arrived at her tent, Hattie looked up at him. "You're an inspiration, Samuel. My consternation over Mollie Pitman is trivial compared to what you've been through."

He shook his head. "I don't know the half of what you're up to, Miss Hattie. But I'm guessing you've made your sacrifices, same as all of us here."

Impulsively, she stuck out her hand. "Thank you, Samuel."

Surprise showed on his face. He looked quickly to the right and left, then gripped her hand, his fingers strong and warm, and shook it. Then, just as quickly, he let go. "Things will all work out in the end, Miss Hattie. We have to believe that."

"I surely hope so," she said.

~ ~ ~

The next day, Major Booth called Hattie in for Mollie's full interrogation. True to what she'd told the arresting officers, she was more than forthcoming, incriminating herself at every turn as she spoke of where she'd come from, her connections with General Forrest, and posing as a man so she could fight with the Confederates. She went on to say that if Major Booth would send her out with ten of his men, she'd lead them to General Forrest so they could capture him. And if that wasn't enough, she hinted that the Federals should enlist her to spy on their behalf.

Listening to her go on in this vein, Hattie became increasingly frustrated. Though she knew it shouldn't matter, she couldn't help but feel as if Mollie was intentionally stealing her thunder. By giving herself up and telling Booth everything he wanted to know, she was making Hattie's involvement irrelevant.

At last, the interview was finished. Booth sent Mollie off with the guards, then turned to Hattie. "Well, Miss Thomas. What have you to add to the evidence?"

Hattie leaned forward. "The testimony Miss Pitman gave aligns with what she revealed to me. But that doesn't mean she's being truthful, only consistent in her story."

Booth raised an eyebrow. "I appreciate your observation, Miss Thomas. But I see little reason to doubt Miss Pitman's word."

Hattie could scarcely contain her anger. "She's a Confederate spy. Surely that's reason enough for doubt."

"But you heard what she said. She's committed to the Union now."

Hattie suppressed a sigh. "Major Booth, I understand your wanting to believe Miss Pitman if only on the general understanding that her womanhood precludes her from deceiving you. But I remind you that a spy's work is predicated on deception."

He tapped his pencil end over end. "What about Miss Pitman's offer to lead us to General Forrest?"

"She says he's her uncle. Do you truly think she'd betray him? It's a trap. Your men would be ambushed, and she'd escape."

He nodded. "What about her claim that Forrest will attack within the week, with the intent of liberating her?"

Hattie shook her head. "She's grasping at straws. She has told me all along that General Forrest plans to attack this fort. Why would that now hinge on liberating her?"

"Maybe she only means that he now has additional motivation."

There he went again, giving Mollie the benefit of the doubt. Hattie didn't know which part of this she should attribute to the major's kindness and which part she should credit to Mollie, who in her oddly frank and disarming way seemed to be winning him over. Either way, it was time to put an end to it.

Hattie drew herself up, holding the major's gaze. "Miss Pitman harmed the Union by operating as a Confederate spy. She will harm it even more if she's allowed to pretend she's in our service."

He raised an eyebrow. "You think we should reject her offer to spy for us."

Hattie pressed her hands flat on her lap. "Absolutely. You've got quite enough evidence to convict her at trial."

"You'd see her hanged?"

His blunt wording took Hattie aback. "See her come to harm is not my intent, sir. I only wish to see her and others like her kept from damaging our chances at victory. So if I may, I'd like to get on with my testimony and get back to Nashville."

The major set down his pen. "I hope I haven't misled you, Miss Thomas. I am not equipped to organize a trial here at Fort Pillow. In the morning, I intend to send Miss Pitman to St. Louis to stand trial. If you'd be so kind as to escort her, you may give your full testimony there."

Hattie hesitated. She had little interest in St. Louis and even less in escorting Mollie. "I really should be returning to Nashville," she said. "I could write up my statement, and you could send a soldier with Mollie."

"With Bolivar in Rebel hands, you're better off going back via St. Louis," he said. "Plenty of trains you can catch between there and Nashville."

She smoothed her skirts, reminding herself that compared to all that Samuel had been through, very little was being asked of her. "Very well. I don't suppose a day or two will matter one way or the other."

~ ~ ~

After a fitful night's sleep, Hattie woke the next morning at dawn. Rain had fallen off and on during the night, and while the sound of it beating on the canvas tent was soothing, she'd been startled awake each time it started up. No reason for jitters, she told herself. If anything, she should be excited to be moving on. A short trip downriver, and she'd be rid of Mollie Pitman for good.

She rose from her cot and got dressed. As she fastened her saddlebags, she heard men's shouts followed by rounds of gunfire. Lifting the tent flap, she saw soldiers scurrying about. Spotting a familiar face, she called out, "Samuel!"

He hurried toward her, and she saw the alarm in his eyes. "Forrest's men. They're here. Major's sending out a skirmish line. You stay put for now, Miss Hattie. Long as our lines hold, you'll be safe."

Nodding, she withdrew into her tent. Perched on her cot, she heard the firing increase. It was only the garrison's response, she told herself, securing the fort as Major Booth had said they would. The Union troops were disciplined and ready. They'd turn the Rebels back.

Still, Hattie's heart raced. According to Mollie, many of Forrest's newest recruits were hate-filled and ruthless. Then again, this might be yet another of Mollie's deceptions. And how convenient, Hattie thought, that Forrest's men had swooped in on the very day she should have been transferred to Memphis.

Rising from her cot, Hattie went again to the tent flap and peered out. Hattie began to pace. The gunfire sounded even more intense, including what sounded like artillery fire coming from directly below the fort on the Mississippi River. Union soldiers dashed from earthwork to earthwork, taking position to fire on the advancing enemy.

None could be spared to guard Mollie, Hattie realized. In the confusion, she could easily escape. Ignoring the sinking feeling that she was already too late, Hattie ran from her tent. The pop-pop-pop of gunfire filled her ears. A cannon boomed, and she ducked beside a tent, her hands covering her ears.

She rose to see a soldier stumble past, clutching his bloodied arm. She reached for him, wanting to help.

"Get away, miss," he said. "Get as far away as you can."

As he staggered toward the hospital tent, Hattie began running again. A bullet whizzed past her shoulder, too close for comfort. Finally, just inside the second ring of earthworks, she reached Mollie's cabin. As she'd suspected, no one stood guard.

She burst through the unlatched door. Startled, Mollie looked up from where she sat on her cot. "You shouldn't be here," she said. "They're coming for me."

"No one's coming for you." Hattie crossed her arms at her chest. "And you're not going anywhere."

Mollie tipped her chin in her odd way. "I didn't say I'd go with them. I'm on your side now."

"You needn't keep up your ruse with me," Hattie said. "I've seen through it from the start."

Mollie shot up from where she sat. "It's not a ruse."

Hattie's fisted hands went to her hips. "You're only trying to avoid punishment," she said.

Mollie shook her head with a child's wild abandon. "Not true."

"If anything, you intend to help the South more by trying to learn our secrets. You might be able to hoodwink Major Booth, but you'll never convince me."

Mollie's eyes flashed. "You have a lot of nerve, telling me—"

Samuel burst into the cabin, cutting her off. "Miss Pitman, Miss Thomas. Sure glad you're both all right. I've come to take you to the river."

"But Major Booth—" Mollie began.

"Major Booth is dead." Tears glistened in Samuel's eyes. "Riding the lines, encouraging us soldiers, he took a bullet."

"Dead." Hattie echoed, struggling to take this in.

"Major Bradfield is in charge now," Samuel said. "They've got us outnumbered, three to one. We've repulsed two attacks already, but I'm not so sure we can hold back a third. Can't get our guns depressed to where they're shooting from."

Hattie glared at Mollie. The Rebels knew exactly where to position themselves because of what Mollie had told them.

"You ladies best follow me down to the river," Samuel continued. "There's boats there, and we're loading up as many noncombatants as they can hold."

"I'm not leaving," Mollie said defiantly. "If General Forrest sees me boarding a riverboat, he'll attempt a rescue, and that will only put the other evacuees in danger."

Hattie grabbed her by the arm. "You're in no position to call the shots, not when it's your intelligence that gave Forrest the upper hand. You're coming with me to Memphis, and I'm turning you over to the authorities there. Your little run of make-believe is over."

Chapter Nine

APRIL 12, 1864

C lutching Mollie's arm, Hattie ran as fast as her skirts allowed, following Samuel toward the bluff. It was hard to tell for sure amid all the confusion, but it looked as if Federal soldiers were retreating behind the innermost embankment.

As they neared the bluff, Mollie froze in place, refusing to go any farther.

Turning, Hattie saw flames shooting up from where they'd left.

"Forrest's men," Mollie said numbly. "They'll set fire to everything that will burn."

"There's nothing to be done for it now." Struggling not to lose sight of Samuel, Hattie tugged her forward.

At the bluff's edge, they joined a stream of camp followers picking their way down a rock-strewn path to the river. A few of the women wailed, but most were silent, their faces hardened in the way of battle-worn soldiers. Partway down, Hattie lost her footing, and Samuel had to grab her by the arm to keep her from slipping.

When they got to the riverbank, Hattie saw the other noncombatants, many of them Negroes, huddling near the water. One by one, soldiers were helping them aboard the *New Era*, a paddleboat which, according to Samuel, made regular runs between Memphis and points upriver.

Hattie glanced about for Mollie, fearing she might escape in the chaos.

"Right here." Mollie waved her hand in the air, looking almost bemused. "You needn't worry. Even if I was inclined to, there's no escaping from here."

Gesturing for them to follow, Samuel led them toward the *New Era*. But as they neared the vessel, two crewmen pulled up the gangplank.

Samuel waved his arms at them. "Two more here!"

"No room," a crewman yelled from the deck. Black smoke puffed from the stack, and the boat pulled away from the shore, bullets from above pinging the water all around.

At Samuel's urging, the three of them retreated to the base of the bluff. Huddled at its face, they were shielded from the worst of the gunfire.

"Forrest's sharpshooters," Mollie said. "They're well-trained."

A barrage of bullets zinged over their heads, blanketing the path down the bluff. "You'll never get back up there alive," Hattie said to Samuel. "You've got to come with us." She pointed to a smaller paddle wheeler downriver from where they stood, hugging close to the bank. "Do you think we can convince that boat to let us on?" Hattie asked Samuel.

"Worth a try," Samuel said, sweat beading on his brow. "Stay here much longer, and we're target practice for the Rebels."

Running along the base of the bluff, they came within shouting distance of the smaller paddle wheeler. With the *New Era* taking all the fire, this vessel, the *Silver Cloud*, sat thirty yards from shore.

Stepping away from the bluff, Samuel again waved his arms in the air. "Transport to Memphis," he yelled.

A crewman on deck shook his head. "Not coming to shore," the man yelled back. "Too dangerous."

Hattie tugged Samuel's sleeve. "Can you swim?"

He nodded curtly.

"So can I." She turned to Mollie. "You?"

"Yes," Mollie said.

Hattie hitched up her skirts. "If we get in the water, we'll be harder to hit. And if we get to the boat, they surely won't turn us away."

Samuel eyed the top of the bluff. The gunfire was still tracking the *New Era* as it steamed upriver. But once the bigger vessel was out of range, the guns were sure to turn on the smaller one.

"Better hurry," he said. "Before they reposition."

Hattie didn't have to be told twice. She waded into the river. Lapping at her ankles, the water sent chills up her spine. The river mud sucked at her slippers, but they held fast as she went in up to her calves, up to her knees. Behind her, she heard splashing. Mollie and Samuel, she hoped.

"Hey, there!" yelled the crewman from the *Silver Cloud*. "You can't swim in those skirts. You'll drown."

He was right. Hattie's dress and petticoat were dragging her down. "Throw a line!" she called out.

With a wild-eyed look, the crewman grabbed a life ring from the boat's stern and tossed it toward Hattie. She sloshed toward it, going in up to her waist. She grabbed hold, and the crewman pulled the rope hand over hand, reeling her toward the boat like a big fish on a line. Moments later, she was floating alongside the vessel, clinging to the life ring. A second crewman joined the first, and together, they pulled her aboard.

Dripping wet and chilled to the bone, Hattie stood on the deck. Some threw a blanket around her shoulders, and she hugged it tightly. Near the boat's bow, she saw Mollie, clinging to a second life ring. The crewmen rushed forward to hoist her out of the water.

But where was Samuel? Swimming, he should have reached the boat first. Her hand shielding her eyes from the sun, she searched the water. Seeing no one, she turned her gaze toward the riverbank. Dodging bullets, Samuel was scaling the bluff.

Watching him, her every muscle tensed. After what he'd said yesterday, she should have known he wouldn't retreat. *Please, keep him safe. His wife and their little girl, they're—*

A barrage of gunfire interrupted her silent prayer. In horror, Hattie saw Samuel straighten, then fall from the bluff to the beach. A sob caught in her throat. If he would only get up, perhaps he could crawl to the base of the bluff.

But he lay silent and still, his face turned toward the sky. From above came another round of gunfire, bullets piercing his body, spraying up blood all around him.

Hattie turned away, and her sobs overcame her. For Samuel. For his wife and daughter. For every life lost in a war that seemed as though it would go on forever.

The *Silver Cloud*'s engines fired up, and the boat's paddle began to turn. As the boat started downriver, the sound of gunfire receding in the distance, a stranger helped Hattie to a bench.

Samuel knew the risks, Hattie reminded herself. *Said he would sacrifice his life for the benefit of his race.* But he'd died because of her, because of Mollie. And to be shot over and over and over—no one deserved that.

Her tears finally spent, Hattie wiped her eyes with her sleeve. War was personal. She knew that all too well, whether it meant losing the one she'd loved most in all the world or losing a good man she'd only just met.

~ ~ ~

By the time the *Silver Cloud* docked in Memphis, Hattie had gathered her wits about her. Much as she'd like to get back to Nashville, she owed it to Samuel, and to every soldier who had tried to defend Fort Pillow, to deliver Mollie Pitman into the custody of Union officials and provide the evidence she'd amassed against her.

Her clothes still damp, she descended the plank behind Mollie. "Don't even think about trying to get away," Hattie warned. "Or I'll have every soldier within fifty miles of here on your trail. I'm sure there's plenty who'll be out for blood when they learn what's happened at Fort Pillow."

Glancing back at her, Mollie gave a derisive look, but she made no retort. All around the docks, people were already talking about what they'd learned from refugees of Forrest's attack. Not a battle, people were saying, but a massacre, and it was the Negro soldiers who were getting the worst of it.

In stony silence, Hattie steered Mollie toward a waiting carriage. She instructed the driver to take them to Fort Pickering. Climbing inside, she was forced to look Mollie face to face for the first time since they'd left the riverbank.

"You're not the only person feeling bad about Samuel, you know," Mollie said as the carriage rolled into the street.

"If you cared about him or any other Negro, you'd never have spied for General Forrest," Hattie shot back.

"You saw how many times he was shot," Mollie said. "I warned you it would be like that. There's nothing that inflames a Confederate more than a Negro soldier."

"Is that all that matters to you?" Hattie said. "Being right?"

"I'm only saying my insights can be useful if a person chooses to listen to them."

"That person won't be me."

Arms crossed at her chest, Mollie fell silent. For the remainder of the ride, she kept quiet, which was fine by Hattie.

As at Fort Pillow, Confederate troops had taken control of Fort Pickering at the start of the war, only to see it fall to the Union with the rest of West Tennessee. But as Hattie saw when the carriage driver pulled up at the main entrance, the Memphis fort was far more expansive than Fort Pillow, with buildings and fortifications stretching nearly as far as the eye could see. It would take a lot more spies than Mollie Pitman to give Forrest enough intelligence to successfully retake it, Hattie thought, though after his success at Fort Pillow, she suspected he'd try it someday.

After some wrangling with the guards, she and Mollie were admitted past the gates. A sullen young soldier escorted them through the fort, where Hattie noticed many Negroes employed in all sorts of tasks, from laborers to soldiers. Escaped slaves, Hattie thought, as Samuel had been. She wished there was some way for her to track down his wife in Memphis. Hard as it would be to deliver the news of him being shot, it would be better coming from someone like herself who had known him if only for a short while.

The soldier deposited them at the Provost Marshal's office, headquartered in a long brick building with oddly ornate lattice-work framing the veranda.

"I'll do the talking," Hattie warned Mollie as they were ushered inside.

"You always do," Mollie muttered. But she kept her mouth shut as Hattie explained to the marshal, a plump, gray-haired officer, how they'd ended up in Memphis.

The marshal looked Mollie up and down. "She doesn't look like a smuggler. Or a spy."

"Well, she is," Hattie said. "If not for her, General Forrest might have had a much harder time at Fort Pillow."

"I gave myself up before the attack," Mollie said, breaking her silence.

"But not before passing along everything she'd observed to Forrest and his men," Hattie said.

"My loyalties lie with the Union now," Mollie said, looking only at the marshal.

"So she says," Hattie added.

"Enough." The marshal held up his hand, palm out. "The fact is, she belongs in St. Louis. You'll have to take her there. I'll telegraph ahead, let them know you're coming."

"I'm not her nanny," Hattie protested. "Surely you can spare a soldier to escort her. I'll make a written statement of the evidence against her."

He shrugged. "Suit yourself. But I don't know how much weight a written statement would carry. If you truly want to see her punished, you're better off delivering her to St. Louis yourself."

Hattie sighed. When Elliott had proposed this assignment, she'd been certain she could pull it off without a hitch. Now it all seemed to be going wrong.

"Fine," she said. "I'll take her to St. Louis tomorrow. Until then, your men can keep watch over her. I've had quite enough of her."

~ ~ ~

The provost marshal agreed to send Mollie over to Irving Block Prison for the night, leaving Hattie free to roam about the city. But she couldn't get Samuel's death out of her mind. From the news circulating in Memphis, hundreds more soldiers, most of them Negroes, had been slaughtered at Fort Pillow. Many had been trying to surrender, folks said, and the Rebels shot them anyhow, often multiple times as they'd done to Samuel. Such hatred, Hattie thought. It was hard to fathom.

Bedraggled and still a bit damp from the river, she checked into a hotel. Stripping down to her chemise, she laid her clothes about the room to dry, then fell into bed and slept straight through till dawn. When she woke, her first thought was how thankful she was that she had not relived the massacre in her dreams. Many who were there would be reliving it for years to come, she knew.

Her clothing was dry but stiff and pungent with the smell of river water, but having nothing else to wear, she put them on and set out for Irving Block Prison. Even at this hour of the morning, the air was humid, the sky heavy with the promise of rain.

At the prison, she inquired after Mollie. Moments later, two guards hauled Mollie out, one on each arm. Mollie's hands were cuffed at her waist. At last, Hattie thought, someone besides me recognizes that for all her talk, she's a Rebel through and through.

"Behaved herself," said one of the guards as he removed her handcuffs. "I'll give her that much."

"And why wouldn't I?" Mollie shook her wrists free of the cuffs. "As I told the warden, I'm on your side."

Hattie was tired of arguing the point. Eying the handcuffs, she wondered if she should ask the guard to put them back on in case Mollie tried to escape. No, she decided. That would only draw undue attention, and Mollie had generated enough of that already.

"Wretched place," Mollie muttered as they left the prison. "Filthy, and no order or discipline."

"Maybe Alton will be more to your liking," Hattie said, naming the large facility near St. Louis.

Mollie eyed her disdainfully, but at least she did not repeat her refrain about being loyal to the Union now.

As they proceeded to the waterfront, Mollie walked placidly beside Hattie. To a stranger, they would seem to be two friends out for a morning stroll, Hattie thought. Nearing the riverfront, they passed a dress shop. Normally, Hattie gave little thought to her clothes, but given the sorry state of her current dress, she gazed longingly at the blue silk frock in the window.

"Look," Mollie said. "Something's caught fire."

Turning from the window, Hattie saw a plume of black smoke billowing toward the sky. "Something on the water," she said. "I hope it's not our boat."

Just then, she heard a woman's voice, calling out to Mollie by name. Mollie turned, and Hattie with her. On the steps to a waterfront hotel stood a woman in a pale green dress, flounced and hooped, her dark hair falling in ringlets to her shoulders, her features sharp but not unattractive.

But it was the man at her side who got Hattie's attention. Broad-shouldered and handsome, his bright smile faded when he saw Hattie. She pressed her lips firm, trying not to reveal her shock and outrage. What was Anne's husband doing in Memphis, an attractive woman clinging to his arm?

The woman started down the steps toward them, dragging Franklin along with her. "I declare, Mollie," she said as she descended. "You do get around."

"Belle Edmondson," Mollie said. "I figure if I was in Memphis, sooner or later I'd run into you. What have you been up to?"

Reaching street level, Belle looked up at Franklin, her eyes sparkling. "Why, this delightful family friend is visiting over from Indiana. We've just been catching up."

Hattie had never seen Franklin looking less in control of a situation. Then, seeming to gather his senses, he pulled his arm from Belle's and stepped toward Hattie. "What a surprise to see you, Hattie. What brings you to Memphis?"

"Business," she said coolly.

"Same as I," Franklin said.

"How fortunate that you've got a friend in the city," Hattie said.

"As do you," Franklin said, nodding at Mollie.

"We aren't friends," Mollie said bluntly.

Belle's laughter was like the tinkling of wind chimes. "Ever one to say what's on your mind, aren't you, Mollie? We were just enjoying coffee here at my hotel when we heard about the fire." She gestured toward the horizon, where the black plume had grown. "Of course we had to come out for a look."

Franklin squinted into the distance. "They say it's a steamboat."

"Commissioned for military transport," Belle said with an odd sort of glee. "How unfortunate."

Shifting side to side, Franklin seemed to mostly have recovered himself. "I'd best be heading out now. Good to see you, Hattie."

"Likewise," she said, locking eyes with him. "I assume you're headed home soon. Do give Anne my best."

He tipped his hat. "I most certainly will. And what shall I tell her of you? I'm sure she'll want to know what you're doing in Memphis."

She held his gaze steady. "Anne knows I had business in Tennessee. I'm surprised she didn't mention it to you."

Mollie tugged her sleeve. "Our boat," she said. "It's departing soon."

"Headed for St. Louis, I suppose. You do seem to love that city." Belle gave a wry smile. "I hope your boat doesn't go up in flames too."

With a glare that she hoped imprinted in Franklin's memory, Hattie murmured her goodbyes. Walking briskly, she and Mollie proceeded toward the docks.

"Who is that woman?" Hattie asked once they were out of earshot.

"A spy and smuggler in the service of the Confederacy," Mollie said. "And it seems the two of you have a friend in common."

Hattie shot her a look. "An acquaintance. Have you seen him with her before?"

Mollie shrugged. "Belle has any number of male companions. Hard to keep track. But trust me, if he's associated with her, he's not to be trusted."

"I'll be the judge of that," Hattie said.

"Right," Mollie said. "Because you won't believe a word I say anyhow."

This didn't merit a response, and so Hattie didn't give one. As they proceeded toward the docks, she fell silent, wishing she could erase the encounter with Franklin from her mind. He'd said Belle was a family friend. She should take him at his word. If she was also a spy and a smuggler, that didn't mean Franklin knew anything about it. Hattie wasn't going to discredit him on Mollie's say-so. She owed Anne that much.

The smoke in the air thickened as they approached the river. Fire wagons were at the scene, pumping water from the river, trying to douse out the flames.

"Belle sure seemed pleased about that fire," Mollie said as much to herself as to Hattie. "I wonder if she was involved in having it set."

Hattie shook her head. She'd had quite enough of Mollie's suppositions and lies.

It was almost enough to make Hattie wish that it had been their steamboat that had caught fire. But that was wrongheaded thinking. She would see this through to the end, and when she got to St. Louis, she'd make sure the authorities understood in no uncertain terms that a turncoat was not to be trusted.

Chapter Ten

APRIL 13, 1864

A s in towns in other border states, Hattie sensed a general restlessness in St. Louis. Outwardly, the Federals controlled the city, but the undercurrent on the streets leaned decidedly toward Dixie.

"My fourth visit here in as many months," Mollie said, pointing the way to the provost marshal's office. Not knowing the city, Hattie was forced to follow her lead, but she wasn't happy about it.

Provost Marshal John Sanderson did not keep them waiting long. As a clerk ushered Hattie and Mollie into his office, he rose from his desk. Balding, he had gray whiskers and grandfatherly blue eyes.

"So this is the spy I've been told about," he said. "Or one of you is, at any rate. The woman who has now taken up with the Federals."

Mollie offered a half-smile. "That's me, sir."

"Well, then." He turned his gaze on Hattie. "And you must be the woman who found her out."

"And quite proficiently too," Mollie said.

Hattie glared at her. The last thing she wanted was Mollie's praise. "Lieutenant Elliott of Nashville's Army Police dispatched me with orders to apprehend her."

"Except I turned myself in," Mollie said, looking pleased with herself. "I no longer wish to be associated with the Confederates except in such capacity as would aid the Union."

"That's what she told Major Booth." Hattie paused, overcome for a moment with remembering that horrific day.

Sanderson shook his head. "Tragic, what happened to him. To all his men. Simply outnumbered." He gestured toward the chairs in front of his desk. "Please, ladies. Sit. When I received the telegram from St. Louis, I cleared my afternoon to meet with you."

Mollie sat, arranging her skirts about her.

Hattie remained standing. Despite her efforts, Fort Pillow had fallen, and in the most disastrous way. If she was truly going to prove herself going forward, she needed to make sure her concerns were heard. "Sir, if I may, I'd like a word with you in private."

Sanderson looked from her to Mollie and back again. "Very well. Excuse us please, Miss Pitman."

He led Hattie out the door, then closed it behind him. She followed him to the end of the hallway, where they stood in front of a large window draped with heavy red velvet curtains. The afternoon sun warming her shoulder, Hattie faced the colonel. "You strike me as a sensible man, Colonel Sanderson. I expect you see through this ruse of Miss Pitman's."

He studied her, his gaze kind but searching. "You don't believe she has truly switched sides."

"I do not. Before the attack, I shared with Major Booth all she'd confessed to me about her spying and smuggling, much of it here in this city. It was only when he sent soldiers to arrest her that she professed a sudden change of heart. I ask you, Colonel, could you so easily abandon your loyalties to the cause you've fought for these many years?"

His slumped shoulders straightened. "I could not."

"Nor could I. It seems clear to me that Mollie Pitman is only professing a change of loyalty to keep herself out of prison. But Major Booth, God rest his soul, seemed rather persuaded by her claims. I hope that you will scrutinize them more closely."

He glanced out the window, where an oak bough danced in the wind, adorned with the fresh green of springtime. "You have evidence that Miss Pitman cannot be taken at her word?"

Hattie shook her head. "Only my suspicions, sir. She has not been especially forthcoming with me since her arrest."

He stroked his side whiskers. "I understand she gave warning of the Fort Pillow attack."

"She did," Hattie said. "But when the attack was underway, she had to be forced to leave. I believe she was counting on Forrest's men to carry her back into their fold."

"What else?"

Hattie jutted her chin. "Well, nothing except that, as I'm sure you recognize, she could do great damage by ingratiating herself here. Not just by sharing misleading information but also by gathering facts about our side that she could easily slip to the enemy if she's allowed any sort of freedom. As far as I'm concerned, she should be locked up at the military prison at Alton for the duration of the war."

"But you do understand, Miss Thomas, that I have a duty to extract as much information from her as I can. In doing so, I will make my own assessment."

"Understood." It took some effort for Hattie to keep her voice even. Again it came down to her word against Mollie's.

"Which is not to say I don't value your assistance," the colonel added. "I'd like you to sit in on my interviews to help verify whatever claims Miss Pitman makes."

"I am at your service, sir," Hattie said. So much for a swift return to Nashville. But if meant keeping Mollie from doing any more damage, it would be worth it.

Colonel Sanderson led her back to his office. Hattie took the chair next to Mollie. Sitting at his desk, the provost marshal nudged up his sleeves, took up his pen, and began his interview. "Suppose you tell me a bit about yourself, Miss Pitman, and how you came into service with the Confederacy."

Mollie glanced at Hattie, then proceeded to give more or less the same account she'd shared in the days leading up to her arrest, about growing up poor on a Tennessee farm and losing family members one by one to illness and accidents. When she got to the part about dressing as a man and helping raise a contingent of guerrilla fighters under General Forrest's command, the colonel's eyes widened. But he took notes on all she said, including how she'd abandoned her soldier's uniform to take up spying for the Confederacy at her Uncle Bedford's request.

Sanderson put down his pen. "Your uncle, you say?"

"On my mother's side. Her half-brother, actually. They weren't especially close."

Taking up his pen again, he made a note. "And yet when Federal soldiers came to arrest you, you gave yourself over willingly. Why is that, Miss Pitman?"

Mollie leaned forward, her hands in her lap. "When I started out in the war, I had a most intense prejudice against the people of the North, having been exposed to many defamatory notions as to their character, views, and purpose. But during my service with the Confederates, especially during my trips to this city, I came to understand that those notions were wrong."

The colonel glanced at Hattie, who raised a skeptical eyebrow. Then he looked back at Mollie. "Tell me more about this change in sentiment, Miss Pitman."

"Just look around this city," Mollie said. "Business is flourishing. People are thriving. Everything is entirely unlike conditions in the South. I felt compelled to trust my own observations and impressions over what I'd been led to believe. Once I opened my eyes to the truth, I saw that Union officers and soldiers are not the desperadoes I'd believed them to be."

At this, the colonel sat up straighter. "We do our best to maintain the discipline that aligns with our principles."

Flattery, Hattie thought ruefully. The oldest trick in the book. Turning to Mollie, she said, "Yet you must have seen that our goals and aims are not at all aligned with the ones you risked your life for."

Mollie looked at Hattie as if she was a child seeking an answer that was altogether obvious. "Wars start with goals and aims. But at the heart of the conflict, it's the people who matter. You of all people should understand the impact a Northerner's kindness has had on me. You rescued me twice, once when my horse was stolen and again by insisting I leave Fort Pillow before I was burned to death in my cabin."

So now Mollie was using her as proof that her change of heart was legitimate. Hattie could not let that stand. "I only offered what kindness I'd extend to anyone under those circumstances," she said, speaking as evenly as she could manage.

Mollie shrugged. "Nonetheless, your kindness had a transformative effect."

This assertion, too, the colonel recorded in his tidy, compact script. Hattie feared he was already softening toward Mollie, much as Major Booth had.

"If you were so convinced of the goodness of Northerners, why didn't you desert long ago?" Hattie asked. "Why wait until Federal soldiers came to arrest you?"

Mollie held her head high. "Desertion is a dishonorable act. I would do nothing to disgrace myself."

"And changing sides is honorable?" Hattie asked.

Mollie turned her dark eyes on her questioner with more intensity than Hattie had seen from her before. "Once I determined I had a duty to tell the truth and do what I could to atone for my past, I resolved to throw myself at the mercy of the Government. And for the most part, I've not been disappointed in the results."

The colonel's lips turned in the faintest of smiles. "And so shall you continue to be treated, Miss Pitman, provided you prove as honest and forthcoming as you're being now."

~ ~ ~

Leaving the provost marshal's office, Hattie had much weighing on her mind. Her inability to once and for all convince the men in charge that Mollie was duping them. Her troubling encounter with Franklin Stone in Memphis. The massacre of Fort Pillow's brave soldiers, including Samuel, deaths that she wished desperately she'd been able to prevent.

Of lesser consequence was that even after she'd given over all her evidence against Mollie, Colonel Sanderson had asked her to stay on another day or two while he continued to question Mollie. Reluctantly, Hattie had agreed. She'd come this far. Might as well see it through to the end, though what that end would be, she couldn't yet tell.

Hattie had left Nashville longing for direction, for purpose, for a means of proving herself. But with each passing day, that aim seemed to slip further from her reach. What had made her think she was destined for any sort of accomplishment? She was a woman, after all, and women were rarely taken seriously. Unless, it seemed, they professed to be other than what they were, as Mollie Pitman did.

At least Colonel Sanderson had freed her of the burden of watching over Mollie. Despite his softening toward the Rebel spy, he had ordered his guards to take her to the women's prison on Gratiot Street, across from the larger men's facility.

That left Hattie feeling freer than she had in days. Walking through the commercial district near the St. Louis riverfront, she passed office buildings and stores, many with stone or cast iron facades. Proceeding past the Grand Opera House, she thought fondly of the brief time she'd spent filling in at the box office of Grover's National Theatre in Washington. She'd always loved the stage, and she'd enjoyed even the brief stint she'd had in Nashville, onstage with Pauline. Acting a part, she could forget her troubles, her past. And there was a genuine camaraderie among the actors that she felt wistful for now.

She wondered about Alice Gray, the actress she'd grown close to during her time at the National. Did she ever tour this far West? Alice's beau, John Wilkes Booth, had played to an adoring audience in Nashville shortly before Hattie's return there, but as far as Hattie knew, Alice hadn't been with him. Perhaps Booth's wandering eye had brought an end to the relationship.

Rounding the corner to the Everett House Hotel, Hattie stopped and bought a paper from the newsboy shouting out headlines. Then she proceeded to her room, where she sat on the bed, happy to be off her feet. Taking up the paper, she thought she might find an announcement about the shows playing at the Grand Opera. Attending a performance might ease the loneliness she was starting to feel.

Briefly, she scanned the headlines, which were mostly about Lincoln's dismal chances for re-election in the fall. She also saw an article about the trouble the Rebels were causing in East Tennessee. With horses being robbed and the necessities of life stripped from them, the correspondent questioned how the half-starved people there would survive the year. Hattie's thoughts drifted to John Elliott, who'd come to Nashville from East Tennessee after Rebel guerrilla Champ Ferguson murdered his wife. Would he return there after the war, she wondered, or were there too many painful memories there?

She shook off the thought. What John Elliott did or did not do when the war ended was none of her concern.

Paging further, she found a small item saying the Opera House was currently closed for renovations, with an expected reopening next month. So much for an evening's diversion from her troubles.

She glanced down at her dress. Instead of dreaming of a night at the Opera House, she should have been scouting out a place to purchase a fresh change of clothes. Just her luck, prison officials would see to Mollie getting clean garments, and Mollie would upstage her in that too.

But if they didn't...An idea began to percolate in Hattie's mind. Mollie had all sorts of connections around St. Louis, people who had aided her smuggling and spying. If she was going to continue to pass along Union secrets, she'd need to align with her network in the city. That would be hard to do from prison—her cohorts likely didn't even know she'd been apprehended.

But a shopping trip on the streets of St. Louis for a much-needed change of clothes would provide just the opportunity Mollie needed to reach out to her fellow smugglers and spies. Of course, she'd need an escort. Hattie would volunteer, then catch her in an act of betrayal, proving once and for all the danger she posed if Union officials continued to allow her to dupe them.

Hattie smiled to herself, pleased that she might finally be one step ahead of Mollie Pitman. Tomorrow, if Mollie didn't propose an outing to procure a change of clothes, Hattie would offer, seeing as how she, too, needed a new dress. The trap would be set.

With this plan in place, Hattie returned to flipping through the newspaper. She was about to set it aside when a small headline caught her eye: *Miss Dr. Edith Greenfield Heard From.*

Eagerly, Hattie read through the item:

A letter from Castle Thunder, Richmond, has been received by the mother of Dr. Edith Greenfield, who from all appearances is bearing her imprisonment lightly. "I am a prisoner of war," she writes. "But I hope you will not grieve me. I am living in a brick 'castle' with food enough to eat and a clean cot to sleep on. I have a roommate, twenty years of age, from Mississippi. I am much happier than I would be in such circumstances as other ladies might envy. The officers are kind and gentlemanly, and I expect to be released on exchange before long."

This didn't sound at all like the Castle Thunder experience Hattie had endured, with wretched food, filthy linens, a flimsy cot, and an army of rats lurking in every dark corner. But in a letter to her mother, she understood why Edith would paint a bright picture so as not to cause worry. At any rate, Hattie was glad Edith was well enough to write and gladder still that there was hope for her release.

~ ~ ~

When Hattie arrived at the provost marshal's office the next morning, Mollie was already seated in front of Colonel Sanderson's desk, chatting amiably with him. She looked refreshed and composed, not at all like a woman who'd spent the night in prison. But she had on the same dress she'd been wearing, an indication that the trap Hattie had planned just might work.

As Mollie and the colonel greeted her in turn, Hattie had the distinct feeling of having intruded. What was it about Mollie Pitman that charmed men so? She was not unattractive, but there was something disarming about her gaze, as if she was quietly assessing one's every move. Perhaps this keen attention played to a man's ego, Hattie thought.

She took her seat beside Mollie. Sanderson moved a stack of papers to one side of his desk, then took several clean sheets from his desk drawer. He cleared his throat. "I've looked over your papers, Miss Pitman, and I don't see that you've taken the Oath of Allegiance."

Mollie offered one of her rare, sweet smiles. "Only because no one has offered to administer it."

"Then we shall remedy that situation. Miss Thomas, if I can prevail upon you to hold the Bible." He nodded at the volume sitting on one corner of his desk.

Hattie picked up the Bible and held it in front of Mollie. The Rebel spy placed one hand flat on its cover and held the other in the air. Phrase by phrase, Sanderson delivered the lines of the oath. Phrase by phrase, Mollie repeated them. "I solemnly swear that I will henceforth support the Constitution of the United States, and defend it against the assaults of all its enemies; that I will hereafter be, and conduct myself as a true and faithful citizen of the United States..."

Hattie found herself unable to attend to the words, which she knew were blithely administered far too many times by Union officials who failed to understand that their enemies, taking to heart that platitude about all being fair in love and war, had no qualms about swearing to something that they in no way intended to adhere to.

"...so help me God," Mollie said, concluding the process. She had a knack for looking sincere, Hattie had to admit.

Hattie returned the Bible to the colonel's desk, and Sanderson started in with his questions. His first focus was on the trips Mollie had made to St. Louis earlier in the year. Mollie repeated much of what she'd told Hattie about obtaining supplies from local merchants and transporting them by steamer to the South, where other operatives had delivered them to Forrest's troops. Responding to the colonel's queries, she was forthcoming with the names and addresses of the St. Louis merchants who'd assisted in the enterprise. Hattie made a mental note of these. They'd be the ones Mollie would try to connect with if given a chance.

"You would testify against these men in court?" Sanderson asked.

"Certainly," Mollie said. "Though I would want to do so under an alias. I'd rather my former associates didn't know I'd been arrested."

So you can keep passing them secrets, Hattie thought.

"You fear retribution from General Forrest?" Sanderson asked.

"I'm not inclined to fear anything, sir. I wish only to serve the Union, and I can best do so if my identity isn't compromised."

A veiled offer to spy for the Union. Hattie shot the colonel a warning look. Surely he realized the disasters that would follow if he took Mollie up on her offer.

"Anything you'd like to add, Miss Thomas?"

Only that Mollie Pitman is a charlatan and a danger to the Union, Hattie fumed inwardly. But she had a plan in mind, and this was her opening. "I wonder if Miss Pitman would be willing to return to some of those merchants. Additional evidence might be forthcoming."

The colonel pressed his hand to his chin, seeming to consider this. "That could be helpful. Miss Pitman, are any of your former contacts aware of your arrest or your change of heart regarding the Confederacy?"

Mollie shook her head.

"Then we could send you around to speak with them. You'd need an escort, of course, and a pretext for bringing that person along."

"Miss Pitman and I both need a change of clothes following our ordeal at Fort Pillow," Hattie said. "We could go dress shopping. That would provide the necessary cover."

The colonel nodded slowly. "A reasonable plan. Miss Pitman, if I were to send you out with Miss Thomas as an escort, could you go round to some of these merchants under the pretext of shopping?"

In her curious way, Mollie tilted her head, studying Hattie. "I'd have to think about it," she said.

"Fair enough." Sanderson jotted a note. "I'd like to move on to another line of questioning, one that's of great interest to me. Are you aware of any secret order here in the North, Miss Pitman? One by which its members recognize each other by a series of signs or handshakes?"

Mollie frowned. "If I were to belong to such a group, would there be any honor in my telling you about it?"

"There are obligations binding only upon the technical points of honor," Sanderson said. "And I believe the fates of war have decreed a special destiny for you, Miss Pitman. So, yes, I think there is honor in your telling about it."

"I've sworn an oath to protect those involved," Mollie said. "If I ignore it, that's no different than ignoring the oath of loyalty I've just taken here."

"The fact is, Miss Pitman, that a good many of those you feel bound to protect are likely known to me already." He tapped the stack of papers he'd moved to one side of his desk. "You have no moral obligation to shield them when they pose a peril to this nation by virtue of their involvement with a dark and secret order."

A dark and secret order. Hattie thought of the Knights of the Golden Circle tickets she'd found in Franklin Stone's desk drawer.

Mollie sat a moment, silent and still. Then she spoke, quietly but firmly. "A great many Federal officers, present and former, belong to this order you mention. One I captured back when I was disguised as a Confederate guerrilla. When I recognized his value to the South, I let him go." She paused, staring at Hattie. "Another I encountered just a few days ago in Memphis."

Franklin. But was he a true danger, or was Mollie only making this accusation because Hattie knew him?

Sanderson held his pen poised over his notes. "And their names, Miss Pitman?"

Mollie shifted in her seat. Again her gaze fell on Hattie, who did her best to look uninterested. Then she looked back at Colonel Sanderson. "The secret order goes by different names in different parts of the country. The Knights of the Golden Circle. The Order of the American Knights. And of late, the Sons of Liberty."

Sanderson nodded curtly. "They have an elaborate structure, do they not? Supreme council, grand commanders, temples. The

most extreme Copperheads, harboring dark plans to defeat the
Union."

Not Franklin Stone, Hattie thought. Yes, he was a Copperhead,
advocating for the South to rejoin the Union on its own terms,
including slavery. And with the tickets she'd found, he might have
some peripheral association with the Sons of Liberty, if that was
what the secret order called itself now. But dark plans to defeat the
Union? That couldn't be. Whatever Franklin's complaints about
how the Union was conducting the war, he wouldn't so wholly
turn on his former comrades in arms.

Mollie smoothed her skirts. "The Sons of Liberty claim an innocuous purpose. They want to protect civil rights and bring a
swift end to the war."

The colonel frowned. "By which they mean embracing the enemy, by violent means if necessary. Isn't that so?"

"Perhaps," Mollie said plainly.

"And you are a member of this secret order, Miss Pitman?"

"Yes. One of thousands, including Jefferson Davis," she said,
naming the Confederate president. "But I'm profoundly disgusted
with it now. I wish I'd never joined."

"The supreme commanders," Sanderson said. "Who are they?"

"In the southern section, a general who has plans to retake Missouri for the South. In the northern section, a senator from Ohio."

Sanderson raised an eyebrow. "Names?"

Mollie averted her eyes to the floor. "I'd rather not say."

The colonel tapped the end of his pencil on the paper. "We'll
come back to that. These sections, they work in tandem—is that
correct?"

Looking up, Mollie nodded. "They pass information back and forth. I've carried it myself. Some is Union army strategy, gleaned from spies. The rest involves plans they intend to carry out on their own."

The colonel frowned. "What sorts of plans?"

"Riots and demonstrations in Union cities, coordinated with the Confederate army. They want to open a new set of battlelines in the North."

Sanderson nodded tersely "For instance?"

Mollie was silent a moment. "I've passed information about a navy man who will be heading north to organize a raid by water on a Union prison. He intends to release thousands of Confederate prisoners of war so they fight with the Rebels."

How much of this was true, Hattie wondered, and how much was Mollie fabricating to convince Sanderson she had truly switched sides?

Sanderson scribbled a note. "This navy man—would he be the person you encountered in Memphis?"

Mollie shook her head. "I know little about the man in Memphis. Only that he has some involvement with the Sons of Liberty."

"But you know his name?" Sanderson said.

Hattie inhaled deeply, invoking calm. Franklin's name had not passed between her and Mollie. Likely she didn't even know it.

A pained look crossed Mollie's face, though Hattie couldn't tell if it was true or feigned. "Colonel Sanderson, I have given you what information I can. But you must understand that I took an oath to this group, even if I regret it now, and as a woman of my word, I cannot reveal names or signs. I trust you have sufficient knowledge from your various sources to unravel the rest. As to this man in Memphis, there is another in this room who can tell you his name."

The colonel turned to Hattie. "Miss Thomas, you know the man in question?"

Hattie gave Mollie a sharp look. So this was her way of repaying Hattie's mistrust, by putting her on the spot.

"Miss Pitman is referring to a distinguished Union officer," Hattie said, meeting Sanderson's gaze. "He was wounded at Fredericksburg. He was in Memphis on business and went by to visit a family friend."

"Belle Edmondson," Mollie said. "A Confederate spy."

"Miss Edmondson had a rather keen interest in a fire aboard a steamship docked in Memphis yesterday morning," Hattie said.

"Almost as if she'd set it herself," Mollie said.

"Ah yes. The fire." Sanderson shuffled through his stack of papers, bringing one to the top. "Lieutenant Geery of the US Police in Memphis sent a telegram about it. He mentions your name, Miss Pitman, in connection with the fire."

Mollie jutted her chin. "Belle must have put him on my trail to divert attention from herself. She knew I was headed for St. Louis."

Sanderson turned to Hattie. "Miss Thomas, you had charge over Miss Pitman in Memphis. Would she have had an opportunity to engage in arson?"

Hattie struggled not to show the ire that rose in her throat. Mollie was trying to turn her shady associations into an indictment of Hattie's competence.

"I went to West Tennessee charged with making sure Miss Pitman was apprehended," Hattie said. "After turning her over to the authorities, my only remaining duty was to share the evidence I'd gathered against her. Due to the attack on Fort Pillow, I had little choice but to see her to Memphis and then on to St. Louis. In any case, I assure you that while I've had charge of her, I've not let her out of my sight."

With a brusque nod, Sanderson pushed aside his paper. "Very well. Enlightening as this interview has been, I've other business to attend to. Miss Pitman, I'll have a guard take you back—"

"Pardon me, Colonel," Hattie interrupted. "Aren't I to escort Miss Pitman around the shopping district so she can expose her associates there?"

The colonel stroked his whiskers. "Right. We discussed that. I'm a bit surprised, Miss Thomas, that you're proposing giving Miss Pitman free reign in the city."

"With me at her side," Hattie said. *To spy on the spy, and catch her in the act of betraying the Union, which she surely will.* "I'll return her to the women's prison by nightfall."

The colonel turned to Mollie. "Miss Pitman, I assume this scheme Miss Thomas proposes meets with your approval. Seeing as how you were forced to flee Fort Pillow without your belongings, I will provide funds for you to procure an additional frock. In the course of moving about the city, you will engage with your former associates, passing along any evidence that would lead to their arrests."

Gazing at Hattie, Mollie was silent a moment. "I appreciate the offer, Colonel Sanderson. I indeed need a new frock, and I certainly have no problem implicating my former associates, provided all is handled discretely. But I've found it's better not to rush such things. If it's all the same to you, I'd like to request an immediate transfer to Alton Prison."

The colonel raised an eyebrow. "You wouldn't rather stay here in the city?"

Mollie shook her head. "Too many Rebel eyes and ears in this city. Send me to Alton, let some time pass. Then you can have me return here to go around to the merchants as Miss Thomas proposes."

Sanderson tapped his pencil on his desk. "I see your point. And I take it you're not concerned about..." He brushed his hand in the air, vaguely indicating her clothes. "About your frock."

"I'm sure the warden at Alton can furnish a change of clothes."

Hattie could scarcely believe her ears. Mollie had taken her clever trap and turned it in her favor. She'd wait till Hattie was long gone, and then she'd get free reign of the town, no doubt sharing Union secrets everywhere she went.

Hattie turned to the provost marshal. "Colonel Sanderson, I urge you to keep a close eye on Miss Pitman. She is cleverer than you might think."

Mollie gave a wry smile. "Should I take that as a compliment?"

Hattie glared at her. "Take it however you like."

His chair scraping against the wood floor, the colonel stood abruptly. "Ladies, I see you have your differences. But frankly, that's none of my concern. Miss Thomas, I'll have my clerk issue you a ticket back to Nashville. Miss Pitman, I'll arrange your transfer to Alton, effective immediately."

Once again, Mollie Pitman had gotten the upper hand.

Chapter Eleven

APRIL 15, 1864

Hattie supposed she should have telegraphed ahead to let John Elliott know she was returning to Nashville, but as things had turned out, she couldn't get out of St. Louis fast enough. She was washing her hands of Mollie Pitman, who seemed determined to best Hattie at every turn, as if to make clear who was the better spy.

Much as Hattie had wanted to prove herself, she wasn't going to keep butting heads with someone like Mollie Pitman to do it. And in truth, the whole idea of proving herself was starting to seem untenable. She'd done what she could, and it hadn't been enough to stop the massacre at Fort Pillow. It hadn't been enough to stop Mollie Pitman either. She'd only managed to wriggle into a position where she had the potential to do even more harm, especially if she managed to keep hoodwinking Federal officials.

Entering Nashville's Army Police Headquarters, Hattie stood tall, foreswearing her uncertainty. Lieutenant Elliott had given her an assignment, and she'd completed it. Not to the standards she'd set for herself, but she hadn't failed either. She'd put her skills to good use. She had nothing to be ashamed of. But she also knew it wasn't shame that made her uneasy. It was her jumbled feelings.

At this early hour, the headquarters was nearly empty. She went to the end of the hallway and rapped on the lieutenant's door.

"Who goes there?"

Elliott's brusque tone caught her off guard. "Hattie Thomas," she said.

Why had she spoken so softly? Habit, she supposed, from when she'd been better known around Nashville as a Secesh sympathizer, a role Pauline had devised for her.

But Elliott must have heard Hattie, because she heard footsteps inside, and then the door opened to reveal his smiling face. "Thank God. Having sent you east, I was worried you'd gotten caught up in that awful business at Fort Pillow."

"I did." She felt color rising in her cheeks, a response to the genuine concern his eyes conveyed. "One of the Negro soldiers saw me to safety." She bit her lip, remembering. "And lost his life doing so."

Elliott's smile faded. He glanced over his shoulder, and she saw a lanky, bespectacled soldier sitting beside his desk, poring over a set of papers.

"General Sherman is preparing to issue orders about what can be published in the newspapers," Elliott explained, turning back to her. "No speculation concerning planned campaigns. No letters from the front indicating the strength or location of our troops. No notices about the arrival or departure of regiments. He's asked us to amass evidence from Nashville's papers to demonstrate the need for such restrictions. It hasn't been hard to find, I'm afraid."

"People won't be happy," she said. "Families scour those reports for news of their loved ones.

Elliott rubbed the back of his neck. "True. And such restrictions also have a way of snowballing into others. But for some reason, General Sherman didn't consult with me before releasing his order."

She stepped away from the doorway. "I should have known you'd be busy. I'll go back to the hotel and write up my report and await further instructions."

"You'll do no such thing." He turned, addressing the man at the desk. "Micah, I've got business to attend to. Keep at it. I'll spell you when I return."

He exited the office, shutting the door behind him. "You'll have tongues wagging," she said. "Leaving headquarters at such an early hour. And with a lady, no less."

"A lady who's on my payroll," he said, sounding almost mischievous. "It's my duty to keep tabs."

She followed him out the back door. "Unless you have genuine qualms about scandal, there's a lovely bench under that big oak tree." With a sweep of his hand, he gestured toward it. "I retreat there now and again."

"That looks lovely," Hattie said, having spent far too much time in offices as of late.

She and Elliott settled on the bench, the oak tree casting welcome shade on what was already promising to be a warm, humid day. From the upper branches, a robin warbled a cheery song, a

welcome counterpart to the nearby street sounds of the city stir-
ring to meet the morning.

"I should have warned you I was coming," she admitted.

His smile warmed her. "I'm just glad you're here."

She glanced down at her hands, then back up at him. "Mollie
Pitman is under arrest," she said. "But I'm not sure what good
it will do." She explained as best she could about how when the
soldiers had come to arrest Mollie, she'd claimed to have switched
sides.

Elliott's brow furrowed. "I've never known a spy to switch
sides."

"Nor have I," Hattie said. "It seemed all too convenient once
she knew she was going to be arrested. Loyalties aren't so easily
abandoned."

He rubbed his chin. "You don't think she could have had a
genuine change of heart?"

Hattie shook her head. "Not on something so significant. The
arresting officers took her to Fort Pillow, and I went along to
give my evidence. But the major there seemed to think she could
be trusted. Before I could convince him otherwise, the fort came
under attack." She glanced at the leaves overhead, quivering in the
breeze. "It was awful, what those Rebels did to the Negro soldiers."

Looking back at him, she saw his gaze soften. "I'm sorry you had
to go through that."

She sat up straighter. "I feel I owe it to those soldiers to stay the
course, doing what I can for the Union. But I'm not sure how
much use I am, truthfully."

"Of course you're of use," Elliott said. "You secured the arrest of
a Rebel spy."

"A spy who's likely talking her way out of prison as we speak. From Fort Pillow, we escaped by boat to Memphis, and the marshal there sent us on to St. Louis. That's where Mollie claims to have conducted much of her smuggling and espionage."

Elliott nodded. "I've met Colonel Sanderson. He takes such matters seriously, preparing a report for the War Department on treasonous activities."

"He did show a strong interest in what Mollie had to say about secret orders operating in the North."

Elliott raised an eyebrow. "The Sons of Liberty?"

"Yes. Mollie was cagey about what she told him, and yet he seemed entirely convinced of her sincerity. If she's asked for the keys to his office, I rather think he'd have turned them over."

"Never underestimate a woman's powers of persuasion."

"It's not that she's seductive," Hattie said. "But people seem inclined to give her the benefit of the doubt."

"Not you, though?" Elliott asked.

She shook her head. "To be fair, Mollie has been quite forthcoming, first with me and then with Union officials. Only..." Hattie glanced toward the street, where a wagon had stopped, letting off a contingent of blue-uniformed soldiers.

"Only what?" he asked.

Hattie hesitated. Admittedly, her assessment was not as objective as it should be. "She's an odd one."

He considered this a moment. "We all have our oddities, I suppose."

"True, but I've never met anyone quite like Mollie Pitman. I swear she's always scheming, trying to get one step ahead of me."

He laughed. "From what I've observed, that's no easy task."

Hattie smiled in spite of herself. "Well, she managed it, now and again."

"Even so, you accomplished what you set out to. Well done."

She shook her head. "I wish I could've done more. Pretending to be on our side, Mollie Pitman can do more damage than ever."

"Don't be hard on yourself, Hattie. You're more valuable than you know, in any number of ways. You can't be expected to fix everything." He pressed his hands to his knees. "I should let you catch your breath before proposing a new assignment. But you should know I've got one in mind. The wealthiest woman in Tennessee has just returned from Louisiana."

"Adelicia Acklen," Hattie said. Everyone in Nashville, it seemed, knew of Adelicia, who owned the magnificent Belle Monte estate outside the city.

Elliott nodded. "She managed to dispose of an entire crop of cotton from her Louisiana plantations without coming under Federal or Confederate scrutiny. To the tune of a million dollars, some say. Officials have no idea how she accomplished it or what she's done with the money. I'm thinking you could find out."

"Befriending Mollie Pitman wasn't that difficult," she said. "But I can't imagine anyone of Miss Acklen's stature trusting me with her secrets."

"If anyone can manage it, it's you."

A plan began taking shape in her mind, one that might even give her a much-needed respite from trying to prove herself. "I suppose I could try."

He stood. "I knew I could count on you. See my clerk about your expenses. There should be funds for you..." He cleared his throat. "For you to enhance your wardrobe."

Standing, Hattie held out her skirt. "You're suggesting Adelicia Acklen would be unimpressed with a dress I've worn four days in a row after wading through the river in it."

"Something like that," he said. "Although I had no idea about the river. A story for another day, I'm afraid. General Sherman is waiting for my report."

"Then you'd best not disappoint him," Hattie said. "I'll see your clerk as you instructed."

He gazed at her awkwardly, as if he had something more to say but couldn't find the right words. For the first time, she found herself hoping it was personal, perhaps an invitation to dinner or the theatre that night.

But then he glanced toward the street, and when he looked back at her, his expression was all business. "Take your time with Miss Acklen," he said. "Little gets past her."

"Understood," Hattie said.

He nodded, then turned and strode toward the back door of the headquarters. Swallowing back her disappointment, Hattie set off quickly in the opposite direction.

Chapter Twelve

APRIL 18, 1864

The carriage Hattie hired to take her to Adelicia Acklen's Belle Monte estate stopped at the foot of a wide walkway. The driver helped Hattie out, then asked if she wanted help with her satchel. She thanked him but said she could manage it herself.

As the carriage rolled off, Hattie surveyed the property. At the top of the walkway stood a mansion statelier than any she'd seen before. Corinthian columns in the Italianate style towered on either side of the entrance, with similarly designed columns supporting twin balconies. Wings in a style that mirrored the central part of the mansion jutted gracefully from it. At each front corner of the roof, a statue was positioned, and an elegant observation tower rose from the top.

The villa was striking in every detail, and Hattie could only imagine how elegantly it must be furnished inside. But it was Belle Monte's grounds that nearly took her breath away, spreading out from the hilltop in every direction. A tiered fountain of white marble graced the walkway leading to the mansion. Beyond this stood a gazebo of wrought iron lacework. Fanning out from there were manicured gardens on such a grand scale that they might have been attached to a castle.

Scattered about the grounds were several smaller buildings, each in the same style as the house. Hattie was looking from one to the other, trying to imagine what purpose they might serve, when something hit her leg, throwing her momentarily off balance. Looking down, she saw a young girl who she guessed to be four or five years of age, her cherubic face gazing up at Hattie.

"Pauline! Dis-elle desolée," a woman called out. She moved quickly toward them three boys trailing behind.

With a curtsy, the girl made her apology. "Desolée, madame."

Hattie patted the child's dark curls. "C'est rien," she said, reassuring her. If Hattie was to be hired on as a seamstress, she knew she would have to claim Paris credentials. But she hadn't counted on others here speaking French. She wished she'd paid more attention to Madame Girard's French lessons at the Ladygrace School for Girls.

The woman who'd scolded the girl came up beside her. She was petite and slender, with fiery red curls piled atop her head, mischievous green eyes, and a flawless complexion. "Pauline, il faut que tu—"

Pauline stamped her foot. "I don't understand."

The woman sighed. "You must be more careful," she said in accented English. "I've told you before."

The girl stuck her bottom lip out in a pout. "But I saw a butterfly. A beautiful blue one."

"That is no excuse. Now go join your brothers." The woman gestured toward where the three boys had veered off the path and were now crouched, examining something in the grass.

"Mon Dieu." The woman wiped her brow with an exaggerated swipe of her hand. "Some days they do try my patience."

She couldn't be the children's mother, Hattie thought. She was far too young. More likely a governess or a tutor. Either way, she might have some influence with Mrs. Acklen.

"I've come to see about a position as a seamstress," Hattie said in the best French accent she could muster. "I know all the latest fashions from Paris."

With a toss of her head, the woman laughed, a melodic sound. Then she leaned close, speaking in what amounted to a stage whisper. "Lucky for you, chérie, Madame's French is not the best." She looped her arm around Hattie's. "Come with me."

Hattie fell in step beside her as she strode toward the mansion. "Mes enfants," she called over her shoulder. "Come along now. We must get back to your lessons."

Glancing back, Hattie saw the biggest boy get up. He scuffed the ground with his foot, then gestured for the other children to follow him along the path.

"It is my own fault," Hattie's companion said as they ascended the steps to the portico. "But how can I keep them inside on such a glorious day? And our excursion to the ménagèrie was magnifique."

"There truly is a zoo, right here on the property?" Hattie had heard people speak of this in the city, but she hadn't believed it.

"Mais oui." The woman waved her hand vaguely in the direction she and the children had come from. "Though les enfants say the specimens are not so many as before the war. Still, there are the monkey and the bear. And the alligators." She gave an exaggerated shiver. "And the birds. So many birds. They are my favorites, though I detest them being caged."

"Is there a bowling alley here too?" Hattie asked, repeating another rumor she'd heard.

"Certainement," the woman said. "It's still under construction, but the children are allowed in. I've played a time or two, but in truth, boules is not my game." She reached to open the towering front door, and they stepped inside.

The air in the foyer was cool and welcoming, a respite from the humid morning. An elegant white marble fireplace stood ahead of them. Hanging above the mantle was a huge, gilt-framed portrait of a slender, dark-haired woman, a young girl clinging to her hand. Though the child looked the same age as Pauline, her eyes were dark while Pauline's were pale blue.

"Wait here," Hattie's companion said. "I'll find Madame." She started toward a doorway to the side of the fireplace, then turned. "But how shall I introduce you?"

"Hélène Thomas," Hattie said, pronouncing it the French way.

"Hélène of Marseilles," the woman said conspiratorially. "That will explain your strange accent. And more recently of Paris, where you have learned to sew the latest fashions." She stepped closer, lowering her voice even further. "The rest we can fabricate, but on the sewing, you must perform, or you'll make a fool of me."

"I shall," Hattie said, hoping very much that her latent sewing skills combined with the hours she'd spent poring over Godey's Lady's books these past two days would be enough to make good on her promise.

"And I am Elise Cardeau," the petite woman said. "The governess, recently of New Orléans, by way of Paris."

"Enchantée," Hattie said, making a little curtsy.

Elise pressed her hand to Hattie's forearm. "You can't imagine how lonely I've been since I came here. This is all très élègant. But I've no friend my age."

With a swoosh of her wide skirts, Elise proceeded across the foyer and through the doorway. As she disappeared, footsteps pounded up the stairs. The children burst in, the middle two boys shoving one another playfully.

Bringing up the rear, the oldest boy shut the door. "Shush!" he said, rising his finger to his lips. "We don't behave like that indoors."

The boys quit their shoving, their expressions sober. Turning to Hattie, Pauline grinned. Hattie smiled back. Then the oldest boy marched the others through the same doorway Elise had used, leaving Hattie alone again.

Moments later, Elise returned, gesturing for Hattie to come forward. "Madame is taking her tea in her sitting room," she said. "She asked me to bring you up." Elise winked. "I've spoken highly of you, as if you were my sister, not someone I met ten minutes ago."

Leaving the foyer, they crossed an expansive salon and proceeded up a grand staircase. At the top of the stairs, Hattie paused to ask where the children had gone.

"The playroom, I hope," Elise said, leading Hattie down a hallway. "They take their lessons there. I'd best get back to them soon, or there's no telling what mischief they'll get into. Joseph will be headed to military school in the fall, so I rely on him to keep order.

But he's of an age where he can easily be swayed by the antics of his brothers, the little imps."

Coming to an open door, Hattie followed Elise into a well-appointed sitting room. Seated near a tall window, the mistress of the house turned as they entered. Hattie saw that she was the same woman depicted in the portrait, though she looked older now. Her features seemed both delicate and sharp, her gray eyes soft but her gaze keen. The length of her face, while not distracting, gave her a thoughtful, serious look. The lines at either side of her mouth weren't the sort that formed from years of smiling, Hattie thought.

"So this is the seamstress you've brought me." Adelicia spoke softly, but there was no mistaking the authority in her voice.

"Oui, Madame." Elise spoke crisply. "As I said, she comes highly recommended. And now, if you'll excuse me, I'd best see to the children."

"Of course." Adelicia set down her teacup as Elise backed out of the room, shutting the door softly behind her. "Come forward, Miss Thomas," she said, pronouncing the name the way Hattie had given it. "And tell me how it is that you've come to me in my hour of need."

Hattie stepped toward where Adelicia sat. Standing in a square of rose-colored light projected through the red-tinted glass at the top of the window, she curtsied. "I have but recently returned to Nashville," she said, mindful of not overdoing the French lilt in her voice. "Among my acquaintances here is Madame Ford. She sends her greetings." Hattie reached in her pocket and withdrew a slip of paper penned in Felicia Ford's careful script.

She handed Adelicia the paper. Here was one benefit, at least, of the stratifications in Nashville's social order, which not even war could erase. Felicia Ford, who'd been the bane of Hattie's existence during her last stint in Nashville, had been only too happy to flaunt the fact that she knew Adelicia, if only in passing. Felicia had known Hattie as an actress, but Hattie had little trouble convincing her that she'd come on hard times and needed to fall back on her sewing skills.

Adelicia's lips moved silently as she read what Felicia had written:

Miss Thomas comes to you with my highest recommendation. She is bright and talented. I have witnessed her skills in our Society's sewing circle, stitching uniforms for our beloved soldiers, and she has proven herself trustworthy at every turn.

Adelicia refolded the note and returned it to Hattie. "I know Mrs. Ford only by reputation. But I suspect her judgment can be trusted. However, I don't need uniforms, Miss Thomas. I need children's clothing, and I need it right away. Imagine my horror at returning to Nashville and finding that the only seamstress I trust here had closed up shop."

"I've trained in Paris, Madame," Hattie said with a hint of feigned outrage that her skills would be questioned. "I can sew all manner of clothing in the latest fashions."

Adelicia picked up her teacup. Rather than drink from it, she held it up, studying the red roses painted on the porcelain as she fingered the delicate handle.

Should she offer further credentials, Hattie wondered. No, she decided. Adelicia seemed a woman who took her time with a decision. Better to remain silent and let her sort through whatever was on her mind.

Hattie clasped her hands at her waist, waiting for the verdict. Adelicia sipped her tea once, twice, three times. Then she set the cup on its saucer.

"With so few options these days, one must make do," she said. "You may take a week, Miss Thomas, to demonstrate your skills. I'll provide the necessary fabric. You will choose a project from the list I provide. Should your work prove satisfactory, I will keep you on until the children's wardrobes have been updated to my satisfaction. I will pay you by the piece, and you may occupy a room downstairs while you're in my employ. I hope that arrangement will be satisfactory."

"Yes, Madame. Merci." Hattie curtsied again.

Leaving Adelicia to her tea, she inhaled deeply. After all her consternation with Mollie, Belle Monte would be a welcome respite.

Chapter Thirteen

JULY 4, 1864

The weeks at Belle Monte flew by. By Independence Day, Hattie had stitched three pairs of boys' knickers and two sailor tops for the middle boys. For Pauline, she'd sewn two pairs of pantalets and one printed cotton dress with a wide neckline and capped sleeves. Now she was working on a similar style dress in a mint green fabric Pauline favored. After that, she'd start on her greatest challenge, amassing a wardrobe for Joseph, Adelicia's eldest son, who'd grown six inches in as many months, to take to military school in New Jersey.

That Adelicia would send her oldest son to school in the North was one of several contradictions Hattie had observed during her time at Belle Monte. In many ways, Adelicia Acklen seemed the quintessential Southern woman, demure and refined. But Hattie had also observed her keen intelligence and pragmatism. She suspected both traits were at the heart of what she'd been sent to discover, how a seemingly helpless Southern widow had sold off a fortune in cotton when such sales were strictly forbidden.

Lieutenant Elliott had urged her to take her time here, and she was finding it quite easy to do so. Belle Monte was a comfortable setting, to say the least. Here, it was easy to forget what she had or hadn't accomplished and whom she had or hadn't loved. She passed her days measuring and snipping and stitching. Even alterations felt easy and satisfying.

When a pang of guilt struck and she felt as if she wasn't doing enough, she reminded herself that while it might not be obvious, with each garment she finished, she gained a bit more of Adelicia's trust. Elise was helpful in this, too, as Adelicia already seemed to trust her implicitly.

And Elise was good fun. Downstairs in the servant's quarters, she regaled Hattie with tales of growing up in the Montmartre quarter of Paris. Her mother had died when Elise was young. Her father, a sculptor, had been too wrapped up in his art to bother remarrying or, for that matter, to tend to his daughter. So Elise had gotten into all sorts of mischief, at least until her father's sister intervened and got her some proper schooling. It was with this aunt that she had traveled from Paris to New Orleans to deliver one of her father's sculptures to Mrs. Acklen. Eager to get out from the aunt's watchful eye, Elise had jumped at the chance to tutor the Acklen children.

It was Elise who explained that the child in the portrait that hung in the foyer was one of six children who had died within a span of ten years. "Quel domage," Elise had said, expressing sadness over how one woman, never mind her wealth could have suffered such sorrow. Adelicia never spoke of her dead children by name, Elise said, but she'd admitted once to feeling sad that she would never hear their sweet prattle again.

In marriage, too, Adelicia had endured loss after loss. While attending the Nashville Female Academy, she'd been engaged to marry at age seventeen, but her fiancé had died before the wedding. Five years later, she married a wealthy plantation owner more than twice her age.

"If the first was love," Elise whispered to Hattie, "the second was money. He traded in slaves." Elise shook her head. "All this beauty out of something so ugly."

After seven years of marriage, Adelicia's husband had died, and she'd inherited a fortune. "She's no fool," Elise said. "When she married again, she insisted on keeping control of that fortune. Mr. Acklen even signed an agreement." Elise's eyes sparkled. "True love, non?"

True genius, Hattie thought. Women generally gave up all control of their assets—and for that matter, their lives—when they married. Getting Adelicia to give up her secrets would be no easy task.

Not long after Elise shared this information, Hattie found her first clue. Adelicia was in the city, making social calls, and so Hattie wandered into the library under the pretense of having misplaced her scissors. Rifling through the desk drawers, she'd discovered a letter from Adelicia's second husband, Joseph, who'd died of fever last fall. In it, Joseph wrote that he wanted nothing more to do with enslaving Negroes.

But this declaration might not be what it seemed, Hattie knew. Working in Allen Pinkerton's Washington mailroom, she'd learned that senders might intentionally draft misleading messages, knowing they would fall into enemy hands. In another desk drawer, she found a ledger recording transactions from the last months of Acklen's life. Nothing there indicated he'd let go of any of the people he and Adelicia enslaved.

Hattie wasn't sure what favor Joseph Acklen had hoped to gain by foreswearing slavery, but she was certain that's what he'd done. And even if only through the letter, Adelicia must know it too. To make her illegal cotton sale, she may have done something similar, convincing Union officials she was other than what she seemed. A wealthier, more refined version of Mollie Pitman, Hattie thought as she'd replaced the letter and ledger.

But part of the benefit of this assignment was that in the ease and comfort of Belle Monte, Hattie did not have to think about Mollie. Nor did she have to think about Franklin or Thom Welton or even John Elliott. She just had to cut and fit and sew with her eyes and ears trained on any clues to how Adelicia had managed to sell a fortune in cotton when the Federals and the Confederates both disallowed it.

Before she knew it, Independence Day was upon them. Last year, she'd spent part of the holiday extricating John Elliott from the saloon where he'd been nursing his sorrows. Today, she was madly stitching up a last-minute project, a bonnet for Pauline to wear with her fanciest dress at the party her mother was throwing. She'd modeled the hat after one Adelicia owned, with a large asymmetrical brim and a large flower stitched out of silk and fastened to the top.

Pauline was thrilled about the bonnet. In fact, she was thrilled with most everything Hattie did, following her about the estate like a puppy. The child had begged Hattie to teach her to sew, and Hattie had obliged with moderate success. More than once, she'd wished the two Paulines could meet. The younger would be awed by the older's swagger and sword, Hattie thought, and she suspected her friend would have a soft spot for the precocious little girl.

Thanks to the brilliant weather, resplendent with sunshine, Hattie was able to work on the bonnet's finishing touches without Pauline's pestering her, the child having gone off to ride her pony. The day being too beautiful to stay inside, Hattie had found a bench in the circular gardens where she could sit and do her stitching. In the sun's bright light, the work was easier on her eyes than it was in the house, where Adelicia favored candlelight over gasoliers, which she found crass.

Aside from the strain on her eyes, Hattie was surprised at how much she enjoyed doing the work of a seamstress. In finishing school, she'd hated needlepoint, which seemed to her a pointless pursuit. But designing clothes was a challenge she enjoyed, working from a set of measurements and an assortment of fabrics and ribbons to create a garment that matched a mental image. Granted, it wasn't the puzzle she'd come here to solve, but it had gotten her in the door. She was hoping tonight's party would allow her an opportunity to slip away and conduct a thorough search of Adelicia's papers, which had eluded her so far.

A robin serenading her from the branch of a nearby tree, Hattie attached the final swaths of ribbon to Pauline's bonnet. Tucking her work in her basket, she started for the stables, knowing Pauline would want to try it on. She met up with workers coming from the rose garden, their arms brimming with colorful blooms destined for tonight's fete. Circling the dairy house, she came upon more workers toting cans of cream and wedges of cheese.

At the corral next to the stables, she found Adelicia's only living daughter trotting a circle with her pony. Elise stood at the fence. "Pas si vite!" she called to her young charge. "Not so fast."

Pauline slowed the pony, but only a little. Then she spied Hattie. "Hélène! You've finished my bonnet?"

Coming alongside Elise, Hattie nodded. "Oui, Mademoiselle Pauline. You may try it on."

"And then we must get back to your lessons," Elise said.

Pauline trotted the pony up to them. "But it's a holiday," she complained.

"A holiday for the Federals," Elise said. "This household is of a different persuasion."

"Then why is Mama having a party?"

"Your maman takes her social obligations seriously," Elise said. "And that includes giving her Nashville friends a respite from the rather raucous celebrations of the Federal soldiers."

"And you shall be the talk of the party in your new bonnet." Fishing the bonnet from her basket, Hattie held it up for the child to admire.

Letting go of the reins, Pauline reached her chubby hands toward the hat.

"Careful!" Grabbing her arm, Elise swung her down from the pony.

Pauline scuffed the dirt with her riding boot. "No one ever lets me do anything for myself."

Hattie opened the gate. "Come around this way," she said. "And the bonnet is yours."

The girl ran through the opening, then planted herself in front of Hattie. "Here I am."

Elise shook her head. "Mon Dieu. A whirlwind."

Hattie held out the bonnet. Pauline snatched it from her, then planted it on her head. Crouching beside her, Hattie adjusted its angle, then tied the satin ribbons under the child's chin. Standing, she smiled at the effect.

"Magnifique!" Elise clapped her hands twice. "It brings out the blue of your eyes."

"You'll be the talk of the party," Hattie said.

The child beamed. "Then I shan't take it off, not ever."

"You shall take it off now." With a firm tug, Elise undid the bow. "Mademoiselle worked her fingers to the bone, finishing in time for the party. And she won't have time to fix it if you have some disaster." She plucked the hat from Pauline's head and handed it to Hattie.

"Go along to the house now. Mademoiselle and I must attend to our own party clothes."

"But I'm not—" Hattie said.

"Yes you are," Elise interrupted. "Madame says two of the ladies she invited have sent their last-minute regrets. You and I are to fill in for them." She linked her arm through Hattie's. "We have but a few hours to make ourselves presentable."

~ ~ ~

The evening felt magical, the grand salon transformed with flowers and finery into a place beyond war and even beyond time itself. This was clearly Adelicia's intent, as indeed was her intent with all of Belle Monte, that it be a place to cast off the cares of the world for those who could afford to do so.

It was easy to get swept up in the splendor of it all. Carriages came and went, traversing the white clamshell drive to the mansion's grand entrance. The women who emerged from them wore finery that rivaled anything Hattie had seen in Godey's Lady's Book. Only the dress uniforms of the Confederate officers in attendance hinted at battles being won and lost in lonely outposts not so far from here.

Inside, the bounty of food and flowers seemed endless. Floral scents filled the ballroom, wafting from huge vases filled with tasteful arrangements of roses, azaleas, verbenas, saxifrage, and begonias. As the food was brought in, the smells of roast capon, fried sole, blancmange, and raspberry cream overtook the floral scents.

After dinner, Adelicia's guests wandered the salon, its columns and windows creating the illusion of a marbled terrace overlooking a park. Contributing to the effect was the trickling water from a cast iron fountain situated within a bay of tall windows. On the soaring, barrel-vaulted ceiling was painted an open sky.

It felt odd to mingle among Nashville's wealthiest people, but Elise assured Hattie that this was Adelicia's expressed wish, provided the two of them could do so without letting on that they were actually among the hired help.

Elise seemed entirely in her element, laughing and flirting with every man she encountered, young or old, uniformed or not. Hattie was more reticent, hanging back near the bay windows and observing the interactions of Adelicia's guests. This was the way of life the South aimed to preserve, she thought, and yet it was a scene only the most privileged Confederates would ever enjoy. Most Rebel soldiers fighting and dying for the cause had likely never seen such elegance.

As the sunlight streaming through the windows turned golden and then dimmed altogether, servants moved ghostlike through the room, lighting hundreds of candles that cast a warm glow over the scene. In one corner of the salon, a small orchestra began tuning up.

"You've found a splendid place to hide." Wearing a gown flounced in varying hues of blue, a young woman approached. Freckles dotted her otherwise clear complexion. "I hope you won't mind if I share it. If we stand side by side conversing, there's less chance of a gentleman's asking either of us to dance. I assume you, too, have a beau who can't be here tonight."

Color rose in Hattie's cheeks. "Not exactly," she said coyly, pushing aside the image of John Elliott that had arisen against her will.

"Well, I do," the woman said resolutely. "Aunt Adelicia knows that full well, and yet she insisted on my attending tonight. She wants to give her guests someone to gossip about besides herself."

"I wouldn't know," Hattie said.

"Then you're the only one who doesn't then." She turned to face Hattie full on. "Sorry. That's not the sort of introduction we were taught to make at the Academy. I'm Sally Acklen," she said, offering her hand. "Adelicia's niece by marriage."

Hattie grasped her fingers firmly, using her left hand, as was the French way, the left hand being nearer the heart. "Hélène Thomas."

"You're new here?" Sally said.

Hattie shrugged. "Passing through."

"Me too. Or I was. I was sent here from the South after Uncle died last fall. He was my guardian, and now Aunt Adelicia is. She enrolled me in Nashville Female Academy to ensure I came out a proper lady. And still I've managed to disgrace the family name." A smile lit her face. "I'm engaged to marry a Union officer."

Hattie tipped her head, her lips turned in a slight smile. "It is a wondrous thing to be in love," she said. "But I suppose you've felt compelled to carry out your courtship in secret."

Sally leaned close, her wide skirt brushing Hattie's. "Aunt Adelicia found out last week. She has her own secrets, you know, and I suppose that's made her alert to mine."

"I've heard talk of cotton," Hattie said casually.

"Oh, yes!" Sally exclaimed. "Bales and bales of it, back in Louisiana. They'd brought me there, you see, and—"

At that moment, the orchestra struck up a valse à deux temps. Hattie waited, hoping Sally would finish her thought. But almost immediately, two men in Confederate uniform approached.

"So much for your hiding place," Sally whispered. But she smiled brightly at the soldier who asked her to dance, her Union officer momentarily forgotten as she followed him to the dance floor, where couples had begun to glide in half-circles.

Aware of the second man's gaze on her, Hattie watched as Sally's partner circled his arm about her waist and they took up the waltz.

"I could look at you all night," the stranger in gray said. "But I'd rather we dance."

It was not only his flirtatious words that made Hattie think of Franklin Stone. It was his dashing good looks and the fruity scent of the Macassar oil he'd used to comb back his hair, a product Franklin also favored. too. She glanced around for Elise, hoping she was close enough to rescue her. But Elise, too, was dancing, circling the floor with a tall, white-haired man who looked old enough to be her grandfather.

The soldier at Hattie's side bowed. "Colonel Nathan Hildebrand." When he looked up, she found herself looking into eyes that matched the blue of the painted sky overhead. In the candlelight, Hildebrand's features seemed perfectly proportioned. If not for his warm smile, he might have been mistaken for one of the marble statues gracing Belle Monte's grounds.

He held out his arm to her. Hattie started to shake her head, an excuse forming on her lips, when she noticed that Adelicia, standing near the bay windows in a resplendent lavender gown trimmed in purple ribbons, was watching her intently.

Not wanting to arouse Adelicia's suspicions, Hattie took the colonel's arm. "Enchantée," she said, and she followed him to the dance floor.

She hadn't danced since before the war, and even then it had been in the company of clumsy boys who were more conscious of their feet than anything else. In contrast, Colonel Nathan Hildebrand kept his transfixing blue eyes on her. When the notes of the waltz gave way to a varsouvienne, he kept his arm so firmly about her waist that she had little choice but to let him guide her through those steps too. At each measured pause in the music, he smiled with teeth so even and white that Hattie wondered whether he'd ever suffered the deprivations of war.

When the varsouvienne ended, she tried to break away, saying she needed to rest her feet. Hildebrand took this as an invitation to escort her out of the salon and onto the portico. Settling on a far bench, she had to admit the breeze felt refreshing. Overhead, stars were beginning to show themselves.

As Hildebrand claimed the space beside her, Hattie was grateful for her wide skirt, which kept him from sitting too close. "Your first time at Belle Monte?" he asked in a voice that matched the evening's velveteen softness.

"I came here some weeks ago. I'll be leaving soon," she said, hoping to discourage his interest.

"So it is with all the beautiful ladies. The war has made transients of us all."

He leaned back. Silhouetted in the moonlight, there was something familiar in his posture, his shoulders square and his head erect. She'd noticed him earlier, she realized, silhouetted in candlelight as he'd followed Adelicia down a hallway to her study.

"Are you long acquainted with the Acklens?" she asked.

He shrugged. "Not especially. It's only because of a favor that I'm here."

This piqued Hattie's interest. "It seems we all owe more favors now than we did before the war."

"Some more than others." Even in the light of the rising moon, his smile was brilliant. "I've oft observed that such obligations are proportionate to one's wealth and status."

"It is hard to fathom a person of Mrs. Acklen's prestige and wealth owing a debt to anyone."

"She is indeed formidable. I learned as much last winter."

"While she was in Angola," Hattie said, naming the Southern town where Adelicia had arranged her illegal sale. "I understand she saw a good deal of her cotton crop brought in."

"Harvested, transported, and sold, never mind what the laws say. Not what you'd expect of one of our fragile Southern women, is it?"

Hattie feigned surprise. "But what laws would forbid her from managing her plantations after her husband died?"

Hildebrand shrugged. "Depends who you ask. The Yanks don't want Southern folks selling cotton, knowing a portion of the profits would circle back to the war effort. But our side doesn't want it sold either. We're desperate for England and France to support our cause, and cotton's our best leverage. So we have to make sure they can't get it until they embrace our side."

"I had no idea," Hattie said, though John Elliott had explained as much before sending her here. "I can't fathom Mrs. Acklen managed it."

"I've never known a woman who so successfully got folks to do her bidding. In fact, it's what brought me here."

Hattie smiled. "You don't strike me as a man who'd be easily influenced, Colonel Hildebrand."

"I'm not." He leaned close. "But between you and me, Mrs. Acklen has been playing a very deep game. I had orders to burn her cotton. But as I made preparations to do so, she approached me with secrets gained from Union officers she'd entertained at her home."

Hattie's eyes widened in surprise that was only partially feigned. "Mrs. Acklen is a spy for the Confederacy?"

Hildebrand's lips turned at the corners. "I wouldn't let her hear you say so, and you aren't hearing it from me either. Let's just say the officers were loose-lipped in her presence, and she paid more attention than they were aware."

Hattie suppressed a smile. Men did tend to blather on, as the colonel was doing now, showing off what they knew with little regard for a woman's capacity to understand or retain it.

"It's all so confusing," Hattie said. "Why would Mrs. Acklen entertain Union officers when she supports the Confederacy?"

"Because she was playing both sides, as I later found out. She passed Union secrets to me, and she passed our secrets to the Union officers who came to the mansion. Not that I would ever confront her with that fact."

Hattie straightened. "But you could have had her arrested."

"Indeed. Instead, I ordered my men to stand guard over the wagons that brought Mrs. Acklen's cotton to the barge for transport. Union wagons, no less, and a Union barge."

"And here you are, all because you did her a favor."

He laughed. "Several favors. First by not burning her cotton, then by guarding its transport, then again by not exposing her duplicity. And now I've even delivered her the bill of sale rendered when her shipments reached London." He tipped his head at her. "But it seems Mrs. Acklen has done me a favor, too, for how else would I have met such a lovely lady as you?"

~ ~ ~

Returning to the ballroom on Nathan Hildebrand's arm, Hattie took care to show no enthusiasm over his revelations. No doubt he assumed they'd gone in one of her pretty little ears and out the other.

She saw that Elise had moved on to yet another partner while Sally was nowhere to be found. Given what she'd said about her engagement, Hattie suspected she'd retired to her room at the first opportunity. The orchestra struck up a new tune, and the colonel led Hattie onto the dance floor. His eyes fixed on her, he led her through the promenades and pivots of a schottische and then through a lively redowa.

Concentrating on her steps, Hattie was able to at least partially calm her excitement. A bill of sale. That was the proof John Elliott had asked for. She just had to find it before Adelicia concealed it beyond reach. Hattie had seen Hildebrand follow her to her study, so it must be there, at least for the moment. She needed to look for it now, while Adelicia and her servants were occupied with the party.

The redowa wound to an end, the orchestra playing its final notes. "You've been a fine dance partner, Colonel Hildebrand," Hattie said, still a bit breathless from the lively dance. "But I must excuse myself. All this activity has tired me, I'm afraid."

A trace of disappointment crossed his handsome face. "May I escort you to the guest wing?"

"That won't be necessary," she said.

"Then allow me the pleasure of seeing you in the morning before I leave."

"As you wish," she said, knowing that to put him off entirely might cause him to make inquiries about her. "Good evening, Colonel."

As she left the ballroom, she felt his gaze on her. Smiling to herself, she wondered which would disturb him more, to learn she was among Adelicia's hired help or to learn she was a spy.

She passed through one of the dining rooms, then circled back toward the study. In the candlelit hallway, the entrance was dark. Trying the knob, she found the door unlocked. No surprise—the family used the room frequently.

Slowly, she opened the door and slipped inside. Lit only by moonlight, the room looked different than it did in the daytime. With the windows closed, the air was still. Adelicia's marble busts faded into the gray, the detailing on the Egyptian revival wallpaper likewise lost to the night. A linen cloth had been placed over the birdcage, so instead of the usual warbling, there was only silence.

Hattie checked the desk drawers and, finding nothing of interest, pulled out a drawer in the room's circular table. Nothing there but a few small trinkets. She looked about the room but saw no more drawers where Adelicia, in her haste to get back to the party, might have stashed the bill of sale. Then her gaze landed on a bookshelf. She'd known books to contain coded messages. Why not a bill of sale?

Starting on the top shelf, she pulled out the leatherbound books one by one, fanning the pages for a slip of paper concealed inside. She had reached the bottom shelf, flipping through a gilded edition of Plutarch's lives, when she found a slip of paper. In the dim light, she could make out only two of the words, but they were the right ones: *Received. Collected.*

Holding the paper to her nose, she inhaled the fruity smell of Hildebrand's hair oil. This had to be it. Clutching the paper in her hand, she returned the book to its shelf.

Elated at her discovery, she turned to leave. But then the door opened, and she saw a woman's figure silhouetted in the flickering candlelight from the hallway.

"Is that you, Hélène?"

Hattie reached for Pauline's doll, which lay prone on the circular table. "Oh, it's you, Madame. What a fright you gave me. Pauline was looking for her doll. I told her I'd fetch it."

Snatching up the doll, she balled the paper in her hand.

Though the light was dim, Hattie saw Adelicia smile, serene and controlled as ever. "How kind of you," she said.

Head held high, Hattie crossed the room toward the door where Adelicia stood waiting, her eyes steely. What had prompted her to come here?

"A splendid party, Madame," Hattie said. "It was kind of you to allow me to attend."

"I could not disappoint our soldiers by having too few ladies in attendance," Adelicia said coolly. "And Colonel Hildebrand seems especially pleased to have met you. He told me so himself, shortly after you left the ballroom."

Hattie's heart leaped. Did Adelicia know what he'd told her?

"I was careful not to let on the fact of my employment," she said.

"I knew you could be trusted on that count." Adelicia crossed her arms at her chest. "I have enough black marks against me, at least in the eyes of some, without adding another little scandal to the mix. I'd wager half my guests frown on my doing what any mother would do to ensure that her children were cared for."

"Of course, Madame," Hattie said.

Adelicia tipped her chin, and her gaze seemed to intensify. "A woman's first loyalty must always be to herself, Hélène. Remember that."

Hattie resisted the urge to look away. "Quite so, Madame."

Adelicia nodded brusquely, then glided into the hallway. Behind her, Hattie shut the door, the doll clutched in one hand, the bill of sale crumpled in the other.

"I presume we've reached an understanding, Miss Thomas."

Hattie swallowed hard. "Yes, Madame. Of course."

Chapter Fourteen

JULY 28, 1864

After the party, it seemed to Hattie there were two Belle Montes. One featured the tranquil, ordered luxury that kept the world at a distance. The other was dark and filled with secrets, overseen by a mistress who kept a close eye on Hattie's every move.

A woman's first loyalty must be to herself. Along with their spying, Hattie thought Adelicia Acklen and Mollie Pitman must have this in common too.

Hattie would have liked to have left the mansion immediately, but that would have only affirmed Adelicia's suspicions. Instead, she penned a copy of the bill of sale, then slipped the original back where she'd found it. After that, she went back to sewing Joseph's wardrobe for military school. Every so often, she'd notice her fingers trembling, but she told herself that was only the pressure of finishing the clothes, not the fear that Adelicia knew what she'd done.

Still, it was a relief to finish the last shirt and pack her satchel. The morning of her departure was oppressively hot, and in the humid air, the edges of the gardens and even the mansion itself seemed to shimmer.

Elise and the children came to see her off. Adelicia was noticeably absent. As a cabriolet from the carriage house pulled up to take her back to Nashville, Hattie found it harder than she'd expected to say goodbye. Little Pauline clung to her skirts and would only let go after Hattie promised to write. Even the boys looked sorry to see her leave.

Tears glistening in her eyes, Elise hugged Hattie hard, then slipped her a paper with a Paris address. "I intend to return to France when the war ends," she whispered. "Stay in touch. One day, we'll arrange a visit."

A lump forming in her throat, Hattie nodded, though she couldn't fathom traveling across the ocean. "I'll miss you."

As the cabriolet rolled down the driveway, Hattie waved goodbye to them all. Already, her time with them seemed like a dream. But in her purse was her copy of the bill of sale she'd taken from the study, proof that the time she'd spent at Belle Monte had been both real and purposeful.

~ ~ ~

Illusory as life at the Acklen mansion had been, the swarms of blue-uniformed soldiers on Nashville's streets—and the disdainful looks townspeople bestowed on them—left no doubt that the war was as real as ever. In the heart of the city, Union soldiers were congregating in especially large numbers around the railroad station. She wondered if General Forrest was threatening a raid.

She hoped Mollie Pitman hadn't talked her way out of prison so she could ease his way with Union secrets.

The driver dropped her at the City Hotel—not Nashville's finest, but it fit her budget. She checked in, deposited her satchel, and set out for the Army Police Headquarters, eager to share what she'd gleaned at Belle Monte.

Arriving at the headquarters, she went around to the back entrance. Seeing John Elliott's open door, her heart quickened. This was only from professional interest, she told herself. She strode briskly down the hall, her hand on her purse where she'd tucked the bill of sale for Adelicia's cotton. Elliott would be pleased to see her, she knew. Pleased, that is, that she'd accomplished what he'd sent her to do.

But when she reached his office, the man who looked up from the desk wasn't John Elliott. Tall and lanky, he was the young soldier she recognized from the last time she was here, the one who'd been helping Elliott compile evidence for Sherman's restrictions on newspapers. Looking up at Hattie, he pushed his spectacles higher on his nose and pressed his lips in what seemed a forced smile.

"Oh," she said, careful to sound nonchalant. "I was expecting Lieutenant Elliott."

"He's changed offices," the soldier said. "Two doors down. But he's in a meeting with Colonel Truesdail right now. Not sure when they'll be through." The soldier shook his head. "Plenty to keep us busy these days. Something I can help you with?"

"That's alright. I'll stop by another time. Just let him know that Miss Thomas was here with the information he was after."

Retreating toward the back door, she scolded herself for feeling disappointed. She wasn't a child, needing the lieutenant's approval for a job well done.

Outside, she paused a moment in the shade of the spreading oak tree, near the bench where she'd sat with John Elliott the last time she was here. On this hot July day, the air beneath the tree felt cool and welcoming. With its thick trunk and spreading branches, the oak had surely been in this spot for hundreds of years. There was some comfort in knowing that, even with the war's upheaval, it would endure.

The question of what Hattie would do next had not been far from her mind these past few days. Now, as she gazed into the green canopy of leaves, it pushed forward again. Eroded by her dealings with Mollie Pitman, her sense of ambition was returning. She had useful skills to offer, and she intended to make the best of them until the war was over.

Looking down from the branches, she saw John Elliott striding quickly toward her. "Hattie!" Nearing her, he held out his hands to her, and without thinking, she met them with her own. His grip was warm and welcoming, as was his smile. "You're back."

She returned the smile, and for once, she felt no conflict, only delight at having someone who welcomed her the way he did. "I've brought the information you wanted." She patted her purse. "I'll explain in your office if you've got time."

"I've always got time for you. But I've been cooped up in meetings all day. Walk with me, and you can tell me what you've learned. Plus your timing is perfect. I've got a surprise for you."

She raised her eyebrows. "A surprise?" Her thoughts went to the dinner invitation she'd hoped for the last time they met.

"All in due time." He offered his arm. She took it, and they set off. In the warm air, they stuck to the shaded side of the street, where the path was less crowded and the soldiers few. In another era, they might have been any young couple out for a stroll.

They turned onto a quiet residential street, and Hattie slowed her pace, sensing this was a good place to talk. "You were right about the cotton," she said. "Adelicia made a fortune on it."

She stopped, and he waited while she fished the bill of sale from her purse and handed it over to him. He looked it over, then gave a low whistle. "That's a lot of cotton," he said, his eyes meeting hers. "A lot of cash sitting in London."

Hattie closed her purse. "I expect Adelicia will head there to retrieve it as soon as the war is over."

He tucked the paper into the inner pocket of his uniform. "It's just the proof I needed," he said as they began to walk again. "However did you manage to get hold of it?"

"I joined the household for a time. As a seamstress. The children needed new clothes."

He shook his head. "Clever, capable, and she sews."

She shot him a look. "Just don't ask me to do needlepoint. Nothing duller. At least clothes have a purpose. And there's a challenge to it."

"So you were the seamstress in the corner of Belle Monte, stitching away and eavesdropping the whole while."

She laughed. "You could eavesdrop all day and night and Adelicia would never give up anything worth hearing. She's far too clever for that."

"But she never suspected you?"

"She may have after she caught me in her study after hours. But she never confronted me about it, and I think I know why." Hattie explained what she'd learned from the Confederate officer at the gala about Adelicia's sharing secrets with both sides.

"Now I understand why Union officials gave her as much latitude as the Confederates did. Not that any of them would admit to it." He patted his jacket pocket. "This is truly helpful, Hattie. We're at such a crucial point in the war. This money would be a big boost to the South if the government got its hands on it. Now that we know where it's being held, we can have our friends in London keep an eye on it."

"You won't arrest her?"

"Probably not. She's too big a fish, as they say, and now that she's completed her sale, she's got no reason to spy."

"That makes sense," Hattie said. "I can't picture Adelicia in prison. It's not just her wealth. She's too savvy. And her estate at Belle Monte..." Hattie's voice trailed off. "It's hard to describe. A place apart. An illusion, almost."

"Not for her enslaved Negroes," Elliott said.

"Right," Hattie said. "I guess that's another reason she felt she had to sell that cotton. When the war's over, she'll have to start paying her servants."

He rubbed his chin. "You're assuming we win."

"Of course we'll win."

"I like your confidence. But if Lincoln loses in November..." He shook his head. "Grant's troops are stalled in the Shenandoah valley. We're all weary of war. It doesn't get much better for a Peace Democrat to prevail in the election."

"And end the war on terms favorable to the South," Hattie said. "Including slavery."

"Exactly," he said morosely.

"So much heartache. So many dead. So many wounded and maimed. What's the use of it if the evils of slavery are allowed to continue?"

"That's Mr. Lincoln's stance as well, which is why there's such an effort to oust him." Elliott's steps slowed. "Well, here we are. Your surprise awaits."

Engrossed in conversation, Hattie hadn't paid attention to their route. Now she saw that they'd arrived at the corner of Broad and Vine. "The Pest House?"

Disappointment must have shown on her face, because he patted her arm and said, "You'll be pleased, I promise."

Instead of mounting the front steps, he guided her around to the back, where a woman was hanging out laundry in what would have been a courtyard before the residence was converted into a hospital for prostitutes. He led Hattie to a side door, then rapped on it.

Footsteps approached from inside. Then the door swung open, revealing a slight woman with a bright, birdlike gaze. She was dressed in the trousered women's attire known as bloomers.

"Edith!" Hattie flung her arms around her. Encircled in Hattie's embrace, Edith patted her back awkwardly.

Hattie stepped back, realizing her effusive greeting was a better fit for lively Elise than for the staid doctor. "I was so worried about you. How did you manage to get out of prison?"

Edith offered a prim smile. "A bit of subterfuge. I wrote a treatise ardently supporting General McClellan's candidacy for President, knowing full well Rebel officials would open and read it. They decided that as an advocate for McClellan, I'd be of more use to their cause outside of jail."

"We were just discussing the plots afoot to unseat Lincoln." Elliott turned to Hattie. "And if I understand correctly, Dr. Greenfield has a related matter to discuss with you, Miss Thomas. I'll leave the two of you to discuss that."

He tipped his hat, then turned and strode quickly away, an abrupt departure that left Hattie feeling momentarily deflated. *Better this way,* she thought. It was all too complex, the dancing she and John Elliott did around their grief-tainted pasts, now complicated even further by the secret she was keeping about Thom Welton.

She wasn't going to think of that now. She turned to Edith. "Are you back to run the hospital here?"

Edith shook her head. "I came here hoping to find you."

Hattie could scarcely believe her ears. She had the greatest respect for Edith Greenfield as both a doctor and a spy. That she'd traveled to Nashville in search of Hattie was praise beyond any she could have imagined. "Lieutenant Elliott said I'd be pleased, coming here. He couldn't have been more right."

Edith brushed her hands together, a gesture Hattie recognized as her way of steering a conversation back on track. "I don't suppose you've got all day, and I haven't either. I'd invite you inside, but this chamber is little more than a closet. But I wanted a place where I'd attract little attention, and in that, it does fill the bill."

With that, she stepped outside, closing the door behind her. The woman who'd been hanging out laundry was gone, leaving the courtyard empty save for the sheets flapping in the wind.

"How did you know you'd find me in Tennessee?" Hattie asked as they started for the courtyard.

"Your friend Pauline," Edith said. "I...ahem...took in her show in Washington City. Quite entertaining, I must say."

Smiling, Hattie shook her head. "I should've guessed. For a former spy, Pauline isn't shy about sharing what she knows."

Seeing how Edith squinted in the sunlight, Hattie suggested they occupy a small stone bench in the shade of the building. As they sat, Edith rubbed her forehead. "I haven't felt entirely myself since leaving prison," she said. "The light bothers my eyes, and I get headaches."

"The papers reported what you wrote to your mother," Hattie said. "You sounded hopeful about conditions at Castle Thunder."

Edith smiled weakly. "I didn't see fit to worry my dear mother with reports of bed vermin and musket balls crashing through the walls and gaslights that burned all night, ruining my eyesight."

"You've lost weight too," Hattie said. "Not that you had extra to lose."

Edith waived away her concern. "Some good came of it. While I was there, I learned of a plot to create a Northwest Confederacy, opening new battlegrounds in the North."

Hattie straightened. "I've heard talk of such plans from a Rebel spy. I didn't believe her, but if you've heard something similar..." Hattie's voice trailed off. If Mollie's testimony on the plot had been accurate, what did that mean for the other accusations she'd made, including what she'd said about Franklin Stone?

"My sources weren't the most upstanding of men," Edith said. "But on this matter, I believe they were truthful, which is why I went straight to General Sharpe about it after my release."

Sharpe was in charge of US military intelligence. If Edith had gone to him, she must truly be concerned. "There's an officer in St. Louis who seems quite interested as well," Hattie said.

"Colonel Sanderson," Edith said. "General Sharpe mentioned him. Said he's preparing a report on the group behind the plot."

"The Sons of Liberty," Hattie said. "Also known as the Order of the American Knights. Also known as the Knights of the Golden Circle."

Edith looked surprised. "The Rebel spy revealed that?"

"And then some." As succinctly as she could, Hattie explained how she'd ended up in St. Louis with Mollie Pitman in tow, then sat in on her interrogation at Sanderson's request. "I don't believe she has truly switched sides," Hattie said. "But Sanderson believes her. If he bases his report on what she tells him, it's likely to be full of false information."

"Then it's a good thing Sharpe dispatched me to learn more. But I told him I needed help. The plot is set to unfold on multiple fronts, the first being Indianapolis. Naturally, I thought of you."

Hattie took a sharp breath. Indianapolis. Franklin Stone.

"Working with Military Intelligence, a man by the name of Coffin infiltrated the secret group there," Edith said. "But the conspirators found him out, and they made threats on his life. I suggested to General Sharpe that under the circumstances, a woman might have better luck uncovering the plot. And you know the city."

"I...I can't imagine they'd take a woman into their confidence." Hattie was buying time, stammering out the first excuse that came to her. The idea of unraveling a plot of this magnitude intrigued her, and even more so if she could work with Edith. But what if Mollie was right? What if Franklin was involved?

"We wouldn't have you try to infiltrate the group," Edith said. "Not after Coffin almost..." Again, the wry smile. "Almost ended up in a coffin. You'd simply be the eyes and ears of our effort, working your knowledge of the city and the Copperheads there. I assume you're aware of a few."

"Well, yes, but—"

"You're much better positioned than I for the task. Besides your knowledge of the town, you dress the part of a lady." She sighed. "One day, women will come to their senses, and my manner of dress will become commonplace. In the meantime, it does draw attention where I'd rather it didn't."

"You could disguise yourself as a man," Hattie said.

"My point is that a woman should be able to dress as she chooses, not that in doing so she should present herself as a man. Lord knows I'm called *sir* more often than I care to mention." Drawing herself up, Edith looked Hattie squarely in the eye. "You're skilled at this work, Hattie. You think on your feet. You can act a part, and yet there's a sincerity about you that wins people's trust."

Coming from Edith, this was high praise, and it landed well with Hattie. An idea began to form, a way that she could honor Anne's wishes while also fulfilling the role Edith proposed. "How soon would I be needed in Indianapolis?"

"Within the week." Edith lifted an eyebrow. "Lieutenant Elliott told me you've been at Belle Monte. I suspect you're ready to do something more substantial after lolling about that wealthy woman's plantation for weeks on end."

"I wasn't exactly lolling," Hattie said. "But yes, I'd like to help you get to the bottom of this Northwest Confederacy plot." If Franklin was caught up in this—and she very much hoped he wasn't—better she was the one to find out. It could put her in a difficult position with Anne, but hadn't Edith just praised her cleverness?

"Then it's settled," Edith said. "You'll proceed to Indianapolis and see what you can learn about the Sons of Liberty and their Northwest Confederacy plot. You send a telegram when you're finished, and we'll determine what needs doing next."

"Without consulting General Sharpe?"

"His office has established the contours of our work. It's up to us to see it through. You send a telegram when you're ready, and we'll proceed from there."

"A telegram? I thought you were coming with me."

"If you can handle Indianapolis on your own, my time would be better spent in St. Louis. I'd like to interview this Pitman woman myself, seeing as how she claims some knowledge of the plot."

Hattie smiled. In no-nonsense Edith Greenfield, Mollie Pitman just might meet her match.

Chapter Fifteen

AUGUST 5, 1864

Returning to Indianapolis, Hattie had hoped she could stay as she had before with Anne's parents. It would be less awkward all around, especially with the delicate operation Hattie had in mind, exposing the Northwest Confederacy plot while making sure not to implicate Anne's husband in it.

But Anne's parents already had guests—Anne's Aunt Patty and her cousin Julia were visiting from Washington City. A few weeks ago, Rebels under the command of foul-speaking, tobacco-spitting General Jubal Early had come dangerously close to occupying the nation's capital. After that, the family decided the Trent women would be safer in Indiana, at least until General Grant's army achieved a much hoped-for victory over the Rebels in the Shenandoah.

If they'd known of the Copperhead plots brewing in Indianapolis, the Trents might have found themselves a different refuge. But on the surface, all seemed well in the city. There was a good deal of activity at Camp Morton, but that was to be expected. Union soldiers were even taking time out from their drills, Anne said, to enjoy cakes delivered by local women.

As it was, Hattie's staying with Anne—a delicate balancing act, to be sure—would soon prove its usefulness. In the meantime, Anne seemed far more eager to discuss Hattie's potential for romance than the details of her spy work.

One evening shortly after Hattie's arrival, when Franklin was out and Jo had gone to sleep and Hattie was helping Anne with her mending, she mentioned that she thought Lieutenant Elliott had finally come to trust her even with assignments involving some risk.

Anne's blue eyes sparkled. "I hope that means you'll finally allow him to court you. From what I gather, he's been sweet on you for a long while."

Hattie pulled her thread into a knot, then snipped it off. "I don't know about that. He's a good man, but..." She left her thought unfinished.

"But he's not Thom Welton." Anne sighed. "Your devotion to Thom won't bring him back to life, you know."

Hattie felt a pang of sorrow. Anne was right, she knew. But to give up on Thom's memory felt too much like acknowledging the truth of the dark secret she carried. "I just can't..." She paused. Can't what? Let go? Admit that what she'd had with Thom had been less than the complete and glorious love she'd thought it was? "I can't see how John Elliott can forget his wife either. You should see the look in his eyes whenever he mentions her."

"Loving another doesn't require forgetting."

Hattie breathed deeply. She'd told Anne she'd come here from Nashville. She'd told her about her frustrations with Mollie Pitman. But she'd said nothing yet about Memphis. "Did Franklin say anything about running into me in Memphis?"

"Why, yes," Anne said. "I can't believe I forgot to mention it. What a small world this is."

"So he told you...I mean, you know about..." Her voice trailed off. She didn't want to hurt her friend, but she had a right to know.

"About Belle Edmondson?" Anne's face brightened. "Oh, Hattie. I see why you're concerned. But honestly, she's just a friend. Her family and the Stones go way back. She and Franklin toddled about together when they were scarcely older than Jo is now. Franklin introduced us once when she was passing through Indianapolis. Quite the lady. Charming, flamboyant. He told me he'd be stopping in to see her when he was in Memphis."

"It's said she's a spy," Hattie said.

"Oh, Franklin told me all about those rumors," Anne said, taking up her stitching again. "A woman like her, well, people talk."

"I suppose he'd know," Hattie said. It was Mollie, after all, who'd told Hattie Belle was a spy, and her motives were questionable as far as Hattie was concerned.

"He does." Anne gazed out the window, where the evening sky had turned a dusky blue. "I wonder when he'll be home." His place at the table was set, though the dinner she'd fixed had long since gone cold.

"He does work some long hours," Hattie said. "His legal services must be in high demand."

"It's a printing project he's been working on lately," Anne said. "With his friend Harrison Dodd, who's so seldom home himself that Mrs. Dodd tells me she's quit making dinner for him altogether."

"What sort of printing?" Hattie asked, trying to sound less interested than she was.

"Nothing nefarious, I assure you," Anne snapped. In the waning light, the creases on her forehead looked deeper than what Hattie remembered. Anne had always been a worrier, but her need to shield her husband was taking a big toll.

Hattie held up her hands in a gesture of surrender. "Just making conversation."

"I haven't pried about your business at Camp Morton," Anne said. "So please don't pry into Franklin's business."

"There's nothing exciting to reveal about my interrogations," Hattie said. This was the reason she'd given Anne for returning to Indianapolis—that she'd been assigned to interview Rebel prisoners held at Camp Morton. "And I only wondered about the printing because of Pauline's memoir."

"Oh, that." Anne's forehead relaxed as she picked up her stitching. "I'd forgotten she was writing a book. Is she still with Barnum?"

"As far as I know," Hattie said. "She sent a card in care of Lieutenant Elliott some weeks ago, saying she'd soon be touring the West."

"Won't that be fascinating," Anne said, looking wistful. Like Hattie, Anne had a spirit of adventure, though admittedly she was more prudent in her approach. Still, Hattie wondered whether if, given a chance to do it over, she'd have been so quick to marry. But of course she had little Jo to think of now. All the more reason for Hattie to make sure that whatever doings of the Sons of Liberty

she uncovered here, any involvement by Franklin Stone stayed out
of it.

~ ~ ~

When Hattie left the Stones' house the next morning, she encountered what felt like a wall of hot, muggy air, the August heat
having diminished little overnight. Fatigued as she was, she'd rather
not have to deal with the heat as well. After she'd gone to bed,
Franklin finally came in last night. He and Anne had argued, their
voices rising until little Jo woke in a fit of tears. Only then had the
house quieted.

By heading out early, Hattie had avoided interacting with
Franklin at breakfast. Though she tried for Anne's sake to be pleasant with him, it wasn't easy knowing how difficult her friend's life
had become since they'd married. But all marriages must involve
some degree of conflict, Hattie told herself. Their troubles would
pass. The war would end, and Little Jo would get older, demanding
less of Anne's attention. They'd have more children, settle into a
comfortable life.

It was a vision of the future Hattie had once imagined for herself
back when Thom Welton was alive. Now she had no sense of what
would become of her when the war ended. Even if she succeeded
as she hoped at the task Edith had set before her, she couldn't
imagine capitalizing on her achievements as Pauline had. Then
again, Pauline had on more than one occasion accused Hattie of
thinking too small.

For the moment, as Hattie slogged in the sticky heat toward
the city's center, she was grateful that Pauline's fame had allowed
her to give a quick answer when Anne questioned her interest in

printing. She would put a different spin on the story with Harrison Dodd, though.

It wasn't difficult to learn the location of Dodd's print shop. Unloading a wagon, a teamster pointed the way. A block from the courthouse, the limestone building was within sight of Statehouse Square. Three years ago, Hattie and Anne had gone to the Square for the sendoff of Indiana's original regiment of Union soldiers, the Zouaves. So much had changed since then. They'd grown up, both of them, though thankfully they hadn't grown apart. Hattie intended to do all she could to keep it that way.

She climbed the stairs to the fourth floor of the limestone building, then followed the signs to Dodd's Printing and Bookbindery. Pushing open the door, she entered an office that smelled of printer's ink and tobacco. Boxes were stacked all along one wall, some labeled "stationery" and others labeled "Sunday School Books." The latter struck Hattie as strange. She'd have thought a printer would label his work by title, not by type.

A stout, dark-haired man wearing a smudged printer's apron emerged from a door at the far end of the room.

"I'm looking for Mr. Dodd," she said.

He bowed rather dramatically. "Harrison Dodd at your service, miss." Despite his jowly cheeks, Hattie guessed him to be in his early thirties, young enough to have been conscripted into the Union Army. She guessed he'd paid $300 to a substitute enrollee to serve in his place.

"Hattie Thomas," she said. "I've come on behalf of a friend with an interest in publishing her life's story. You may have heard of her." Leaning forward, Hattie lowered her voice. "Miss Mollie Pitman."

Dodd cocked his head. "You're a friend of Miss Pitman's?"

She nodded. "I last saw her in St. Louis. Union soldiers recently brought her in for questioning."

He frowned. "If there's any truth to what I've heard of Miss Pitman, they'll get little out of her."

"Indeed. I expect they've tied themselves in knots by now." Hattie's shoulders relaxed. Mollie's professed shift in loyalties must still be a secret to her former associates.

"True to her oath." He straightened, cleared his throat, and spoke what seemed to be memorized lines. "The superior intellectual and physical development of man must progress, even should the subjection of the inferior to a condition of servitude to the superior be necessary."

He was testing her, Hattie realized, by reciting a portion of the Sons of Liberty ritual. "Miss Pitman told me as much herself," she said, a signal she hoped he took for knowing. "Though I have much yet to learn of the sublime creed."

"Well, then," Dodd said, relaxing his stance. "If Miss Pitman is eager to have her story in print, I should be happy to assist her. When the South prevails in this wretched war, people will be clamoring to learn how extraordinary people assured the victory." From the way he puffed out his chest, it seemed Harrison Dodd counted himself in that number. "Bring me her manuscript, and we'll ready it for publication. I hope she's not in a rush though. We have quite a lot in the works at present."

"Oh, Miss Pitman is well aware of that," Hattie said. "She says this month will be a turning point in the war."

"Quite so," Dodd said.

Hattie glanced away, then redirected her gaze at him, hoping to convince him she could be both coy and direct. "I would welcome the opportunity to be of service to the cause while Miss Pitman is indisposed."

Smiling in a fatherly way, he patted her arm. "As a neophyte, you'd have much to learn."

"More than I could ever hope to take in. Only...in her present circumstances, it would be such an encouragement to Miss Pitman if I could bring her some inspired bits of news."

He pressed his finger to his chin, seeming to consider this. "It would be somewhat irregular since you have yet to complete the initiation. But I suppose it wouldn't hurt for you to observe one facet of what we have planned. A quite spectacular demonstration, actually."

She clapped her hands in delight. "I would very much appreciate that."

"Take a stroll along the river on Sunday," he told her. "South of town, around about four o'clock, you'll find me and one of my associates testing our Greek fire apparatus."

"Greek fire," she repeated. "I don't understand."

"You won't need to understand to appreciate the effect," Dodd said. "Entirely memorable, I assure you."

~ ~ ~

A storm blew through Indianapolis Sunday morning, leaving the air dry and warm but not sweltering. The day was so splendid that when Hattie announced she was going for a walk, Anne wanted to go with her, walking little Jo in her buggy. But Jo was teething, and to Hattie's relief, Anne decided to stay home, mind-

ful that a screaming child was not the best company on a Sunday
stroll. Bouncing Jo on her hip, she waved goodbye as Hattie set out.

Hattie walked to the city's center. There she hired a carriage to
take her to the river's edge on the south end of town. After passing
Camp Morton, she noticed fewer soldiers milling about the streets.
As they neared the edge of town, the road turned rough, the pot-
holes too numerous for the driver to avoid. Bouncing jarringly in
her seat, Hattie scanned the riverfront. In the distance, she spotted
Dodd, recognizing him by his stout build and dark hair. Hands in
his pockets, he stood next to a lean, white-haired gentleman.

Not seeing Franklin, she relaxed. Had he been there, she'd have
had the carriage driver turn back. It relieved her to think he was
actually at his office as he'd told Anne he'd be, his association
with Harrison Dodd simply involving a printing project. Even if
that project was political—even if it was some sort of Copperhead
screed—that didn't mean Franklin was entangled with the Sons of
Liberty as Dodd clearly was.

She paid her fare and asked the driver to return in an hour.
Then she set off on foot, the path along the river well-worn but
thankfully dry.

As she drew near, Dodd strutted up to meet her. She took his
arm, and they proceeded toward the older man. Hattie thought he
resembled an older version of Andrew Jackson, the thin, sharp-fea-
tured president she'd seen only in pictures.

"So this is the young lady who wants to see our fire," the man
croaked as they approached.

She smiled. "Mr. Dodd tells me it will be quite the show."

"Indeed it will," the white-haired man said. Dodd introduced him as Dr. William Bowles, a Confederate loyalist who owned a resort property at French Lick Springs, south of Indianapolis.

"I had no idea there were so many like-minded folks across the state," she said. "It gives me hope for a proper outcome to this conflict."

"Oh, there will be a proper outcome," Bowles said. "You can be certain of that."

"As for numbers, we are forty thousand strong," Dodd said.

"And that's in Indiana alone," Bowles said with a lecherous wink. "We've got equal numbers in Illinois, Ohio, and Wisconsin."

"If not more." Dodd slapped him on the back.

Scowling, Bowles recoiled, apparently displeased at Dodd's familiarity. Then he pulled a gold watch from his pocket and popped open the filigreed cover, revealing its face. "Five till four," he announced. "Any minute now."

Shielding his eyes with his cupped hand, Dodd gazed downriver. "Hope they don't run into trouble."

"Does Greek fire often cause trouble?" Hattie asked innocuously.

"That's the point of it," Bowles said. "The usual destruction of fire, but with a twist."

Hattie smiled as if his vague answer perfectly matched her ability to comprehend such matters. "I've heard of Greek sculptures and Greek gods, but never Greek fire."

Dodd set his hands on his hips. "The Byzantines were the first to deploy it against their enemies," he said. "Sulphur, rock salt, ashes, resin, and a bit of quicklime, which must all be handled with the greatest care lest it explode in one's face."

"You must be a man of some learning, Mr. Dodd, to have put together such a complicated mix of substances," she said.

"Don't give him more credit than he deserves," Bowles said.

"But then who—"

An explosive boom cut her off, followed by a whoosh of flames and a plume of black smoke. To the south, it looked as if the river was on fire.

Dodd and Bowles exchanged satisfied nods.

"It looks as if the water is burning," Hattie said.

Dodd chuckled. "And so it is. That's the beauty of Greek fire. Wait till you see its effect on the waters of Lake Erie."

Bowles shot him a look. "I thought you said she hasn't been fully inducted yet."

"She's a friend to Mollie Pitman," Dodd said. "That's good enough for me. And I'll bet she doesn't know the first thing about Lake Erie."

She smiled sweetly. "That's one of the Great Lakes, isn't it? I'm afraid that's all I know." She shielded her eyes, watching the unlikely conflagration. "I sure wish Mollie could see this."

Dodd set his hand on her shoulder. "Don't you worry about Mollie. They won't detain her long. Our people are armed and ready."

"Our soldiers, you mean," Hattie said.

"Our citizens," said Bowles.

Dodd nodded vigorously. "First we take the arsenals. Then we turn loose our prisoners. And with that, the war shifts in our favor."

"But how—"

"How is none of your concern." Eyes narrowed, Bowles held her gaze. "Neither is who, when, or where."

"Just be sure Mollie knows the Sons of Liberty will see to her release."

"Of course," Hattie said. "She'll be grateful to hear it."

"Well, Dr. Bowles." Dodd slapped his friend on the back. "I believe we're all but ready. One more meeting to make sure we've dotted our I's and crossed our T's."

Bowles shirked from his touch. "Thursday, is it?"

Dodd nodded. "Seven o'clock. And Miss Thomas, you'd best bring that manuscript around before then. Once we set our plans in motion, there's no telling where I'll be."

"Oh!" Hattie put her hand to her mouth. "The manuscript—I'm sorry if I gave the wrong impression. With things in such a state of flux, Miss Pitman intends to make some additions before the book is ready."

Dodd chuckled. "A whole new ending if we've got anything to say about it, right, Bowles?"

"Right."

"Well, then. I'll be in touch. Thank you kindly for the enlightening demonstration," Hattie said.

Dodd pointed his thick finger at her. "Watch for the headlines," he said.

She smiled. "Of course." As she turned to leave, she saw out of the corner of her eye how the men struck an odd pose, each man grasping his own wrist as he crossed his arms across his belly. A signal, she thought, for their secret order. A signal, she prayed that was wholly unknown to Franklin Stone.

Chapter Sixteen

AUGUST 8, 1864

Hattie spent the next day and the next turning over in her mind what she should do. Back in St. Louis, she'd thought Mollie's claims about the secret order rather outrageous. But between what Edith had said and what Hattie had seen and heard yesterday, she knew the Sons of Liberty had to be stopped. But how?

She wished Edith were here so they could make a plan together. But Edith was in St. Louis, and this wasn't the sort of thing they could discuss by telegram.

One option was for Hattie to go to the local authorities with the information she'd gathered. If they believed her—and that was a big if—they could break up the meeting on Thursday, arresting Dodd and Bowles and the other local members of the Sons of Liberty leaders before they had a chance to put their plot in motion.

But what if Franklin was there? Hattie didn't want him getting arrested based on the intelligence she'd provided. A promise was a promise, and Anne was her best friend in all the world. There had to be a way to protect Franklin and at the same time, thwart the Sons of Liberty's plans.

At dinner on Wednesday, Hattie was still trying to decide what to do. As she passed Franklin a serving bowl of boiled potatoes, Anne announced that her mother had invited them to dinner tomorrow night. "She's had the cook make gooseberry pie," Anne said. "She knows it's your favorite, Franklin."

"How kind of her," Hattie said. Out of the corner of her eye, she glanced at Franklin, who was cutting into his slice of beef.

"Can't attend," he said, not looking up. "I've got an appointment with a client."

"Another evening appointment." Anne sighed. "Can't you reschedule?"

Franklin set down his knife. Eyes flashing, he said, "I've asked you before to stay out of my work affairs."

Anne's face colored. She glanced in Hattie's direction. Sensing her friend's embarrassment, Hattie feigned a sudden interest in her food.

"I'm not inserting myself in your affairs," Anne said. "I'm simply asking you to arrange for your client to come another night."

"Our business can't wait," Franklin snapped.

"Not even until the next morning?" Anne asked.

"Quit hounding me."

"I'm not hounding. But mother has already had the pie made, and—"

With his fisted hand, Franklin pounded the table. "Enough!"

From her highchair, Jo let out a squeal. She opened and closed her fingers, sticky with bits of potato her mother had mashed for her.

Catching Hattie's eye, Anne offered an apologetic smile, then turned to her daughter. "Such a little piggy." She mashed another bit of potato and offered it to her daughter, who crammed a fistful into her mouth.

"I heard the most curious rumor the other day," Hattie said, eager to rescue Anne with a change of subject. "A man was saying General Forrest had died of lockjaw."

Franklin swallowed the meat he'd been chewing. "People these days will believe anything," he said. "Forrest is just laying low, waiting for his next opportunity to attack."

Then Anne turned the conversation toward the weather, which had turned muggy, and the couple's conflict over Thursday's dinner invitation seemed forgotten.

~ ~ ~

With Franklin so adamant about tomorrow night, Hattie knew what she had to do. But she needed a few moments with Anne, the sooner the better. The problem was that Franklin had been making more of an effort to stay home evenings—other than tomorrow, as he'd made clear—and what Hattie had to say was not for his ears.

Fortunately, little Jo came to the rescue. Having stuffed herself full of potatoes, she should have been sleepy. Instead, she was wide awake and crying inconsolably.

"Maybe we should walk her?" Hattie suggested. "A little motion, a little evening air. It might do the trick."

"Worth a try," Anne said. She tucked the fussing child in her buggy, and she and Hattie set off. Darkening to dusk, the sky had turned a deep shade of blue, and along the path, crickets chirped from the grass.

At first, Anne and Hattie talked about Jo's fussing, which Anne attributed to teething. They also spoke of Anne's brothers, the oldest engaged to be married and the younger one likely to propose to his cousin Julia when she turned eighteen.

Before long, Jo's wails turned to whimpers. Turning to Hattie, Anne's face looked troubled. "I'm sorry you had to witness that spat between Franklin and me."

"No need to apologize," Hattie said. "All couples argue now and again."

Anne sighed. "I fear Franklin and I argue more than most. I do my best to keep the peace for Jo's sake. But sometimes it's hard. He can be so stubborn. And so guarded about his time."

And his secrets, Hattie thought. "He must have some very important clients," she said. "Not wanting to reschedule their meetings."

"I dread telling Mother that he's not coming to dinner tomorrow, especially after she baked that pie. I feel as if I'm always making excuses for him."

They turned a corner. In the buggy, Jo fell silent. Her eyes were still open, but her eyelids looked heavy, and she had the vacant gaze of a child about to succumb to sleep.

It was now or never, Hattie thought, to speak her mind. "You're a good wife, Anne. I see how you protect Franklin, and I understand that, especially with Jo to consider. And I want to honor my promise to leave your family out of my spying. But you should know that a matter has arisen that may require our action."

Glancing at Hattie, Anne raised her eyebrows. "This involves me?"

Hattie nodded firmly. "There's much at stake, and I fear if we don't act, Franklin may get drawn into something bigger than he can handle."

"If he hasn't already," Anne said, and Hattie saw the worry in her eyes.

Slowing her pace, Hattie explained what she'd learned from Mollie and Edith about the Sons of Liberty's plans for a violent uprising to establish a Northwest Confederacy. "Edith is in St. Louis learning what she can from Mollie and an army colonel there who's preparing a report," Hattie said. "And knowing that the group has been active in this area, she asked me to come here and see what I could find out."

"Don't tell me you've been looking in Franklin's desk again."

Hattie shook her head. "I told you I wouldn't. But his friend Harrison Dodd is involved in planning the uprising. He makes little secret of it. On Sunday, I attended a demonstration of one of the weapons they intend to deploy. Dodd was there along with a man named Bowles."

Anne's brow furrowed. "The doctor from French Lick. Franklin brought him to the house once. Rather full of himself, I recall thinking at the time."

"That's him," Hattie said. "They intend to use something called Greek fire in their plot to take control of Northern arsenals and prisons. They'll arm the Confederate prisoners they've freed, and troops will rush North to join them.

Anne glanced at her sleeping child. "They'd bring the war here?"

Hattie nodded. They walked a few paces in silence, the buggy jiggling on the uneven path. Inside, Jo was sleeping at last, a look of peaceful bliss on her face.

Finally, Anne spoke. "You haven't a choice, Hattie. You have to expose their plot. If they succeed, innocent people will be hurt. The war will drag on."

Relief flooded over Hattie. "I agree. But I worry Franklin's involved."

"But you said it was only Dodd and Bowles you met with on Sunday. Just because Franklin knows them doesn't mean he's caught up in their schemes."

"I'd like to think that," Hattie said. "But the Sons of Liberty meet tomorrow night at Dodd's print shop. An important meeting, they said. The last one before they put their plan in motion."

Anne's expression darkened. "You think that's why Franklin refused Mother's invitation? Because he has to be at that meeting?"

"It's possible." Taking hold of Anne's arm, Hattie slowed her stride. "There's a way to find out. And a way to keep him out of it, I think. But I'll need your help."

~ ~ ~

The next morning, after Franklin left for the office, Anne took a quill from the desk. While Hattie bounced Jo on her knee, Anne penned a note. She folded the paper and slipped it into an envelope which she sealed and handed to Hattie. Then she scooped Jo into her arms, and the two of them stood in the doorway as Hattie left the house, Anne lifting Jo's chubby arm to wave goodbye.

A basket on her arm, Hattie proceeded up Virginia Avenue. If by chance she ran into Franklin, she could say Anne had sent her with a list of items to fetch from the market. Even at this early hour, the air was warm and heavy. Not wanting to betray the urgency of her errand, Hattie walked at a pace that behooved a lady. Miss Wickham would appreciate that, Hattie thought with a wry smile. Headmistress at the finishing school Hattie and Anne had attended here in Indianapolis, she'd been a stickler for manners. Had she managed to keep her Ladygrace School for Girls open during these last difficult years? Hattie would have to ask Anne what she knew about that.

Circling the courthouse, Hattie went north on Illinois Street. At the intersection with Market Street, she stopped in front of an unassuming brick house, then climbed the narrow stairs and knocked loudly on the heavy wooden door. Moments later, an older woman cracked the door. Judging from her plain gray dress, she was a servant, Hattie thought.

"I need a moment with Governor Morton," Hattie said.

The woman lifted her chin. "The governor doesn't see strangers at his residence."

She started to shut the door, but Hattie stepped into the threshold. She pulled Anne's note from her basket and thrust it at the woman. "This is from Roger Duncan's daughter. Mr. Duncan is a close associate of the governor. It's an urgent matter."

Seeming unsure what to do, the servant studied the envelope. From behind her, Hattie heard footsteps, and a man she recognized as Indiana's governor, weary-eyed and wearing a rumpled shirt, stepped into view.

"Cynthia is calling for you," he said, addressing the servant. "She wants her medicine."

The servant handed him the note. "This lady says she needs to speak with you. I tried to send her away, but she won't go."

"I've brought an urgent message from Roger Duncan's daughter," Hattie said to the governor.

A woman's thin voice called from upstairs. Hattie couldn't make out her words. "Go tend to her, Betty. I've done all I can."

As the servant scurried away, the governor tore open the envelope and studied Anne's note. Glancing up at Hattie, he gestured for her to come inside. "Roger's daughter says I'm to trust what you tell me," he said. "Important and time-sensitive, she says."

Hattie nodded. "You're aware of the Sons of Liberty?"

His eyes narrowed, his gaze piercing. "Yes. What of them?"

Hattie gave the briefest possible version of what she had discovered about the group's plans to stage riots, take control of arsenals, arm Confederate prisoners, and attack Northern cities using Greek fire. "Indianapolis appears to be their staging ground," she said. "And their last meeting before setting their plans in motion will be tonight."

Morton stroked his chin. "This state is honeycombed with secret societies sufficient to inflict real damage not just here but throughout the North. But we've had a hard time catching up with their leaders, and without specifics, our hands have been tied. You say they're meeting tonight to put the finishing touches on their plans?"

"That's right. Seven o'clock, Dodd's print shop."

He glanced through the doorway toward the street, then looked back at her. "You did well to come to me. What these men are plotting is treason. If I have anything to say about it, the men at that meeting tonight will wait out the end of this war in prison."

All except Franklin Stone, Hattie hoped. She thanked the governor for his time and hurried away, the empty basket on her arm. So far, all was going as planned. But the most difficult part lay ahead.

Returning to the Stones' house, Hattie relayed to Anne her conversation with Morton. Gravely, Anne nodded. "Good," she said simply, but worry showed in her eyes.

Rather than make another visit to Camp Morton, the training grounds and prisoner of war camp named after the governor she'd now met, Hattie busied herself helping Anne with the washing. On the back porch, heat seeming to shimmer up from the ground, she bent over the washtub, scrubbing shirts till her arms ached while Anne rinsed and ran them through the wringer. Having grown up in a household with plenty of hired help, Anne managed remarkably, Hattie thought.

As the afternoon progressed, Jo's fussiness returned. Pegging the clothes on the backyard line, Hattie and Anne exchanged nervous glances. For dinner, Anne set out a plate of cold beef and sliced tomatoes. They took turns holding Jo, who took great delight in smashing bits of tomato between her fingers while Hattie and Anne picked at their food. Hattie kept an eye on the clock. If their operation was to succeed, timing was everything.

At twenty minutes to seven, she got up from the table. She nodded at Anne, who took up a pen and hastily scribbled on a scrap of paper. Anne handed the paper to Hattie, who folded it and slipped it into her skirt pocket.

"Be careful," Anne said. "They're bound to have weapons. If they suspect you—"

"They won't," Hattie said.

Anne's dark expression indicated she wasn't so sure. But she put on a brave face. Her interest in the tomatoes waning, Jo started to cry.

"It's as if she knows what we need from her," Hattie said.

Anne offered a weak smile. "She's always been a cooperative child."

Leaving the house, Hattie tried not to think of all the things that could go wrong. She walked briskly, a woman on an important errand. Checking the time, she took Thom's watch from her pocket. Tonight, there was nothing sentimental in her using it.

On the streets, a few stragglers headed home from work. Near the city's center, soldiers walked their patrols, but they didn't seem to be any more alert than usual. Slowing her steps, Hattie strained to see the face of a man coming toward her, worried it might be Franklin, arriving late for the meeting. But as he neared, she saw he was a stranger. He turned a corner, disappearing from sight.

Sighing with relief, she entered the limestone building that housed Dodd's printery. She climbed the stairs to the fourth floor, then proceeded down the hallways, treading lightly, another skill she owed to Miss Whitcomb and her finishing school.

She stopped short of the print shop's entrance. Wafting from under the print shop's door, the smell of tobacco stung her nose. She heard the men inside talking, though the mix of voices was such that she could only pick out a word here and there.

"Order!" She recognized Dodd's voice, much louder than the rest, followed by the pounding of what sounded like a gavel.

Scarcely daring to breathe, Hattie held still, straining to hear. Beyond the door, the men launched into what she assumed was part of their ritual, with Dodd barking out words and the men replying in unison. Such drivel, Hattie thought as they waxed on about plighted vows and sublime creeds. But drivel didn't make them any less dangerous.

"Divine Essence, so help me that I fail not in my troth," Dodd said, "lest I shall be summoned before the tribunal of the order, adjudged, and condemned to certain and shameful death, while my name shall be recorded on the roll of infamy. Amen."

"Amen!" echoed a chorus of men's voices.

"By order of the Grand Council and our Supreme Commander, I call this meeting to order," Dodd said, and she heard the gavel strike again.

"The United States of America has no sovereignty," he continued. "We recognize our inherent right and imperative duty to resist its officials, and, if need be, to expel them by force of arms." Dodd paused as if to let the impact of his words sink in. "I cede the floor to Major-General Bowles for a report from the military committee.

On the far side of the door, a man cleared his throat. "Our command is organized and ready for action." It sounded like Bowles. "Our men are drilling at such snatched times as they can get."

"Speak to the invention we've tested," Dodd urged. "The Greek fire."

Bowles cleared his throat again. "Sunday last, we conducted a demonstration to the south of this city. "Two fires were set, one with a hand grenade and one with a machine activated by a clock. These fires are devised so that nothing can put them out, even on water."

The men inside the print shop murmured their approval.

"In Louisville, we've already used Greek fire to destroy stores and boats," Dodd said. "And the Confederate government has committed to paying us ten percent of the value of each piece of property we destroy."

"A pretty penny for the Chicago convention center," someone said.

"And for a Lake Erie ferry," Bowles said.

Hattie breathed deep, taking this in. The Confederate government was funding the Sons of Liberty's treasonous plans. With targets so large—the Chicago convention center, a Lake Erie ferry—hundreds if not thousands of innocent people could die.

Dodd thanked Bowles, then launched into his own report. "As you know, I met with Commissioner Thompson last month at the Clifton House in Niagara. The Confederate government is fully supportive of our efforts. In fact, Thompson says we are the South's best hope for victory."

"Here, here!" someone shouted.

"Next week, on August 16, we will dispatch couriers throughout this state to signal the start of our attacks."

"Where do we gather?" a man asked.

"Dr. Bowles, that's your department," Dodd said.

"Here, we'll gather in the field below Camp Morton," Bowles said. "In southern Indiana, at New Albany. In Illinois, at Rock Island, Springfield, and Chicago. In each of those places, we'll seize the arsenals."

"To supplement our supply of Sunday School books," Dodd interjected. Laughter resounded from within the room.

That explained the boxes that were so oddly labeled, Hattie realized. They contained weapons.

"Thus armed, our men will march on St. Louis," Bowles said.

"What about Johnson's Island?" someone asked.

"All in due time," Dodd said. "After we take the state capitals. Here in Indianapolis, I'll convene a political meeting at the state house. Our members will come in wagons, with weapons secreted in the straw."

"What do we do about Morton?" a man asked.

"Get him out of the way," Dodd said. "And put a new man in the governor's house. One of our own."

Applause erupted. Hattie felt the hairs on the back of her neck stand on end. Morton, too, was in danger.

"That will position us well for the convention," Bowles said, referencing the Democratic Convention in Chicago at the end of August. "We'll put up our own candidate for president."

"Depose the Original Gorilla!" someone shouted.

Hattie winced at this derisive name for President Lincoln, who she much admired. Worse yet was the threat of a Sons of Liberty candidate prevailing against him. Restoration of the Union would be a pipe dream, and Lincoln's emancipation of the nation's enslaved people would be no more

"The government cannot be restored without revolution!" Dodd proclaimed. "Seize control of the states, then on to Chicago!"

"To Chicago!" his followers chorused. Shouts followed, men calling out in a growing frenzy. Hattie shuddered to think what damage tens of thousands of them could do at the Democratic Convention in Chicago.

Hattie glanced out a hallway window. Soldiers were amassing at the far end of the street. Shielding his eyes, one of them glanced up at the fourth floor where she stood.

It was now or never. Hattie stepped to the door and pounded on it sharply. She waited a few seconds, then pounded again, louder this time.

The door opened a few inches, revealing a short, squat man with a dark beard and piggish eyes. Bemused, he looked her up and down. "Lost your way, miss?"

"This is Dodd's print shop, isn't it?" she said.

The man tapped the gold lettering on the door. "Ain't no one taught you to read?"

She ignored the insult. "I've got a message for Franklin Stone." She pulled the note Anne had written from her pocket. "It's important."

"So's the major-general's report. I'll see Mr. Stone gets it when he's finished."

Franklin was a major-general with the Sons of Liberty? She had to get him out of there, fast.

The man reached for Anne's note, but Hattie snatched it away, holding it behind her back. Behind him, the crescendo of voices began to fade.

Hattie stepped into the door's opening. "I need to see Mr. Stone. Now."

The man braced his arm against the door jamb, preventing her from entering. "Less you're a member, you ain't allowed in."

She pushed forward, her ribs pressed against his arm. "I'll only be a minute."

The man's eyes widened, his mouth twisting into a grin. "I see what you're after, little lady. Want me to come out and give it to you?"

She stepped back. "You misunderstand me. I only want a moment with Mr. Stone."

All at once, Franklin appeared, towering over the man blocking her entrance. "Who's asking..." Pausing, Franklin eyed her. "Hattie. What are you doing here?"

"Anne needs you." She held up Anne's note. "She sent me with this."

Franklin glanced back at the crowd in the print shop. They'd settled down, and Dodd was explaining how the guns—the Sunday School books—would be distributed.

Shoving the short man aside, Franklin barged past the door. Shutting it behind him, he confronted Hattie "Who told you I'd be here?" he demanded.

"No one," she said. "I went to your office, but it was locked up. Anne said you sometimes had business with Mr. Dodd, so I thought—"

"You shouldn't be here." He reached for the paper.

She glanced at the window. A second contingent of soldiers had joined the first, and they were marching this way.

"Outside," she said. Briskly, she walked toward the stairs. Gathering her skirts, she started down them.

Franklin quickly caught up with her. He grabbed her by the shoulder. "Give me that note," he said. "I've got business to attend to."

She broke free of his grasp. If the soldiers met them on the stairs, they'd know they'd come from the meeting, and Franklin's fate would be sealed. "Your business can wait," she called over her shoulder, taking the stairs as quickly as she dared.

Within seconds, he was at her side. "I demand to know what's so important that you felt compelled to interrupt my meeting."

"It's about Jo," she said.

Concern flooded his face. Anne was right. Whatever else occupied Franklin's attention, he was devoted to his daughter.

They reached the ground floor. He reached again for the paper, but Hattie pushed open the door. Only then did she hand him the note. She watched his face as he read Anne's words, expressing alarm over Jo. "Fever," he muttered. "Inconsolable." He looked up. "Has she sent for..." His voice trailed off as he noticed the soldiers approaching.

Looping her arm through his, Hattie tugged him away from the building. "We're out for a stroll," she whispered. "Just passing by."

Franklin hesitated for a moment, then fell in step beside her, walking with the limp he'd developed from his war injury. The soldiers clomped toward the building that housed the print shop. At the end of the block, Hattie glanced back and saw they were streaming inside. The Sons of Liberty meeting was about to come to an abrupt end. When the arrests were made, Franklin Stone would not be among them.

~ ~ ~

At breakfast the next morning, few words passed between Anne and Franklin. Hattie did her best to stay out of the way. Franklin was especially silent, studying a newspaper account of last night's raid. The paper recounted how Governor Morton, having learned of a dangerous plot in the making, had dispatched soldiers to Dodd's print shop. From the boxes of "Sunday School Books," they'd confiscated 400 navy revolvers and over a hundred thousand rounds of ammunition. They also made several arrests.

He should be grateful he wasn't among them, Hattie thought.

After breakfast, Anne pulled Hattie aside. "I think it's best if you move on. Before Franklin starts asking questions."

Hattie nodded. She'd been thinking the same. In the back bedroom, she packed her satchel, then slipped out to say goodbye to Anne and Jo.

"Stay strong," she said, pulling Anne into a hug.

Tears glistened in Anne's eyes. "Be careful."

Leaving the house, Hattie prayed that last night's raid was enough to warn Franklin away from the Sons of Liberty for good. But she also knew that in other cities across the Northwest, men like him were plotting violence. And from what she'd heard last night, their next target was the Chicago convention.

On her way to the train station, Hattie stopped at the telegraph office and sent a message to Edith in St. Louis:

Leaving Ind. Meet Chicago convention.

Chapter Seventeen

AUGUST 30, 1864

Hattie moved along with the throng at Chicago's Courthouse Square, Edith at her side.

"I've never seen so many people gathered in one place," Hattie said.

"Nor have I," Edith said.

Hattie nodded at a wagon passing on the street. "There's another one."

"That makes fifteen since we left the hotel," Edith said. "Something's up."

With packed warehouses, a busy harbor, and rail lines crisscrossing the city, commerce was thriving in Chicago, war or no war. Vehicles of all types clogged the city's wide streets. But since the Democratic Convention began yesterday, every other one seemed to be a farm wagon, loaded with straw. Hats pulled low over their eyes, the drivers seemed to seek one another out, pulling up along curbs and climbing down to converse in low tones with one another.

"And look," Hattie said, nodding toward a cross-street. "Three are stopped there, chatting amongst themselves. None of these drivers is a vendor in the city with something to sell. They've got munitions concealed in those wagons, just like the Sons of Liberty said at their meeting. The question is what to do about it."

"We go to the authorities," Edith said. "Now. Before it's too late."

"The Chicago police?" Hattie asked. "Mr. Pinkerton always said they were inept."

"They're the ones patrolling the streets. We just have to convince someone in charge to search a few of those wagons."

"And if we're wrong?" Hattie asked.

"I hope we are," Edith said. "But I doubt it."

~ ~ ~

The Precinct 3 Station was a flurry of activity. Waiting in line to speak to the officer in charge, Hattie overheard complaints about a burglary, a runaway carriage, and a peeping Tom.

When their turn came, Edith explained why they'd come. "There is a plot set to unravel in this city," she said, keeping her voice low. "One that involves the Democratic Convention."

With thick jowls and a graying beard, the officer set down his pencil. "A plot to install McClellan as the nominee and oust Lincoln? Ladies, there's no crime in that."

"A plot involving armed men. They intend to take over the convention, then free the prisoners at Camp Douglas."

The officer shrugged. "Then take your concerns to Camp Douglas."

"By the time they get to Camp Douglas, it will be too late to stop them," Hattie said. "You need to intervene now before the signal is given for the weapons to be unleashed."

"Ah, a signal," he said. "Look, miss, this ain't the battlefront."

"It will be," Edith said, "if the Sons of Liberty have their way."

The officer pushed aside his notepad. "I don't know where you people come up with this nonsense. The Sons of Liberty are a legitimate group seeking a peaceful end to the war."

"You call 400 guns and thousands of rounds of ammunition—" Hattie began.

Edith cut her off. "Perhaps we could speak to the precinct superintendent."

The officer shook his head. "Not in. Even if he was, he's not going to waste his time with your idle speculation. Rumors are a dime a dozen in this town."

It was all Hattie could do to keep from stamping her foot. "These aren't rumors. They're facts."

"Thank you for your time, sir." Edith took Hattie by the wrist. "Good day."

~ ~ ~

Outside the station, a stiff breeze blowing off Lake Michigan fluttered the hem of Hattie's dress. "I can't believe you let him run us off," she said.

Steering Hattie by the elbow, Edith set off toward the lake. "You heard him. He called the Sons of Liberty a legitimate group. For all we know, he's a member. If we'd revealed any more about our suspicions, it would only have tipped them off."

Hattie fell in stride beside her. "What about Camp Douglas? We could try to convince someone there to act."

"Mollie Pitman says Union officers are involved in the plot. If we raise our concerns with one of them, we might end up detained ourselves."

"Mollie says a lot of things," Hattie says. "That doesn't mean they're true."

"I know you're disinclined to believe her," Edith said. "From my interviews, I disagree. I was able to verify much of what she told me."

"For instance?"

"The Sons of Liberty intend to establish a secret police force that would kill Union soldiers on the streets at night. Colonel Sanderson says he's confirmed that. Miss Pitman also says Sons of Liberty members are responsible for several assassinations of Union soldiers and their supporters in northwestern Missouri. Sanderson says that checks out too. And after meeting with her in St. Louis, even President Lincoln's private secretary found her credible."

"She may be convincing," Hattie said. "But I still say she's no friend of the Union."

"At any rate, our immediate problem is not Miss Pitman. It's those wagons and what's hidden under the straw."

As she said this, another wagon rattled past, headed toward Courthouse Square. Hattie shook her head. "Speculation. Rumors. I don't see how we convince anyone in charge that this has to be stopped. Unless..." Her steps slowed. "Unless we spread some rumors ourselves."

Edith straightened. "And confuse the matter even further?"

"Confuse it for the ones involved in the plot. If we're right, these wagons have come here from across the Northwest. But now that they're in the city, they have little means of communicating, right?"

"They don't need to," Edith said darkly. "Their guns will speak loud and clear."

Hattie grabbed her arm. "Hear me out. We approach the drivers of these wagons, alerting them that the plot has been uncovered and the authorities are poised to arrest them. The rumor spreads from one to the other, and they back off."

"What makes you think they'd believe us?"

"We pose as women spies in their ranks."

"Not we." Edith gestured at her bloomers. "You. Those men won't believe for a moment a woman dressed like me would be among their ranks."

She had a point. "Then I'll do it," Hattie said. "And I know the perfect costume for it."

"You'd best be quick about it," Edith said as another wagon rolled past. "Those conveyances are multiplying like rabbits."

~ ~ ~

Edith groused about the cost of the widow's garb Hattie purchased. "General Sharpe does not have a fortune to invest in this enterprise."

"It's money well spent." Looking in the mirror on the wall of their hotel room, she adjusted the black veil to fully cover her face. "No one will recognize me."

"They wouldn't anyhow."

"But if I'm part of their group, I'd want to make sure I go unrecognized while not standing out too much." Hattie pulled on one black glove and then another. "Plenty of widows these days—nothing stands out about that. And my face is hidden. Remember me telling you how Pauline was poisoned last winter?"

"Of course. You came to me for help, and I prescribed ipecac."

"Well, Pauline maintains to this day that it was a veiled woman in widow's garb who brought her the cakes that made her ill. A Confederate spy, Pauline says."

"And you think the Sons of Liberty will mistake you for her?"

Hattie thrust her hand through the strings of her black beaded purse. "We'll soon find out."

The rest of the day and into the evening, Hattie flagged down the driver of every straw-filled wagon she encountered. Nearly every one of them stopped and heard her out.

"The plot has been compromised," she informed them one by one. "The authorities know about the wagons and the guns. Go home and await further instructions."

To the few who questioned how she knew this, she said she'd been dispatched by the major-general. That seemed to satisfy them, especially when she crossed her hands at her waist and held her wrist, the signal she'd seen Dodd and Bowles use at the end of the Greek fire demonstration.

One driver even mentioned the Greek fire, saying he'd been looking forward to the spectacle. Another driver thanked her by name. "You take care now, Miss Slater," he said. "We need you now more than ever."

Slater. Hattie filed away the name to mention to Pauline the next time she saw her, a possible identity for her veiled woman.

By nightfall, there were noticeably fewer wagons on the streets. The next day, when the convention was expected to wrap up, Hattie and Edith scarcely saw any at all.

"The power of rumors," Hattie said as they made their way to Courthouse Square that night. "I should thank that officer for giving me the idea."

Edith shook her head. "I had my doubts when you proposed your scheme. But it seems you've pulled it off."

"We can only hope," Hattie said. But as they arrived at the square, merging with the thousands already gathered there, she felt on pins and needles. If the rumor had failed to reach the Sons of Liberty's leaders, there could still be trouble.

Above a platform in the center of the square flew a banner heralding the Democratic ticket, with General George McClellan for president and George Pendleton as his running mate. Chosen by delegates earlier in the day, the ticket was a compromise between the more radical Copperheads, who favored giving the South what they wanted, and the so-called war Democrats, who wanted to oust Lincoln and fight to the finish. Near the platform, a band played a bright, rousing tune, and all around flew flags that read *McClellan and Liberty*.

The band wound down, and party officials took to the platform one by one to make rousing speeches. Amid cheers and hurrahs and shouts of "For the Constitution!" and "McClellan, our leader!" Hattie scanned the crowd. All around was the "generally swell mob" a news writer had joked about, with more than a few plug-uglies and shoulder hitters. But there were plenty of respectable folks, too, gentlemen and ladies alike.

Beside her, Edith was doing the same. As the crowd erupted into applause, she leaned toward Hattie. "I see nothing out of the ordinary."

"Nor do I," Hattie said.

Still, they continued their watch. Finally, the speeches ended, and the multitude broke into a rousing rendition of a Yankee favorite:

John Brown's body lies a-moldering in the grave

John Brown's body lies a-moldering in the grave

John Brown's body lies a-moldering in the grave

But his soul goes marching on

With the last line, another round of cheers rose from the crowd. Then there was a loud boom. Hattie and Edith both whirled around, looking to see where the shot had come from. Another boom sounded, and then another. Then Hattie glanced up and saw that the explosions were coming not from guns or the dreaded Greek fire but from a display of fireworks erupting in brilliant sprays of red, white, and blue overhead.

Her shoulders relaxed. Like Edith, she turned her face to the sky, entranced by the display. A fitting ending, she thought, even if what the two women were celebrating was a success few would ever know about, averting a potential disaster.

~ ~ ~

By the time she and Edith got back to the hotel, Hattie was bone-weary from all the activity, not to mention dodging revelers in the streets, many of them drunk on some combination of spirits and the prospect of Lincoln ceding the presidency to Little Mac, as General McClellan was affectionately known.

But as she and Edith approached the hotel's entrance, Hattie stopped short. Under the gas lamp at the street corner stood two men in deep conversations. One was short and slight, scarcely larger in frame than Hattie herself. The other was tall and broad-shouldered. There was something familiar in the way he carried his head, cocked a little to one side, as if bemused.

Then he turned slightly, and in the lamplight, Hattie saw the flash of his smile. Her heart skipped a beat. Taking hold of Edith's arm, she steered her into the hotel's entrance. In the lobby, Edith pulled away, giving Hattie a sharp look. "What has gotten into you?" she asked.

Flustered, Hattie stumbled over the most innocuous explanation she could think of. "There's a man out there I recognize," she said. "From my past."

Edith frowned. "A dangerous man?"

"No, not at all," Hattie said quickly. "It's just that...I'd rather not converse with him at present."

"Then come along to the room," Edith said matter-of-factly. "I'm half-dead on my feet."

Hattie hesitated. After he'd been spared from arrest in the Indianapolis raid, she'd hoped Franklin had disentangled himself from the Sons of Liberty. Maybe he was only here for political reasons, nothing to do with the group and their plans. But what if, after everything, he was still involved?

Tired as she was, she had to find out. "You go on upstairs," she told Edith. "I'll be along in a few minutes. There's something I need to check on."

Edith tilted her head. "Suit yourself."

She continued up the stairs while Hattie perused the lobby. There was an empty settee situated between the hotel's entrance and the registration desk. Situated as it was, it would allow her to keep her back to anyone who entered the lobby from the street while still enabling her to eavesdrop.

Approaching the settee, she tucked a few loose tendrils of hair beneath the brim of her hat, tipping it to conceal as much of her face as possible. If only she were wearing her widow's costume—Franklin would never suspect her in that. But for the evening's festivities, she'd had no need for it.

Aside from the clerk, there was only one other person in the lobby, a small, white-haired woman in a black silk mourning dress. Perched in a wide wing-backed chair across from the settee, she looked like a tiny queen on an oversized throne. She watched, birdlike, as Hattie took her seat.

"So much coming and going," the woman said, her voice thin and reedy. "All those drunken men in the streets. And those blasts." Pressing her fingers to her temples, she shuddered. "Impossible to sleep."

Hattie commiserated, saying that she also felt too wound up with all the excitement to go up to bed yet. The woman went on to tell Hattie quite a lot about herself. Widowed last winter, she'd come by train from Galesburg to visit her sister in Chicago. She hadn't realized that her visit would be during the Democratic Convention, nor had she realized that her sister's husband had become so obnoxious in his old age that she could not stand to be in the same house with him.

"I should have just gone home," the woman sniffed. "But that would've given that horrid man a victory he didn't deserve."

Stifling a yawn, Hattie glanced at the clock behind the registration desk. Ten minutes had passed. Maybe the men under the streetlamp weren't staying here after all. And perhaps she'd overreacted, mistaking a stranger for Franklin.

She was about to excuse herself and go up to bed when she heard the voices of two men as they came in behind her. One spoke energetically. Deeper and more measured, the other man's voice was unmistakably Franklin Stone's.

The woman across from her had briefly paused her chatter when the men entered. Now she returned to a tale that Hattie only half-followed, straining as she was to hear what the men were saying.

"Her cat seized every opportunity to prowl about my roses," the woman said.

"Sandusky," Hattie heard Franklin say.

"Departing Saturday," said his companion. This was followed by something unintelligible, then something that sounded like "bell," and then more distinctly, "Thompson." Their voices sounded farther away now. They must be moving toward the staircase, Hattie thought.

"You can imagine the mess it left beneath the bushes," the woman in the wing-backed chair said. "My husband..."

Cocking her head, Hattie did her best to shut out the woman's voice. Across the room, the men laughed. Then Franklin spoke again, his tone more serious. Among the words she could discern were "fire" and "ferry."

"...the creature will never be back, I assure you," the woman said.

Hattie nodded, feigning interest.

"Set out within the week," Franklin's companion said.

Then, in Franklin's response, she heard clearly and unmistakably words she'd last heard through the door of Dodd's print shop: "Johnson's Island."

"I hope I haven't distressed you," the woman said, her voice rising a notch. "Perhaps you have an affinity for cats."

Hattie glanced toward the staircase in time to see Franklin and his companion give the Sons of Liberty signal. Then Franklin reached in his pocket and pulled out a wad of bills that he handed to his companion, a slight man with red hair, a long mustache, and small, bright eyes.

"Do you?" The woman asked.

"Do I what?" Hattie turned back around before the men saw her looking.

"Have an affinity for cats," the woman said, sounding irritated.

Hattie shook her head. "Never had one."

Across the room, she heard the plodding of footsteps on the stairs, the two men ascending. Allowing time for them to enter their rooms, she entered back into the woman's good graces by shifting the topic to songbirds and the hazards cats posed to them.

Moments later, Hattie wished the woman goodnight, saying she hoped she'd be able to get some rest now. As she climbed the stairs, a rush of energy twined with her weariness. Though unable to discern all the men had said, she'd heard plenty to pique her interest, especially the part about Greek fire and Johnson's Island.

Entering her room, she found Edith lying awake. She turned to face Hattie. In her nightclothes, her face softened by the semi-darkness, she looked far less intimidating than she did wearing her bloomer suit, which never failed to draw attention.

"Well," Edith said. "What have you ascertained?"

"A fair amount." Sitting on the edge of the bed, Hattie slipped out of her shoes. "As I suspected, the man I saw on the street corner was someone I know. He's staying at this hotel."

"And you enjoyed a pleasant reunion in the hotel's lobby while I lay awake, waiting for you to come in?" Edith sounded cross. As Hattie had discovered on this trip, Edith liked her sleep.

Hattie began unfastening her bodice. "He entered the lobby with a companion, but I kept myself turned from them. I'm certain of his identity. His voice was unmistakable."

"And what exactly is his identity?"

Hattie hesitated. If she revealed all she knew about Franklin, including the snippets of conversation she'd heard tonight, Edith might insist on them turning him in. "I'd rather not reveal it."

"If this is some lover—"

"He's not," Hattie interrupted. "He's just a...friend of a friend. I've known him to have some dealings with the Sons of Liberty in Indianapolis."

Edith's gaze sharpened. "I thought all those men were in jail."

Hattie shook her head. "Not all of them."

"Then it's hardly a surprise he's at the convention," Edith said. "Not considering all the armed oafs in wagons we've encountered."

"This man's no oaf," Hattie said. "He and his companion seemed well-informed. Remember what I told you about Greek fire? They brought up the topic. Mentioned in conjunction with a ferry."

"A passenger ferry?"

"I assume so." Hattie slipped out of her bodice, then loosened the laces of her corset. "And there was something about a bell."

"Well, ferries do have bells," Edith said. "I don't suppose you have any idea where this plot might unfold."

"They mentioned two locations," Hattie said. "Sandusky and Johnson's Island."

"Sandusky is in Ohio," Edith said. "On the shores of Lake Erie. I expect a good number of people travel by ferry. But I don't see what advantage these men would gain from burning one up."

Hattie removed her corset, her chest relaxing. "Johnson's Island was mentioned at the Sons of Liberty meeting in Indianapolis."

"And here I thought we'd subverted the threat. Now we'll have to try to persuade the authorities to bring these men in for questioning."

"A waste of time," Hattie said. "After the response we got on the wagons."

"We had no proof on the wagons," Edith said. "On this, we've got specifics, not to mention two potential suspects registered at this hotel."

"The convention is over," Hattie said. "By the time we get to the police, these men will be long gone."

"It sounds as if you know where at least one of them hails from," Edith said. "Tell the authorities who he is and where to find them, and let them take it from there."

"But I thought this was exactly what General Sharpe dispatched you to do," Hattie said. "Foil the Sons of Liberty's plans."

"There was no foiling about it. He asked me to investigate. I'll make my report. He'll assess it along with Colonel Sanderson's report and determine a course of action."

Hattie stood, unfastening her skirt. "And meanwhile, a ferry gets blown up on Lake Erie."

"So extract the details from this acquaintance of yours so it can be stopped before it happens."

Hattie stepped out of her skirt, then unfastened her crinoline. "I can't."

"Why not?"

"It's...complicated."

Even in the dim light from the street, Hattie could see the anger in Edith's eyes. "Quit trying to protect this man, Hattie. You're not doing him any favors."

Tossing aside her crinoline, Hattie stood in her petticoat, feeling both exposed and emboldened. "You don't understand."

"How could I? A clam would be more forthcoming than you've been."

Hattie jutted her chin. "I know what I know. I'm going to Sandusky myself to do what I can to put a stop to this plot. You can come with me or not."

Chapter Eighteen

SEPTEMBER 3, 1864

Hattie stood on the deck of the ferry *Philo Parsons*, river water lapping at the boat's wooden hull as it steamed from Detroit toward Lake Erie. The hour was early, the sun having risen only a half-hour ago, streaking the eastern sky in hues of pink and gold. A hint of fall was in the air, prompting Hattie to draw her wrap tighter about her shoulders.

Beside her, Edith gripped the rail. After chiding her for protecting Franklin, Hattie hadn't expected her to come along. But Edith said that for Hattie to venture alone to Sandusky was simply too big a risk. With so many other Sons of Liberty plots foiled, the secret order would likely be desperate for this one to succeed.

She was right, Hattie knew. And she was glad for Edith's help, valuing the older woman's expertise and presence of mind. She only hoped their efforts weren't for naught, that she hadn't misconstrued the few snippets of conversation she'd heard between Franklin and the red-mustached man. But she also recalled what

Mollie had said back in St. Louis, about a navy man organizing a raid by water on a Union prison. Much as she might want to discount Mollie's information, the pieces all seemed to fit.

And so the morning after the convention ended, Hattie and Edith had put together a plan. Hattie would pose as a wealthy young widow in fragile health. She would claim to be touring the Great Lakes in the company of her private physician, who despite her unusual attire was known to be a fine doctor. They'd travel to Sandusky and see what details of the plot they could uncover in hopes of putting a stop to it.

They'd taken the train from Chicago to Detroit, where they'd booked passage on the *Philo Parsons*. With every mile she traveled, Hattie was grateful for the distance she was putting between herself and Franklin Stone. She hoped the roll of bills he'd handed his companion that night in the lobby was the sum total of his involvement in the Sandusky plot. If she ran into him there, she'd have a good deal of explaining to do.

"You look at ease on the water," Edith said as the city's skyline receded.

"My mother used to take me by riverboat to New Orleans every summer," she said. "Being on the water was my favorite part of those expeditions." She glanced at Edith's white-knuckled hands. "You don't appear to enjoy it much."

"I prefer land. Never learned to swim."

"Perhaps you'd be more comfortable in the cabin."

Edith glanced at the narrow cabin in the center of the ship's deck. "Tight quarters in there," she said. "But I guess I'll give it a try."

With uncertain steps, Edith started for the cabin. Looking down, she nearly collided head-on with a man Hattie recognized— the slight, red-mustached man from the hotel lobby.

"Excuse me," the man said.

Edith looked up. At that moment, the steamer rocked in the wake of a larger vessel as it passed, and her balance faltered.

The man caught her by the sleeve. "Steady there," he said.

"You startled me," she said.

He doffed his hat and bowed. "My sincerest apologies." He regarded Edith quizzically, and after a moment's hesitation added, "Ma'am."

"I should think so." Edith brushed at her sleeve as if he'd soiled it. Then she straightened and, rather unsteadily, proceeded to the cabin door.

The man stepped to the railing, filling the space where Edith had been. Hattie's heart quickened. Was Franklin with him? She resisted the urge to look behind her.

"Bit of an odd duck, isn't she?" the man said.

Hattie smiled pleasantly. "Her manner of dress is unusual. But her medical training is superb."

His eyes widened. Standing close, Hattie saw that they were a striking shade of gray. "That woman's a surgeon?"

Hattie nodded. "With but one patient at present. Myself."

He drew back a bit, looking her over. "But you are the picture of perfection, madam. No illness could mar you."

"You're kind to say so. And indeed, the lake air has already refreshed me, just as Dr. Greenburg promised it would," Hattie said, using the alteration of Edith's name they'd agreed on. "She proposed a town called Sandusky as a good place to absorb its benefits."

"Sandusky!" he said. "Why, that's where I'm bound."

"You make your home there?"

"No, but I've spent a good deal of time there in recent weeks." He fingered the gold watch chain tucked into the pocket of what looked to be an expensive suit. "My position demands a fair amount of travel."

"You must do important work."

He laughed. "So it is, I suppose, to certain persons. It requires cavorting with the well-heeled set, which I must confess is not an entirely dreary enterprise." Letting go of his watch chain, he offered his hand. "Charles H. Cole, secretary of the Mount Hope Oil Company, at your service."

She took his hand. In keeping with her feigned delicate health, she was careful not to grasp it too firmly. "Helen Thomas," she said, using the name she and Edith had settled on.

"Helen, as in the bewitching woman of Troy. It suits you. I was just on my way to say hello to the captain of this vessel." He held out his arm. "If you'd like, I'll introduce you."

Smiling with the sort of reserved charm she'd learned from watching Adelicia Acklen, she took his arm. "I'd like that," she said.

Cole walked her around the aft of the ferry, the smokestack belching black smoke overhead. On the port side, they were forced to walk closer, owing to the narrowness of the deck. At the wheelhouse, he introduced her to Captain Atwood as well as the vessel's co-owner and clerk, a man named Walter Ashley.

Taking care to show she was impressed with his knowledge of the ferry and its crew, Hattie readily agreed to stroll with Cole around the front of the boat, where he introduced her to the ship's mate and its engineer. To a man, the crew seemed quite charmed by Cole and his interest in what others might consider the mundane running of the boat. What was the longest delay the ferry had encountered? Cole inquired. When they ran late, how soon was another vessel sent to check on them? Could passengers be picked up at points on the route that weren't regular stops? How far could the *Parsons* travel without stopping to refuel?

All these questions he asked out of what seemed casual interest. Now and again, he would turn and say he hoped he wasn't boring her with his curiosity about all things nautical.

Not at all, she assured him. But his interest seemed to her less about all things nautical and more about the running of this particular ferry. It was the interest of a man who had a plot in mind, a plot to liberate 2500 Confederate prisoners from the Johnson's Island prison.

But what exactly did Cole and his fellow conspirators, whoever they might be, have in mind? If she and Edith were to stop their plot, there was much they needed to learn.

At least Hattie had Cole's attention. That was a good first step.

Chapter Nineteen

SEPTEMBER 15, 1864

From Sandusky's shore, Hattie looked out over the gray waters of Lake Erie. Overhead, the sun was bright, but autumn was in the air, and winter was not far off. Only last week, the leaves on the maples and oaks towering along the shore had blazed in brilliant hues of red and orange. But already those colors were beginning to dull, and while the trees were far from denuded, fallen leaves swirled at Hattie's feet, a stiff breeze buffeting them along the shoreline.

Across these waters lay Canada. Each time Hattie looked north, she thought of her brother, George. She pictured him as she'd last seen him three years ago, tall and fine-featured, with their mother's piercing blue eyes but none of her meanness. Then he'd gone off to war, and she'd gone to Washington to work for Allen Pinkerton. She hoped George truly was there. It would mean he was safe, or as safe as one could be working as a spy for Lafayette Baker's National Detective Police if in fact that was what George was doing.

Her thoughts also circled, as they often did these days, back to John Elliott. She'd been away from Nashville a long while, and she knew he'd be concerned for her safety. He might not understand why she'd felt compelled to travel from Indianapolis to Chicago to Sandusky. She wasn't sure she fully understood it herself, except that the success which had eluded her thus far might lie across these waters.

Tucking a stray tendril of hair behind her ear, Hattie focused her attention on Johnson's Island. A month ago, she could not have located Sandusky on a map, let alone Johnson's Island. Now she knew about the island's Union prison and the Confederate soldiers held there. Charles Cole, who'd become her daily companion, had even toured her around the facility.

As he had on the *Philo Parsons*, Cole seemed to charm the Union soldiers who ran the prison, though she suspected they also appreciated the cases of wine and boxes of cigars he gifted them with. The facility itself differed little from the prison where Hattie herself had been confined. She counted thirteen buildings, including one the guards called the boar's nest, which was especially hot and stifling.

The prison's sutler shop had recently been moved out, one of the guards told her, and rations had been cut. She wasn't surprised at the fat rats that lurked in dark corners, nor was she surprised by the dazed looks on the faces of some prisoners, especially the younger ones. She took care not to show any dismay in front of Cole, who seemed to treat the tour as a holiday jaunt.

Of one thing Hattie was certain—if freed, the imprisoned men would leap at the chance to get revenge on their captors. This, she knew, was exactly what the Sons of Liberty had in mind. Following the arrests in Indianapolis and the fizzled convention plot in Chicago, they'd pinned all their hopes on Johnson's Island in a plot which, if she was reading Cole's signals correctly, was set to unfold any day now.

If Cole seemed at ease on the ferry and at the prison, he was even more so in the town of Sandusky. He kept accounts at each of the local banks and also went almost daily to the telegraph office, transmitting what he said were communications about the oil business. He frequented local saloons and was generally known around town as a big spender. When prison officials came ashore in their off-duty hours, he wined and dined them. Although Hattie had yet to see it, he hinted that he was on equally friendly terms with the officers of the *USS Michigan*, the ironclad naval boat that plied the waters of Lake Erie, tasked with ensuring the security of both the Johnson's Island prison and the entire Great Lakes region.

A charming, generous man who commanded a large supply of money—that was the impression Charles Cole made in Sandusky. Hattie fingered the pearl choker he'd placed around her neck at dinner last night, the most expensive by far of the gifts he'd bestowed on her, gifts she'd tried unsuccessfully to refuse. But she knew the importance of letting him woo her. She needed him to think she appreciated his affections, and that but for her ill health, she would embrace his advances.

From behind, she heard footsteps. She turned swiftly. Though Cole had yet to even mention Franklin Stone, Hattie still worried he might turn up in Sandusky.

But it was only Edith, gesturing for Hattie to come away from the shoreline. "You mustn't catch a chill," she said. "You wouldn't want to disappoint your suitor."

"He's not my suitor," Hattie said. But she fell in stride beside Edith, walking back to their hotel. Edith was right, of course—not about the chill but about Charles Cole. For all his casual flirtations, Hattie knew he kept an eye on her comings and goings. No matter how entrancing she found these waters that mirrored weather and sky, she didn't want him questioning whether her health was as delicate as she claimed.

"There are the gifts," Edith said. "And quite a number of dinners."

"A number of tedious dinners," Hattie said.

"One must keep one's goal in sight," Edith said.

Easy for her to say, Hattie thought. Edith could come and go as she pleased without worrying that her health might be perceived as overly robust. And no matter how often Hattie reminded herself to be patient, she'd gotten precious little out of her interactions with Cole so far. Mostly, he seemed intent on parading her around town on his arm. She'd sat stiffly in the dining rooms of nearly every well-to-do person in Sandusky, channeling Adelicia Acklen's calm, disaffected demeanor while listening intently for any hint of a plot involving Johnson's Island.

But Cole gave away nothing. True to his story of being a Pennsylvania oil man, he seemed to care less about the war than using his charms to solicit investments. She was beginning to wonder if she'd misread the scattershot discourse between him and Franklin Stone in Chicago. Maybe this whole Sandusky venture was only about money.

But then why the mention of Johnson's Island and the vague allusion to fire? There had to be a plot. She just needed patience, though admittedly, that had never been her strong suit.

~ ~ ~

Two hours later, heads turned as Hattie descended the stairs of the West House Hotel, her face and neck powdered and her hair drawn back. Her dotted silk gown, flounced and ruffled at the bodice, was the most elegant of her dresses. She'd only worn it twice in Cole's presence. On both occasions, he'd raved about how stunning she looked.

Located across from the docks, the five-story hotel was a first-class establishment, surprising for a town the size of Sandusky. Its restaurant was elegant too. As Hattie entered, the maître d' greeted her, then escorted her to the table where Cole was waiting.

He stood as she approached. Taking her hand, he brushed his lips over her fingers. "You look ravishing, my dear."

She smiled, then took the seat the maître d' offered. Immediately, her alarm went up. The table was set for three.

"Are we expecting company?" she asked.

Taking his seat, Cole patted her hand. "We are. A charming gentleman, actually, though I hope not so charming as to steal your affections."

"I'm not so easily moved, Charles," she said lightly, but inside her heart was racing. Franklin Stone could charm a snake off a cliff.

She tried to focus on the menu, but Cole seemed to sense she was distracted. "You mustn't be distressed, darling," he said.

"It's my nerves," she said. "Dr. Greenberg says I should be getting more rest."

He frowned. "I don't know about that doctor of yours. I know a man in Detroit who could see you. A reputable surgeon. I'd be happy to make the arrangements."

She flitted her hand in the air, brushing off his suggestion. "Dr. Greenberg says I'm progressing."

He leaned close. "You do look well, darling. But I'd like some assurance you can withstand an upset."

"But why would there be any upset?" she said.

In the lamplight, his gray eyes sparkled. "Well, there's talk of a war going on, you know."

"Is there?" She smiled at his little joke. "This far north, I'd almost forgotten. Though I do envy folks across the water in Canada, not being caught up in our little skirmish."

"There's some who are quite engaged in our conflict," Cole said. "When I've finished my business here, I intend to travel to Montreal. If you're feeling well enough, perhaps you can join me."

She clasped her hands at her chest. "Oh, that would be delight-ful, Charles. I'll ask Dr. Greenberg what she thinks. Would we go soon?"

"Soon enough," he said.

"You're a hard one to pin down, Mr. Cole."

"The nature of my business requires some flexibility, I'm afraid."

"But surely it doesn't require such secrecy as to keep from me the identity of the man who'll be joining us for dinner."

"Well, he's a navy man, quite experienced on the water. He has made quite a reputation for himself in the East."

"A naval man. How fascinating." Hattie's shoulders relaxed. Franklin Stone had served in the cavalry, not the navy.

"Perhaps he'll regale us with some tales of his exploits." From a crystal decanter, Cole poured himself and her a glass of sherry. "Although I must warn you, he tends to be less than forthcoming on certain details."

"No wonder you two are friends."

"As I said, a necessity of my trade." He held her gaze, his fingers brushing the back of her hand. "I hope you don't hold it against me."

She smiled. "We all have our secrets, I suppose." She sipped from her sherry, its warmth spreading through her veins.

At the sound of footsteps, Cole turned. "Ah, there he is."

As the stranger approached, Cole rose to greet him. With square shoulders and a gentleman's bearing, the man towered over Cole. He had a high forehead, and his brown hair was neatly combed. His nose was straight and regular, and his trim mustache and well-kept whiskers offset his pale complexion. He couldn't have been more than thirty years old, Hattie thought, but he carried himself with the seriousness of someone a good deal older.

Cole thrust out his hand, and the men exchanged a vigorous handshake. Then Cole gestured toward Hattie. "John, this is Helen Thomas. Helen, this is my friend John Beall."

Beall. She'd caught a glimpse of the name on a note Cole had slipped to the hotel's clerk last night, but she hadn't put it together with the extra seat at their table. Nor had she realized it was pronounced *bell.* Going over the words Hattie had overheard in Chicago, she and Edith had thought *bell* must refer to some sort of signal that would be given relative to the plot. Now she understood it referred to the man taking his seat beside Charles Cole.

"Pleased to make your acquaintance, Mr. Beall."

"The pleasure is all mine," Beall said. His low voice struck her as almost musical. But his eyes, small and light blue, seemed to bore into her.

Cole refilled his glass of sherry, then offered the same to Beall. "Helen hails from Tennessee," Cole said. "You know how many loyal supporters we have there."

Beall lifted an eyebrow. "You are a long way from home, Miss Thomas."

"Not so far, really. The lake air is far more pleasant than the stagnant heat we endure back home this time of year. I suppose the ocean is even more delightful. Charles tells me you served in the navy, Mr. Beall. Do you miss the sea?"

"Almost as much as I miss my home in Virginia."

"Then I hope you'll be able to return there soon," she said.

"Unlikely," Cole said. "John ran into some misfortune there."

"On the bay, actually," Beall said, glancing at the menu.

"Chesapeake Bay," Cole said. "John led a company of rangers that harassed Yankee ship traffic there."

Beall glanced at the waiter who was approaching to take their order. "Perhaps this isn't the best place to speak of the enterprise, Charles."

His cheeks flushed from the sherry, Cole slapped his back. "Can't hide a personage of renown."

"Of renown." Hattie cocked her head, showing interest. "How is that, Mr. Beall?"

"Why, John here was one of the most hunted men in the country," Cole said.

The waiter intervened then. As he took their orders, Hattie studied John Beall out of the corner of her eye. He must be the navy man Mollie Pitman had mentioned.

When the waiter left, Hattie picked up the thread of their conversation, using a tone she'd heard from Adelicia any number of times, suggesting mild but genuine interest. "You were saying, Mr. Beall?"

Again his pale blue eyes seemed to bore into Hattie. "Nothing."

Cole twirled his sherry glass at the stem, facets of the crystal catching bits of lamplight, and winked rather conspicuously at Hattie. "She wants to hear about your work with the Volunteer Coast Guard. Otherwise known as privateering."

Beall jutted his chin. "My men were not out to line their coffers. We didn't even get paid."

"Fair enough," Cole said. "But you must admit, my friend, that your men were irregulars, accomplishing on the water what Mosby and Forrest have done so effectively on land, striking a target and then disappearing before anyone can catch them."

"How adventuresome." Hattie suppressed a shudder, recalling her own encounter with so-called irregulars in the wilds of East Tennessee. "What sort of vessel did you sail, Mr. Beall?"

"Our fleet consisted of two vessels, a 22-foot black yawl and a white 28-foot sailing canoe."

"The *Raven* and the *Swan*." Cole's words slurred slightly. He'd nearly drained his third glass of sherry. He liked his liquor, to be sure, but Hattie had never seen him consume so much so quickly. He must be anxious, she thought. *Some trouble is brewing.* "Folks called you...what was it, John?"

Beall shifted in his seat. "The Grey Ghost of the Chesapeake."

Cole elbowed him. "And it was all well and good until you were captured, right?"

Beall glowered. "If it's all the same to you, Charles, I'd rather not discuss it."

His tone had an instant sobering effect on Cole, who sat up straighter and pushed aside his half-empty glass. "Of course, old chap. All I was getting around to is how fortunate we are that your release from prison was secured, integral as you are to our plans."

Hattie's breath caught. If she could get them to reveal even a little of how they intended to pull off their plot, she and Edith might be able to intervene. The key, she knew, was to act as if she was not the least bit interested in the topic.

"I trust you didn't suffer long in prison, Mr. Beall," she said. "Charles took me to see the facility on Johnson's Island. I feel so sorry for those men. The conditions they must endure."

"The Federals complain of the treatment of their prisoners," Beall said. "But from my experience, they do little to see to the comforts of the men they incarcerate."

Cole slapped his hand on the table. "We shall see to their salvation."

"I should hope so," Hattie said.

Beall glanced at Cole. "What have you told her?"

Cole's cheeks colored. "Nothing."

Beall's expression relaxed. "Good."

Hattie looked from one to the other. "They say women keep secrets, but my experience is that they pale in comparison to the confidences you men entrust to each other." She pressed her hand to her forehead. "Just as well. I'm not in the mood for such serious talk."

Cole looked concerned. "Not another one of your headaches, I hope."

She smiled bravely. "Just a small one."

Cole shook his head. "You need to see my man in Detroit."

She tilted her head, considering. "Perhaps I shall."

He grasped her fingers. "The sooner the better. On Monday, I'm to dine with the officers of the *Michigan*. You'd make a fine—"

Beall held his hand up, palm out. "I don't think that's wise, Charles."

Cole's gray eyes danced. "I thought we agreed. I take care of the *Michigan*. You take care of getting your friends here from Malden or wherever you've arranged for them to be picked up."

"The *Michigan* is critical to our operation." Beall's voice was low, his teeth nearly clenched.

"You think I don't know that?" Cole lowered his voice too. "I've got the officers eating out of my hand. Supporters lined up on shore as well." He gestured toward the window. "Three days from now, we'll own that lake.

Hattie felt Beall's gaze light on her as she bent her head, feigning interest in a hangnail. "Miss Thomas, I trust you'll keep in confidence the plans we mention here."

She looked up, meeting his gaze, and offered a befuddled smile. "Sorry. Which plans do you mean, Mr. Beall?"

Cole waved off their exchange. "Only that you're to join me for dinner aboard the *Michigan* on Monday evening. My friends there are eager to meet you."

"They won't hold my allegiance to the South against me?"

"They won't know your allegiance to the South, just as they don't know mine. The ship's officers have an interest in oil, the same as anyone of any importance in these parts." He brushed his fingers to her cheek. "Between now and then, you should see my man in Detroit so he can prescribe some proper medication. I want you at your best. There may be a bit of excitement on board, and I can't have you swooning.

"Charles." Beall shot him a look.

Cole grinned. "I only mean the pyrotechnics. It promises to be quite the show."

Hattie clapped her hands beneath her chin. "How delightful. I love fireworks."

Then the waiter delivered their first course, and the conversation turned to other topics. Beall asked about her home in Tennessee, quizzing her in such detail that she feared he was trying to poke holes in her story. When she mentioned an acquaintance with Adelicia Acklen and the party she'd attended on July 4 at Belle Monte, that seemed to satisfy him.

As it turned out, Beall was betrothed to a woman from Nashville. Martha was her name, and he spoke of her with affection that belied the brutalities he'd committed on the Chesapeake. In this way, he embodied the odd combination of traits Hattie had recognized in her Southern grandfather—genteel in manner and yet capable of much cruelty.

As the meal continued, she kept up her end of the conversation with the sort of empty prattling men expected of women. But all the while, she was thinking of what the men had revealed. Their plot was about to unfold, quite possibly on Monday evening. Beall would be leaving Sandusky and returning by ferry, picking up men across the waters in Malden—men would help in the plot to seize the *Michigan* and free thousands of Confederate prisoners on Johnson's Island.

If Hattie was to put a stop to it, she'd need to be on that ferry herself.

Chapter Twenty

SEPTEMBER 19, 1864

On Monday morning, the Detroit ferry docks were bustling. As Hattie and Edith waited to board, Hattie spotted a familiar face.

"There he is," she whispered to Edith. "John Beall."

Edith harrumphed. After Hattie had shared with her the details of her dinner with Cole and Beall, Edith had thought the more prudent course was for she and Hattie to bide their time in Sandusky, where they could summon the police and potentially even the soldiers guarding the prison at the first sign of the plot's unfolding.

Hattie had pointed out that they'd need more to go on if they wanted the Sandusky authorities to take their concerns seriously. Aboard the ferry with Beall, she hoped to garner evidence sufficient to share with officials when the ferry docked Monday evening. Edith insisted Hattie was spinning too much from too little while Hattie suspected Edith's true concern was not wanting to spend any more time on Lake Erie than she absolutely had to.

But when Hattie held firm to her plan, Edith insisted on joining her. If Beall and an unspecified number of armed men threatened the ferry's passengers, it could well take the two women to fend off the threat, Edith said, even if one of them was a bit green about the gills.

Under the pretext of Hattie's consulting with Cole's doctor friend, they'd traveled by train to Detroit on Saturday. Unsurprisingly, the man's solution for her headaches was a bottle of laudanum. Leaving the surgeon's office, she'd started to pour the bottle's contents into the gutter. Then, considering how useful the substance might prove in her spy work, she recapped the bottle and returned it to her purse.

Detroit felt almost as tense as Nashville. Policemen patrolled the city's streets, alert for potential violence between recent German and Irish immigrants and Detroit's rising population of Negroes who'd fled the south. Edith's discontent added to the overall feeling of malaise, though Hattie told herself it was only her friend's dread of the ferry ride that was making her cranky.

Now that Monday morning had finally arrived, Hattie was relieved to see John Beall joining the ferry line. He seemed nervous, his gaze flitting about the docks. When his eyes landed on her, she waved demurely, a waggle of fingers that signaled recognition. He nodded at her, then resumed his perusing of the activity on the dock.

Once they'd boarded, Hattie ushered Edith into the cabin, where she insisted she stay for the duration of the trip. "I want you in good form," Hattie said, "not staggering about the deck ready to heave up your breakfast."

"And they say surgeons are crude," Edith said, but she seemed glad enough to settle onto one of the cabin's wooden benches.

As the *Philo Parsons* backed away from the dock, Hattie went out onto the deck. Not wanting to seem as if she attached much importance to their passing acquaintance, she did not seek Beall out. Even if his mind was on the plans he and Cole were setting in motion, she suspected he'd come to her eventually if only to make a show of this being an ordinary voyage.

Gazing out over the waters, she grew impatient, but she forced herself to remain at the rail. Finally, as the *Parsons* entered the mouth of the river, Beall came alongside her.

"Good day, Miss Thomas," he said, tipping the rolled brim of his flat-crowned hat. "You look lost in thought."

"I was pondering how close we are to Canada. Have you ever visited our northern neighbor, Mr. Beall?"

He shrugged. "Once or twice."

"I should like to travel there sometime. Expansive, or so they say."

"You should have a brief look today. The ferry will make an unscheduled stop at Malden." He eyed her, seeming to look for any sign that she recognized the Canadian town Cole had mentioned. "To pick up some scallywags, I presume."

"I do hope they don't crowd the cabin," Hattie said. "My surgeon sought refuge there, owing to a bit of seasickness. Unwashed hordes of draft evaders would do little to ease her distress. Though that's a presumption on my part, isn't it—that scallywags forego regular bathing?"

"Your presumption may be truer than you think, Miss Thomas. But we shan't have to endure them for long." He turned, facing her full-on. "I trust that while in Detroit, you were able to see Cole's surgeon?"

"Indeed. That was the reason for my trip. He prescribed laudanum. I'll be in fine form for tonight's entertainment.

He looked at her quizzically.

"The dinner with Charles aboard the *Michigan*."

"He'll be pleased to hear it." Beall tipped his hat, indicating an end to their conversation. "Good to see you again, Miss Thomas. I trust you'll enjoy the voyage."

"Likewise, Mr. Beall."

Turning from her, he proceeded toward the aft of the vessel. For the most part, he'd covered his nervousness. But his fingers had betrayed him, tapping by turns at the railing. The plot was in motion. Hattie was sure of it. The only question was how exactly it would unfold.

She wouldn't have long to find out. Not twenty minutes later, the *Philo Parsons* pulled alongside the dock at Malden, on the outskirts of Windsor, Canada. From the bow, Hattie studied the men lined up to board, glad to see that Franklin Stone was not among them.

She counted close to thirty men, a rag-tag group. Each paid his fare in greenbacks, she noticed, and the only luggage they brought aboard was a large black trunk tied with ropes. As the *Parsons* pulled away from Malden, steaming into the open waters of Lake Erie, Hattie strolled about the deck, hoping to see whether any of these new passengers were interacting with Beall.

But Beall was nowhere to be found, so she went to the cabin to check on Edith. At the piano, she spotted one of the more respectable of the new passengers—a Scotsman, judging from his accent—singing along and turning pages for a lady who'd sat down to play.

Hattie slid onto the bench next to Edith, who was tapping her foot in time with the rousing rendition of "Pretty Polly Perkins."

"They've come aboard," Hattie whispered. "Beall's men. That's one of them." She nodded at the Scotsman.

"Armed?" Edith asked in a low voice, not missing a beat.

"I haven't seen any guns," Hattie said. "But they boarded with a big trunk."

Edith raised an eyebrow.

"I'm going to inform the captain. Urge him to inspect the trunk."

Edith nodded. Not wanting to draw undue attention, Hattie clapped along with the music until the song ended. Then, amid the scattered applause, she left the cabin to wander the deck again. The noontime sun warmed her skin, and she was grateful for the cool breeze blowing across the water.

Some of the new passengers seemed to be growing restless. Keeping her distance, she followed one of them around the ferry's perimeter. He seemed keenly interested in things that wouldn't attract a normal passenger's attention—the sidewheel, the lifeboats, the ladder that hung off the boat's stern, the hatches that opened to belowdecks. When she came closer, hoping to see if he had a gun holstered beneath his coat, he turned and glared.

She fell back. The last thing she wanted was to spark a confrontation in the middle of the lake. In the distance, she could see the hazy outline of Middle Bass Island. Turning from the man she'd been trailing, she looked about for Beall, hoping she might strike up another conversation that would add to her understanding of what he and Cole had planned. But he had yet to reappear. *The Gray Ghost,* Hattie thought, recalling the moniker from Beall's exploits on the Chesapeake.

As Middle Bass came more fully into view, Hattie decided she knew enough to feel out Captain Atwood. Heading toward the pilot house, she passed through a gauntlet of men who'd boarded in Malden. Feeling their eyes on her, she rapped on the pilot house door.

Behind her, she felt someone's hot breath on her neck. Whirling around, she found herself eye-to-eye with a stout, swarthy man in a long coat too warm for the weather.

"If it's the captain you're after, he's gone below," the man said.

Her heart skipped a beat. Had some harm come to Atwood? "I hope all is well."

The man offered a crooked smile. "Packing up, that's what I'm told."

"But we can't sail without a captain."

He laughed. "There's plenty aboard that can get this ship where she needs to go. And there's no cause for alarm. It's the captain's overnight at Middle Bass Island. Mate Nichols takes charge from there."

"I see," she said. "I'll seek out Mr. Nichols then." As she raised her hand to rap on the pilot house door again, a second man broke from the gauntlet and grabbed her wrist.

She shook free of his grasp. "A gentleman does not touch a lady without her consent."

The man held up his hand, palms out. "Sorry, ma'am. But the approach to Middle Bass can be tricky, and the mate is still learning it. I don't recommend interrupting his lessons, or we could end up on the rocks."

Hattie pressed her palms, damp with perspiration, against her skirt. She squared her shoulders, looking from one man to the other. "Very well. I'll find a more suitable time to speak with him."

"A wise choice." The politer of the two, the second man tipped his hat at her. "Here's to smooth sailing."

She turned, holding her head high as she passed again through the gauntlet, now seemingly populated by nearly all men who'd boarded at Malden. Some leered as she passed, but others chatted among themselves, ignoring her.

As the ferry approached the dock at Middle Bass, she went around to the port side, gripping the railing to steady herself. Were the waters here truly rocky, or was that a ruse to keep her from talking to the captain's replacement? She had no idea.

Minutes later, the vessel bumped to a stop at the dock, and there was the usual flurry of activity as passengers got on and off the ferry. She thought she might be able to corner Captain Atwood before he departed, but by the time she spotted him, he was already halfway down the plank, his eyes trained on a woman and a gaggle of children who grinned and waved wildly at him.

It would be another two hours before the ferry was due to arrive in Sandusky, Hattie reminded herself. Plenty of time for her to convince Nichols to have the trunk searched. If there were weapons inside, that should be evidence enough for the authorities at Sandusky to detain Beall and the Malden men for questioning.

Twenty minutes after it had docked, the *Parsons* pulled away from Middle Bass dock. Intending to consult with Edith in the cabin, Hattie headed round the aft of the ferry. Hearing Beall's voice, she stopped. Ahead on the hurricane deck, Beall stood next to the ship's mate, Nichols

Hattie stepped behind a lifeboat suspended on a set of ropes, hoping it would shield her from Beall's view.

"You have charge of this boat now, do you not?" Beall asked.

"I do," Nichols said.

"I am a Confederate officer. There are thirty of us aboard this vessel, and we are well-armed. I am seizing this boat and taking you prisoner. You must pilot the boat as I direct." From beneath his coat, Beall showed his revolver. "I want you to run down and lie off the harbor at Sandusky."

Hattie drew a sharp breath. She'd thought Beall and his men were only using the ferry as transportation to Sandusky, where the real action would take place. She hadn't expected them to take over the *Parsons.*

A scuffle on the bow drew her attention. Revolvers drawn, four of the so-called scallywags surrounded the *Parsons'* clerk. "Don't resist, or we'll shoot," one of them yelled.

Ducking out from behind the lifeboat, Hattie rushed to the cabin. On the deck ahead, she saw the black trunk that had been brought aboard at Malden, the rope now undone and the lid open. Inside it, she glimpsed revolvers and hatchets in quantities sufficient to arm all the men who'd come aboard at Malden and then some.

Hattie burst into the cabin. The scene was much as she'd left it, the lady still plunking away on the piano. But the Scotsman who'd been with her was gone.

Spotting Hattie, Edith jumped to her feet. "What is it?"

"The men—the ones who got on at Malden—they just—"

Coming through the cabin's doorway, two of Beall's men shoved past her, both aiming revolvers at the passengers.

"Keep still, and no one gets hurt!" one of them shouted.

A woman screamed. Another let out a frightened yelp. Others only stared at the men, stunned into silence. One of these women, obviously with child, clutched her protruding belly.

From the ship's deck, a shot rang out. Through the open doorway, Hattie saw the ferry's fireman run past. In close pursuit, a man with a cocked revolver yelled, "Get down the hatch, or I'll fire again."

"To hell with you!" The fireman swung himself onto a ladder that led to the upper deck. Another shot rang out, the bullet thankfully missing its mark.

Moments later, the fireman was scrambling down the ladder. At the bottom, five armed men now waited for him.

Another three men tromped into the cabin, barking orders for the male passengers to proceed to the fire hold. The passengers complied, Beall's men escorting them out at gunpoint.

Crowded together, the remaining hostages, all of them women and children, murmured among themselves.

"We shall all die!" an older woman said.

"Not if we do as we're told," said another.

Hattie edged toward Edith. "I tried to speak with Captain Atwood," she whispered. "But he got off at Middle Bass. Two of

Beall's men prevented me from speaking to the mate who has charge of the vessel now. I suspected trouble, but I had no idea they'd seize control of the ferry."

"Well, they have," Edith said. "The question is what we do about it now."

Nearby, a woman gasped. Turning, Hattie saw that the pregnant woman had slumped to the floor. Edith shot up from where she sat. She grabbed her medical bag, which she carried with her everywhere.

"Make way," she said, pushing past the women who were crowding around the fallen woman. "I'm a doctor."

As Edith tended to the pregnant woman, Hattie edged toward the open doorway. Guarding it was the Scotsman who'd been at the piano. He scowled at Hattie, clearly no longer in the mood for cheerful tunes. "Inside, Missy," he said, gesturing with his revolver.

Hattie pressed her hands to her throat. "I'm feeling faint. I need some air."

The man glanced over to where Edith was tending the woman who'd swooned. "Christ almighty," he said. "The trouble you women cause. You can stand at the rail. But you'd best stay where I can see you, or you'll find yourself in a permanent faint."

She nodded meekly, then slipped past him to the railing. Breathing deep, she tried to get her bearings. It looked as if they were traveling east of the ferry's usual course. From the engine room, the firemen shouted up at the pilot house. "Three hours of wood. That's all we've got."

Beall's voice drifted down through the open pilot house window. "Three hours won't do," he called back to the fireman.

"We've got business at Johnson's Island. We need at least six hours' worth."

"Then we've got to go back to Middle Bass and refuel, sir." The man who spoke from the pilot house must be Nichols, the mate in charge, Hattie surmised. "Otherwise, we'll end up adrift."

"Then turn back to Middle Bass," Beall barked. "Load up on fuel."

Slowly, the ferry turned. Hattie strained her eyes, searching the horizon. In the distance, the *U.S.S. Michigan* came into view.

From the pilot house window, she heard Beall inquiring how the *Michigan* might be boarded from the water. There was a ladder, the mate said, attached to the gunship's stern. That was all he knew.

Hattie realized how the plot would unfold. Twenty-five hundred prisoners couldn't escape Johnson's Island with the *USS Michigan*'s fourteen guns at the ready. But now that the renegades had taken over the *Parsons*, they planned to use it to seize control of the *Michigan*, giving themselves all the firepower they'd need to take over the prison.

Brought aboard the *Michigan* and the *Parsons*, the freed Rebels would wage war at every major town along the lakes. From there, they could easily terrorize the Atlantic seaboard. Countless lives would be lost, and the trajectory of the war might well turn in the South's favor, which was of course the ultimate aim.

The question was how to stop them. The refueling stop at Middle Bass might provide an opportunity, Hattie thought. In the flurry of activity, she might be able to break away from the ship and summon help. Captain Atwood was on Middle Bass, and there must be others who'd come to the vessel's aid. But at what hazard to themselves? From what she'd seen in the black trunk, the Rebels had plenty of arms to be trained against any who tried to stop them. And then there was the additional threat of Greek fire, the components of which might well be concealed in the bottom of the trunk.

The Scotsman interrupted her thoughts, grabbing Hattie by the shoulder. "Back inside," he said.

She felt the cool metal of his revolver against her back as he nudged her toward the cabin. Inside, she saw that the crowd that had gathered around Edith and the pregnant woman had mostly dispersed, the ladies now huddling in small groups on the benches. Edith was perched beside her patient, who now lay prone on a bench apart from the others.

As Hattie approached, the pregnant woman winced, clutching her stomach. Blinking, she turned to Edith. "How long?"

Edith checked her watch. "Ten minutes since the last contraction. They're slowing. You say this is your first?"

The woman nodded.

"Then there's a chance these pains are only a false alarm. You may be days away from delivering."

Relief flooded the woman's face. "Thank the Lord."

"Then again, this may indeed be the start of things. Time will tell."

The woman's bottom lip quivered. "I was supposed to be with my mother and sisters when the baby came. They were to tend to the birth."

"And they may well still," Edith said. "In the meantime, try to get some rest."

Her patient closed her eyes.

Seeing Hattie, Edith stood. Heads together, they discussed in low tones the ferry's return to Middle Bass for fuel and Hattie's theory about Beall and his men taking over the *Michigan*. "That will give them the firepower they need to overtake the prison," Hattie said. "Especially with Greek fire added to the mix."

Edith was quiet a moment. "The male passengers—might they get back control of this vessel?"

"They're locked in the fire hold," Hattie said. "Armed men are guarding the hatch. Middle Bass is our best hope. While we're refueling, I'll look for a way to slip off and find Captain Atwood. If he can gather enough men on the island, they may be able to take back this vessel."

Edith shook her head. "I don't like the idea of you escaping by yourself."

"There's no other option." Hattie nodded at the woman on the bench, whose eyes were fluttering open. "You need to stay with her."

"The pirates have used their guns already. I don't doubt they'd use them again, even on a woman."

"I've had guns trained on me before," Hattie said. "I've yet to be shot."

"Under these circumstances, the first time may also be the last."

"That may be," Hattie said. "But I have to try."

Chapter Twenty-One

Returning unscheduled, the *Philo Parsons* caused a good deal of excitement at Middle Bass Island. Once the ferry was secured at the dock, Hattie tried again to get past the Scotsman guarding the cabin door, but this time he rebuffed her claim of needing fresh air.

"No one goes out till we get the say-so from Captain Beall," he said. "'Less you plan on going out toes up."

Hattie relented but didn't retreat. Through the doorway, she watched the crowd that had begun to form at the dock. Shouts about wood were made from the vessel. Seeming to sense trouble, the woodyard's owner refused to allow any wood to be loaded. A volley of shots rang out from the ferry, causing the woodyard man to duck from sight and the villagers to scatter.

Hattie backed away from the doorway. Even if she managed to slip off the ferry, there was no one on shore to help.

Crossing the cabin, she saw that Edith had gotten the pregnant woman to a sitting position. Holding a tin cup to her lips, the doctor was encouraging her to sip some water. The woman reached for the cup, but then she winced and cried out, clutching her swollen belly again. Edith remained calm, but the furrows on her brow betrayed her concern. In the cramped quarters, Hattie saw there was nowhere for her to attempt a proper examination to determine how the labor was progressing.

As Hattie drew near to Edith and her patient, a ship's whistle shrilled. Through the windows on the far side of the cabin, she saw a vessel come alongside the *Parsons*. Veering toward the windows, she recognized the *Island Queen*, a smaller boat that ferried passengers between Sandusky and the islands.

Thinking someone from Sandusky, sensing trouble, had sent the little boat to investigate, Hattie's heart leaped. But then the *Island Queen*'s crew began setting the usual planks to ferry cargo and passengers across the *Parsons*' deck to the dock, and she realized that this was only an ordinary stop for the boat.

She pounded on the window, hoping to get the attention of one of the *Queen*'s crew. But shouts from around the *Parsons* drowned out the sound as several of Beall's men made a rush to board the *Queen*. Startled, the smaller ferry's crew stopped what they were doing. A bell rang, and Hattie saw one of the Queen's crew lunge for the ship's throttle.

"Shoot the son of a bitch!" one of Beall's men shouted.

A shot rang out, and the man who'd tried to reach the throttle slumped over, blood streaming from his face. Two of the swarthier renegades took hold of him, one on each arm, and dragged him onto the *Parsons* and into the vessel's hold.

Guns drawn, Beall's men forced the *Queen*'s passengers across the planks to the *Parsons*. They ushered nearly all the male passengers into the fire hold, save a few who they escorted at gunpoint to the unattended woodyard, shouting instructions for them to load up the wood and be quick about it.

The women from the *Island Queen* crowded into the cabin with the women from the *Parsons*. Some were hysterical, causing a good number of the *Parsons* passengers to begin weeping and moaning again. Edith had gotten the pregnant woman to stand and was trying to walk her around the cabin, but crowded as it was, she was having a hard time making a path.

The situation seemed hopeless. Once the *Parsons* had refueled, nothing could stop Beall and his men from crossing the lake to overtake the *Michigan* and the Johnson's Island prison. There was only one thing left to try.

She went back to the Scotsman, still at his post. "I need a word with Captain Beall," she said.

He looked at her quizzically, no doubt puzzled at how she'd know Beall's name and unofficial rank. "Captain's busy."

"I'll only be a minute." She glanced back at Edith and the pregnant woman. "He's a friend, and I've got some information he'll wish to know."

The Scotsman's gaze sharpened as he looked from Hattie to Edith and back again. "Information, you say?"

She swallowed hard. "Information that could prove vital to his enterprise."

He squinted hard at her. "You'd best be telling the truth, lass."

She jutted her chin. "Captain Beall will vouch for my honor. And I daresay he won't be pleased if you keep me away."

The guard sighed. "Wearing me down, you are." He waved over a younger man who stood at the boat's aft, gun in hand. "Take this lady to Captain Beall," he said. "She wants a word with him. But be quick about it, the both of you."

The Scotsman stepped aside, allowing Hattie onto the deck. The younger guard stepped behind her, his drawn revolver pointed at her back. "Captain's on the hurricane deck," he said.

She proceeded toward the stairs, the guard following at close range. On the dock, it looked like the loading of wood was nearly complete. She didn't have much time.

Reaching the steps, she gathered her skirts, thankful she'd chosen a simple plaid morning dress instead of a fancier hooped skirt for the voyage. Even so, she had to tread carefully on the narrow steps, the hem of her dress obscuring her view of her feet. Yet another reason to envy Edith and her bloomers.

Reaching the uppermost deck, she found Beall and the mate, Nichols, standing near the ship's bell. They turned as she approached.

"The lady wants a word with you, Captain Beall," the guard said.

"Miss Thomas." Touching his hat, Beall dipped his head toward her. "I trust you haven't been overly inconvenienced by our change of plans. My apologies if it causes you to miss your dinner engagement tonight."

"I'm sure Mr. Cole will understand. I know you've got important work at hand. But I need to alert you to a situation below."

"A situation." Beall glanced over the waters, seeming lost in thought. Then he turned to Nichols. "We sail the moment the last log is loaded. Understood?"

"Yes, sir."

Beall stepped toward Hattie. To her escort, he said, "Proceed to the boiler deck. She'll be down in a minute."

The man nodded, then descended the stairs. When he was out of earshot, Beall said, "Your concern, Miss Thomas?"

"It's the women, Mr. Beall. Conditions in the cabin are far from ideal. There are too many for the space, and some of the frailer ladies are rather disheartened. One is with child, and there are indications she may deliver soon."

He rubbed his chin. "Your doctor—she's able to tend to this woman?"

"Yes. She's with her as we speak. But I've been thinking—if you and Mr. Cole succeed in your enterprise." Pausing, Hattie offered a sly smile. "That is, *when* you succeed, it won't do to have tales circulating of how these ladies have been abused."

"A few hours confined to a cabin is hardly abuse, Miss Thomas."

"Indeed. But you know how the papers can conflate a situation."

The corners of his lips turned. "The papers will have much more to report than the temporary distress of a few hysterical females."

"Even so," she said, "I keep thinking about your Martha—what she'd do if she were here. From what you've told me of her, I believe she'd appeal to your gentleman's sensibilities on behalf of these ladies. And if she's as resourceful as you say, she'd probably come up with a solution that would serve the best interests of all aboard."

His face softened at the mention of his fiancée. "In that you're correct, Miss Thomas. Martha is nothing if not resourceful, and her advice has ever served my interests."

"Then perhaps she'd point out that no harm would come from letting the ladies off here at Middle Bass. As long as you keep the

Island Queen tethered to the *Parsons*, they'd have no means of escape.

"That would get them out of harm's way," he mused.

"And avoid the uncomely prospect of a woman being forced to give birth aboard a vessel you've commandeered."

He gazed out again at the waters. "True enough," he said.

Hattie hesitated, not sure if she should push her luck. "You could offload the men as well, with the understanding that they'd look after the ladies. And after exacting their promise not to interfere in your purpose, of course. Parole them as prisoners of the cause, on the condition they not fight against us until properly exchanged."

"Prisoners of war. That's what they are." He stroked his mustache. "No telegraph on Middle Bass. No means of communicating with the mainland."

"Exactly," she said. "There are only these two ferries."

Calling out to Beall, Nichols interrupted their conversation. "Wood's aboard. Ready to push off."

"Hold up," Beall called back. "I've got some business to tend to first."

~ ~ ~

It took little more than thirty minutes to put ashore all the passengers from both ferries, ladies and gentlemen alike. In exchange for their freedom, all gladly agreed to Beall's terms of parole. As he demanded, they promised to refrain from contact with the mainland for the next twenty-four hours.

Standing among the passengers at the Middle Bass dock, Hattie watched the *Parsons* set out for Sandusky Bay, the *Island Queen* in tow. One by one, villagers began to emerge from their hiding places with offers of food and shelter for the stranded passengers. Captain Atwood arrived with a wagon, saying his wife would put up as many women as could fit in their home.

Urged to the front of the line with her patient, Edith gestured for Hattie to come close. "This was your doing, I presume," she whispered as two of the men helped the pregnant woman into the wagon.

Hattie nodded. "I appealed to Beall's gentlemanly side."

"A weakness of many a Southern man, that he perceives himself brimming with honor even when engaged in the most despicable enterprises," Edith said. "But I don't see how we stop him now that we're stranded here."

"Not entirely stranded." Hattie nodded at three wooden rowboats pulled up on shore.

"Those look about as seaworthy as a paper boat," Edith said. "You can't possibly intend to row yourself to Sandusky."

"Not to Sandusky," Hattie said. "To the *USS Michigan*." She glanced at the western sky, where the sun was sinking fast. "And I'm not so foolish as to think I can row myself. But surely someone here can. I just hope they can manage it in the dark."

Chapter Twenty-Two

Waves lapping at the sides of the rowboat, Hattie tried not to think about what Charles Cole had told her about Lake Erie being the most treacherous of all the Great Lakes. Collisions, fires, storms, rogue waves—he'd named all sorts of reasons ships foundered. And here, in the Erie Island area, the lake's waters were especially dangerous.

Small wonder that none of the grown men on Middle Bass Island had volunteered to row Hattie across to the *Michigan*. The trip would take hours, they told her, and while the waves weren't especially bad at present, autumn storms could descend without warning, churning the waters. And aside from the Marblehead lighthouse, positioned to warn ships away from an extraordinarily rocky shore, there would be only the moon's light to guide them. On top of that, anyone rowing to the *Michigan* risked discovery by Beall and his men, not to mention the hazards posed by Greek fire, should they choose to set it, a blaze no amount of water could extinguish.

But after Hattie explained why she had to reach the *Michigan* at the earliest opportunity, two brothers, ages sixteen and seventeen, had been quick to volunteer. Their widowed mother had taken some convincing, but when Hattie made clear all that was at stake, she relented. For their journey, she'd packed a basket of bread, cheese, and apples, shoving it at her boys after hugging them tightly and exacting their promise to be careful. She'd also insisted Hattie take her warm cloak.

As Hattie soon discovered, the boys, Nick and Delos, had voracious appetites. Within an hour of pushing off from Middle Bass, they'd emptied the basket of food. Politely, they'd insisted Hattie eat a portion. Hunger gnawing at her stomach, she'd been grateful for the offering, but she took only a small apple and even smaller hunks of bread and cheese, knowing the boys would need every ounce of nourishment they could get for the hours of rowing ahead.

An hour later, the sun dipped below the horizon, painting the western sky in shades of purple and pink. Taking turns at the oars, the brothers amused themselves exchanging good-natured jabs and complaints. Delos, the older brother, accused Nick of bad form in his rowing. Nick reminded Delos of the time he'd tipped over their boat, a tale Hattie could have done without hearing. Delos countered that it had been well worth the dunking since it had been the result of his reeling in one of the biggest sturgeon ever caught by an islander. Nick pointed out how the sturgeon got bigger every time Delos told the tale. And so it went, the topics of contention shifting from which of them was better with boats to which was better with horses to which brother had more luck with the girls.

Darkness set in, the stars coming out in all their glory. Delos lamented that in their haste to depart, they'd neglected to bring a lantern. But Hattie was glad to be without a light. Bobbing over the dark waters, the rowboat would be hard to see.

As the Milky Way spread across the night sky, the boys quit their bantering and rowed in silence. Soon the beam from Marblehead's light came into view. After some discussion, the brothers had agreed that the best approach to the *Michigan* was to come hard at the lighthouse, then hug the peninsula's coast, coming around to the back of the gunship. After delivering Hattie to her destination—how she'd board the ship remained to be seen—they planned to retreat to their cousins' farm on the peninsula, where they'd spend the night.

It seemed a good plan, if a bit sketchy on details, and in any event, it was all Hattie had. But now, as they approached the rocky shore near the lighthouse, the wind picked up, the waves doubling in size. At the oars, Delos seemed to be struggling to keep on course.

Hattie pulled her cloak tight, grateful for the warmth. Looking out over the dark waters, she fingered the pearl choker Cole had given her. The appointed time for her to meet him at the Sandusky dock had long since passed. She hoped he'd taken her failure to show up in stride, chalking it up to another of her headaches.

Squinting into the darkness, she looked for any sign of the *Philo Parsons*. She didn't think Beall would bring the ferry directly to Johnson's Island, not until the *Michigan* was under his control. Exactly how that would happen, she didn't know. Meanwhile, she assumed the *Parsons* was hovering somewhere in the night.

As Delos rowed into Marblehead's swath of light, Hattie tensed. Silently, she urged him to row faster. But between the wind and the waves and the overall exertion, his pace seemed to slow.

After what seemed an eternity, the boat rounded the point, shrouded once again in darkness save for the glow of a gibbous moon. Ahead, Hattie spotted a row of distant lights.

On the seat across from her, Nick was dozing. She nudged him, and he opened his eyes. "Huh?" he said.

"Those lights—is that Sandusky?" she asked.

He leaned forward, looking where she pointed. "Yup."

"See that dark shape between here and there? It looks like it's at the entrance to the bay. Could it be the *Parsons*?"

"Maybe," Nick said. "Probably."

A wave slammed into the boat rocking it. Gripping her wooden seat, Hattie kept an eye on the silhouette. It didn't seem to be moving, but in the dark, it was hard to know for certain.

Now out of the worst of the wind, the rowboat began closing in on Johnson's Island. It looked much as it did from shore, with gaslights illuminating the perimeter of the prison. Beyond it was the hulking shape of the *USS Michigan*.

"Can you row around to the back?" she asked Delos.

"Sure," he said.

In silence, they neared the gunboat. Viewed from so low in the water, the ship was massive. It was the US Navy's first iron-clad, Cole had told her, with a clipper bow and a tall smokestack plus three tall masts. In addition to its other armaments, the *Michigan* had four cannonades and two pivot guns.

Coming up on the gunboat's stern, Delos pulled back on the oars. Nick stood, wide-legged, and steadied the rowboat against the gunship's hull. He eyed the ladder. "You going up that?"

"If I can manage it." She stood. After hours folded onto the rowboat's seat, her legs wobbled.

Delos leapt to her aid. "With all due respect, ma'am, that ladder don't look like a good idea."

Hattie craned her neck, looking up at the ship's deck. "I'm afraid it's the only idea I've got."

"Then we'd better hold this boat steady as we can." Reaching up, Nick grabbed a bit of rigging that hung from the *Michigan*'s deck.

With Delos's steady hand on her arm, Hattie sidestepped toward the bow of the rowboat. Reaching the rope ladder, Delos took hold of a rung and swung it toward Hattie.

Grabbing onto it, she turned to the brothers. "I can't thank you enough. I don't know what the outcome of my efforts will be, but I do know that if not for the two of you, this ship would certainly be lost, and with it, the prison and perhaps every town on this lake."

It was hard to tell in the moonlight, but she thought she saw color rise in the boys' faces. "It was nothing," Delos mumbled.

"It's you that's got the hard part now," Nick said. "Maybe one of us should go with you."

Hattie shook her head. "It's better I go alone. I can't let you risk more than you already have. I'm sure your mother needs the both of you back at the farm."

She shifted her weight toward the ladder. Delos let go of her arm, and she reached for a second rung, clinging with both hands as her feet found purchase. She turned as the ladder bounced against the hull, her shoulder and hip taking the brunt of the blow.

Then she began to climb. After sitting inert in the tiny boat, her muscles protested. But her urgent purpose propelled her forward, and soon she was going from rung to rung with relative ease. The little monkey—that's what her brother George had called Hattie when they were young, climbing to his secret treehouse in the woods.

A girl's skirts were less cumbersome than a lady's, though. Twice Hattie stepped on the hem of her petticoat, putting herself momentarily off-kilter. The second time, she heard the fabric rip. No matter. With what she intended to do, she doubted anyone would be paying attention to her hems.

Coming eye level with the deck, she paused to assess the situation. She'd expected sailors to be posted all around, but the ship seemed almost deserted, the only sign of life being the lights that shone from the hull's windows. The dinner party must be in full swing, she thought, and the crates of wine Cole had brought over for the crew's enjoyment had likely already been broken into.

Letting go of the ladder, she grabbed first for a life ring dangling off the boat's stern and then for the railing. Hoisting herself onto the deck, she landed with an awkward sort of bellyflop. Scrambling to her feet, she saw that in addition to her torn petticoat, dirt now smudged her bodice. As best she could, she smoothed back her damp, windblown hair. Presenting herself to the captain, she would hardly come off as elegant. She only hoped that in her bedraggled state, he'd still be inclined to believe her.

All she knew of the ship was what Cole had told—mainly, that the captain's cabin, aft on the main deck, was especially luxurious, consisting of two staterooms, a library, a lounge, and a bath. That area, she noted, was dark. The captain, along with the other officers, must be in the dining room, which she assumed was below, where the windows were lit.

Hoping to come upon access to that area, she started around the deck. She stepped as lightly as she could, but her slippers were soaked with water, and with each step, they made a squishing sound.

On the starboard side, past the captain's quarters, she found a door. Grasping the handle, she was about to open it when a man's voice called out, "Who goes there?"

Looking up, she froze. Light from a lantern came bobbing toward her, accompanied by the heavy sound of the man's footsteps. Dressed in a sailor's uniform, he looked not much older than her, though his hairline was receding. The set of his eyes, drooping slightly at the outer corners, brought to mind the expression of a loyal dog eager to please.

"I am Mr. Cole's guest for the officers' dinner," Hattie said, hoping that in the dim light he wouldn't notice her disheveled state.

"Mr. Cole brought no guest," he said.

"I was unexpectedly detained," she said. "But now that I'm here, I'd be much obliged if you'd point me toward the dining room. I'm sure Mr. Cole is wondering what became of me."

A look of disgust crossed the man's face. "If you ask me, all he's wondering is how much more liquor he can pour down the throats of our crew."

"His gift was of wine, not liquor," she said. "And I don't know why you'd condemn his generosity. At any rate, if you prefer not to direct me, at least step aside and allow me to find my own way."

She stepped forward, but he lifted his arm, bracing it against the side of the cabin in a way that kept her from proceeding. "Perhaps you could explain how exactly you came aboard, Miss—"

"Thomas," she supplied. "Helen Thomas. And I'm afraid I don't feel obliged to share the details of my comings and goings with a stranger."

"Then allow me to introduce myself." His tone was cordial, but he did not crack a smile. "Murray Wilson, gunner's mate first-class."

"Pleased to make your acquaintance, I'm sure. Now if you'll excuse me, I'd just as soon there were no further delays to my—"

"Follow me," Wilson interrupted. Without another word, he turned and started toward the bow. Shoes squishing, she followed with as much dignity as she could manage.

Coming upon another door, Wilson pushed it open. Within, an oil lamp affixed to the wall lit a set of stairs that led below. "After you, Miss Thomas," he said.

Grateful for the handrail and the light, she took the steps slowly. She would need to assess the situation without letting on that she'd been delayed by anything other than a headache, and to do that, she needed to make her entrance with as much aplomb as she could manage.

When they reached the bottom of the stairs, Murray marched her down a narrow hallway and around a corner. There, he opened a paneled door and gestured for her to enter.

The ship's dining room was as elegantly furnished as any hotel's. Oil-painted miniatures adorned the dark wood-paneled walls, and white linens covered a long table lit by white tapers in crystal candleholders. It looked as if the plates had recently been cleared, but the smell of roasted beef hung over the room.

At the head of the table sat a man who, judging from the epaulets on his Naval uniform, she presumed to be Captain Jeremiah Carter, commander of the *USS Michigan*. With him at the table were four men, two of them uniformed officers and two of them dressed as civilians. One of the civilians she knew to be Charles Cole, though like the others, he had his back toward her, facing the captain.

"...foregoing the wine with dinner," Cole was saying as he poured from a crystal decanter into the captain's glass, "you'll enjoy this fine dessert port."

As the captain reached for the glass, his gaze fell on Hattie and Wilson.

"This woman claims to be a guest of Captain Cole's," Wilson blurted out.

At this, the four men at the table turned. She must look a fright, Hattie thought, hoping the candlelight softened the effect.

"Helen." Cole set down the decanter. "How did you get here?"

"Hattie," said a tall man whose handsome face and piercing eyes she'd recognize anywhere. "What a surprise."

Chapter Twenty-Three

I gnoring Franklin Stone's stare, Hattie stepped forward, her gaze fixed on Captain Carter. "Your guests are carrying out a Rebel plot. Their associates have seized the *Philo Parsons*."

"Seized the *Parsons*?" the captain said. "My god. The passengers—are they safe?"

"Safe," mumbled one of the officers at the table. "I dunno..." His voice trailed off, and his head wobbled side to side as if it had become too heavy for him to hold up. Across the table, the other officer slumped in his chair.

Franklin pushed abruptly from the table, toppling his chair, which clattered against the wooden floor. "This woman has no idea was she's talking about."

Hattie locked eyes with him. "I most certainly do. I was aboard the *Parsons*. The renegades forced us off the ferry at Middle Bass. They did the same with the passengers of the *Island Queen*, which they seized as well. Now they intend to take over this ship so they can free the Johnson's Island prisoners and terrorize towns along this lake and beyond."

Cole cocked his head at her. "What a fantastical story, darling. But we assess its veracity, do explain how it is that Mr. Stone knows you by one name and I another."

Franklin pounded his fist on the table, clattering the dishes. "She's a spy, trained with the Pinkertons." His eyes narrowed. "A devious little spy who sheltered under my own roof. No wonder you knew about the goings-on at the print shop."

Hattie straightened. "I serve my country if that's what you mean."

Franklin lunged at her. At the table, the officer who remained conscious tried to stand. Slowly and unsteadily, he reached for Franklin. He swayed, then fell to the floor.

Dragging his bad leg, Franklin hurdled over the man's prone form. In his hand, Hattie saw the glittering blade of a dagger.

She shrank toward the door as Murray Wilson stepped toward Franklin, his revolver drawn. "Stop, I say!"

Franklin shoved him aside. Hattie fled through the doorway and down the steps, running as fast as she could. She could hear him behind her. Despite his limp, he was gaining on her. As she reached the top of the stairs, she felt a tug at her skirts. Her torn petticoat—was he stepping on it?

She pulled away, and there was a loud ripping sound as the lace of her petticoat tore off entirely. Then she heard a scrambling of steps, followed by a thud, and she knew Franklin's feet must have tangled in the torn lace.

She pushed through the door onto the ship's deck, searching wildly for something she could use to bar the door. Seeing nothing suitable, she dashed along the starboard side toward the bow. Behind her, she heard the distinctive sound of Franklin's jagged gait, his good foot hitting solidly and the other scuffing as he pulled it forward.

It was anger that propelled him, she knew—anger at the war that had crippled him, anger at her for uncovering his secrets. Even with his bad leg, she feared he would soon catch up with her, the ship offering little room for escape. She could try to hide, but she'd risk being cornered.

The sound of his footsteps drew near. If she was going to hide, she needed to do it here on the ship's starboard side, shadowed by the moon. Ahead, the passageway narrowed between the smokestack and the starboard paddlebox. Overhead, the bridge darkened the deck even further.

She plunged into the darkness. Reaching out her hand, she felt for the smokestack that rose in the ship's center. With the *Michigan* at anchor, the stack was cool to the touch. Sucking in her stomach, she wedged herself behind it. Pulling her skirts from view, she pressed her cheek to the metal and prayed Franklin wouldn't see her.

His steps came closer. They slowed and then stopped. From her hiding place, she couldn't see him, but she could hear his labored breaths, and she knew he was close, knew he was searching.

She held her breath. In the ship's quiet, she could hear Lake Erie's waves lapping at the hull. By now, someone from the crew should have heard the commotion in the dining room, should have noticed the pounding of footsteps on the center stairs.

But she'd seen what had happened with the officers in the dining room, rendered groggy and then unconscious. Cole and Franklin must have drugged them—easy enough to accomplish, she knew from when she'd worked in Edith's dispensary. Had they done the same to the crew?

Footsteps sounded from the direction of the center stairwell. Franklin clearly heard them, too, because she heard the ragged clomp-clomp of him moving away from the sound.

Peering around the smokestack, Hattie saw a dark figure pursuing Franklin. Retreating to her hiding place, she heard a shout.

"You won't get away with this." The voice belonged to Murray Wilson.

"The hell I won't," Franklin said. "The only question is whether I have to kill you to do it. Now put down that gun."

Hattie felt a shiver of fear, not for herself but for Anne. All this time, Hattie had worried about how to stay loyal to her by protecting Franklin. But there was no protecting him now.

A shot rang out. Hattie's heart sank. *I'm sorry, Anne. I didn't mean for it to come to this.*

Then she heard scuffling, and she realized Wilson's shot must have missed—not so surprising in the dark.

"Arghhhhh!" Wilson cried out. "You bastard!" This was followed by the sound of something clattering to the deck. The gun, Hattie thought. Or the knife.

She leaped from her hiding place and raced toward the aft of the ship. In the moon shadow of a lifeboat suspended overhead, she saw two dark figures. Wilson lay motionless on the deck. Franklin stood over him. With his knife raised, he lunged toward Wilson's gun, which lay just out of reach on the deck.

Hattie kicked the revolver from his reach. Then she bent and retrieved it. Gripping the gun in both hands, she pointed the barrel at Franklin's chest. "Drop the dagger," she said. "Or I'll shoot."

Moonlight glinted in Franklin's eyes. "You wouldn't," he said, but he took a step back.

"I will if I must." She hoped that in the semi-darkness, Franklin wouldn't see how her hands shook, gripping the gun.

He kept the dagger raised, its point now aimed at her. "Anne would never forgive you. She loves me, you know."

"Which is why I made sure you escaped the print shop raid. A mistake, I see now. I let my loyalty to her cloud my judgment."

He laughed, a wicked sound. "Stupid of me, to trust either of you women, knowing you'd worked for Pinkerton."

Prone on the deck, Wilson groaned weakly. Hattie kept her gaze fixed on Franklin. "Don't blame Anne. I'm the one who knows what you and Cole have been up to. You think you'll take the Johnson's Island prison? Not a chance. I've alerted the warden. The guards are ready for your little attack. You and Beall and his men don't stand a chance."

None of what she said about the prison was true. As far as the warden and guards knew, this was an ordinary night.

A hint of doubt crossed Franklin's face. "We've got control of the *Michigan*. The prison doesn't stand a chance against her pivot guns and cannonades."

"You'll hang when it's discovered you've killed the crew."

"They're not dead, just incapacitated. That's what comes of a weakness for wine. If we'd been able to convince the captain and this sorry excuse for a gunner to have a glass, we'd be firing the guns right now."

"So much you didn't take into account." She stepped back, the ship's rail behind her. "Including me."

Franklin laughed. "Our plan's in motion." He moved forward, keeping her within striking distance of his dagger. The moonlight shone full on him, illuminating the handsome features that had caused sensible Anne to fall head over heels for him. "Any minute, Cole will be signaling the *Parsons* to move in. Nothing you can do now will stop us."

"I must pose a threat," Hattie said. "Otherwise, why come after me?"

His moonlit face clouded with an emotion she couldn't read for certain. Anger. Disgust. "I've never liked you," he said. "A pathetic excuse for a woman."

She tipped her head, smiling. "I seem to recall you taking no small interest in me back when we first met."

His mouth contorted, his expression turning ugly. "A grave mistake on my part."

The pistol was growing heavy in her hands. "Speaking of mistakes, I hope you aren't putting too much stock in Mr. Beall and his men. There were some obstacles after taking the *Parsons*."

Franklin's eyes narrowed. "What sort of obstacles?"

She shrugged. "A pathetic excuse for a woman can hardly be expected to know. But I did hear of some grumbling among Beall's men. Some talk of giving up on the plan. Somehow..." She paused, smiling. "Somehow word spread among them that the *Michigan*'s captain had been warned of their attack, and they fear the ship's guns are trained on them."

Another groan from Wilson. Franklin turned. It was hard to see in the shadows, but it looked as if the gunner was struggling to sit up.

Now was her chance. She fired into the air. Franklin looked from Wilson to her. At such close range, she knew he couldn't tell who had fired, Wilson or her.

She shot again, this time aiming toward the lifeboat. The sound of the bullet ricocheted. Franklin's look of confusion shifted to panic.

"I'm not through with you, Hattie Thomas!" He rushed the railing. What he'd done with the dagger, Hattie couldn't tell, but he gripped the rail with both hands and vaulted himself over. With a splash, he landed in the water.

Straining her eyes in the moonlight, Hattie watched Franklin swim from the boat. Anne had told her he was a strong swimmer, having taken to the water after his injury as a way of strengthening his muscles without the pain he suffered on land. He might make Johnson's Island, or even the peninsula, where he could hide in the forest.

Turning, she started toward Murray Wilson. Then, remembering the rope ladder she'd used to climb aboard, she hurried back. Setting aside the gun, she pulled the ladder rung by rung onto the deck, ensuring that Franklin couldn't get back on the boat.

Then she hurried back to Wilson. He lay on the deck, his breathing labored but his eyes alert. Seeing her, he blinked twice. "Are you hurt, Miss?"

"A little shaken, that's all." She crouched beside him. "What about you?"

"Bleeding from the left shoulder," he said. "Where he stabbed me. Must've hit my head going down. Knocked me out for a spell, I reckon."

She touched his shoulder. Her hand came away warm and wet with his blood. She ripped another section out of her petticoat, then wrapped it around and around the wound, hoping to staunch the flow.

"The captain." Leveraging himself on his good arm, Wilson tried to sit up. "Is he all right?"

"I hope so." She looped her arm under his good shoulder and, with some effort, got him to his feet, his back against the cabin wall for support. Where he'd lain, blood stained the decking. But her makeshift bandage wasn't yet soaked through, a good sign.

"I...got that man," Wilson said, catching his breath.

"Cole, you mean?"

Wilson gave a weak nod. "The threat of my gun was...sufficient to subdue him."

"He wasn't armed?"

"Had a...small pistol. But he was...slow with it. Took it from him and...left him...handcuffed. Only..." Wilson paused, gulping air.

"Only others of their persuasion might be hidden aboard this ship," Hattie said.

"They could...overpower the captain." Unsteadily, he stepped away from the wall. "Need...need to get down there."

She set her hand on his chest, stopping him. "You can't manage those stairs. And even if you could, you'd be of no use with that injury."

He eyed the gun in her hand. "I can shoot."

"So can I," she said. Hitting her target was another matter altogether.

She made Wilson promise to stay put, then hurried to the stairs. Bone-weariness was beginning to set over her, but her new worry over hidden conspirators brought a surge of energy. She scampered down the stairs, then burst through the dining room door.

The captain and Cole were sitting where she'd left them. "Well, well, well." Cole tipped his head, seeming jovial as ever. "Look who's back. I'd stand to greet you, darling, but these manacles are a rather tedious impediment." He raised his hands, displaying the handcuffs.

His pistol trained on Cole, Captain Carter pushed back his chair and stood. His demeanor was calm, but the color had drained from his face. "Hearing a shot, I feared for your safety," he said.

"I'm fine," she said. "But the fellow who chased after me stabbed Mr. Wilson. He needs medical attention."

Laughing heartily, Cole nodded at the officer slumped over the table. "There's your ship's surgeon if you can rouse him."

"You poisoned him," Hattie said. "Him and the rest of the crew."

"Not poisoned, darling. I was just explaining to the captain here. I only added a healthy dose of narcotics to enhance the effects of the wine. They're only enjoying a deep and extended slumber."

"And to think I nearly indulged," the captain said.

"It would have served our purposes better if you had," Cole said. "As soon as you were all under the influence, I was to have signaled the Parsons."

"Using Greek fire," Hattie said.

He looked at her quizzically. "Stone told you our plan?"

"Stone told me nothing. And he's no longer part of it. He has, shall we say, abandoned ship."

Looking doleful, Cole shook his head. "A pity. Such well-laid plans we had. Once we seized control of the *Michigan*, the prison didn't stand a chance. And once those men were freed, you can be sure they'd have fought to the death for the South."

"You're the one who won't stand a chance," Captain Carter said gruffly. "Treason. Sabotage. Those are serious charges."

Cole cocked his head, his expression amused. "Ah, but I'm like a cat, Captain. I land on my feet." He turned his gaze on Hattie. "It can't be true, can it, darling? What Stone said about you being a spy?"

"Quite true," she said. "And I'm not your darling."

"Shameful, what the war has done to our women," Cole said.

Despite her fatigue, despite her torn gown and waterlogged slippers, despite the heaviness of the revolver in her hands, Hattie straightened. "Call it shame if you like," she said. "I call it determination to do what's best for our country."

Chapter Twenty-Four

SEPTEMBER 20, 1864

When Hattie woke the next morning, she wasn't sure at first where she was. Then it all came back to her. The bunk in the dark-paneled room belonged to Captain Carter, who'd insisted she try to get some rest after the night's excitement. Despite his age, he claimed an unwillingness to sleep himself, saying he intended to stay awake until every one of the men recovered from the effects of the drugged wine.

Through the wall, Hattie heard Murray Wilson snoring lightly. With her at one arm and the captain at the other, they'd managed to get him down the stairs and into a bunk to await tending by the ship's surgeon.

Turning, Hattie rose from where she lay and went to the basin. The water she splashed on her face took off a layer of grime, but she saw in the mirror that soot from the smokestack still smudged her cheek. Besides the rip in her petticoat, her bodice was soiled and torn, and her skirt had somehow ripped at the pocket.

But she was alive, no small feat considering how close Franklin had come with his knife. Exhausted as she'd been last night, she'd lain awake a good long while in the dark, worrying that he might somehow get back on the ship and come after her. The loyalty she'd felt toward Anne was nothing Franklin understood. Given the opportunity, Hattie had no doubt he'd kill his wife's best friend as readily as he'd kill a stranger.

When she'd gotten herself as presentable as was possible under the circumstances, she followed the smell of biscuits to the dining room. Though haggard, with dark circles under his eyes, Captain Carter was back at the head of the table. The two officers from last night were at the table too. Both looked substantially worse for the wear, as if they'd pulled themselves from the gutter after a hard night of drink.

Carter gestured toward an empty chair. "I hope you slept well."

"Quite. How is Mr. Wilson faring?"

"I washed and wrapped his wounds a few hours ago," said the surgeon, his voice a bit wobbly. "He should be resting comfortably."

Hattie reached for a biscuit, the only fare on the table. She presumed this was the best the cook could manage, considering the state he and his shipmates had fallen into last night. Still, the biscuit was warm and flaky. She slathered it with butter and, in a less than ladylike manner, consumed the whole of it in four bites.

"When do we make for Middle Bass?" she asked Captain Carter.

"As soon as my mate returns from his errand at Johnson's Island."

She raised an eyebrow. "Cole?"

Carter nodded. "If he's lucky, he'll sit out the remainder of the war at the prison he intended to breach. If he's not, he'll hang."

Hattie didn't necessarily wish Cole dead, but she was glad Union officials had charge of him now. "And Franklin Stone—has he been apprehended?"

The captain shook his head. "The lake may have claimed him. Then again, if he's a strong swimmer—"

"He is," she interrupted.

"Then he may well have reached land. The water's cold, but I've known others to survive it if they're young and robust. And the woods offer plenty of places to hide."

"Not to mention Canada," she said. "He'd just need to find someone to ferry him across the lake, and he'd be safe from any consequences."

If that were the case, Franklin might never return to his wife and daughter. Hattie felt awful for Anne, having to deal with the uncertainty. Would she blame her friend? Hattie hoped not. She'd done what she could to respect Anne's wishes. But in the end, she couldn't let her loyalty to her friend keep her from doing what was right.

~ ~ ~

Later that morning, after Carter's mate had seen to Cole's incarceration, the *Michigan* set sail for Middle Bass Island. Gray clouds hung overhead, and owing to a brisk wind, Captain Carter had ordered his crew to raise sails on the ship's three masts.

Despite the chill, Hattie stood at the bow, bracing herself against the wind. The ship's lookout reported no sign of the *Parsons*, but she kept an eye out for it all the same. She watched, too, for Nick and Delos in their little rowboat. Seeing no sign of them, she told herself they must have set out early, knowing their mother needed them at home.

At last, the outline of the island came into view. She wondered how the passengers had fared, isolated and fearful. Edith's calm presence would have helped, but then the doctor must have had her hands full tending to the pregnant woman.

As the *Michigan* neared, villagers emerged from their houses. Captain Carter ordered the anchor dropped offshore, the ship's ten-foot draft too great to allow docking. He directed Hattie into one of the ship's dinghies, and a crewman rowed her toward shore.

As they approached, cheers went up from the crowd. Hattie searched the faces for Edith. Finally, she spotted her, cradling a bundle in her arms. The baby, Hattie realized.

The dinghy bumped against the dock. As the oarsman tied it off, hands reached to help Hattie out.

"Salvation at last!" a woman said.

"And the *Michigan* unharmed," said the man next to her.

"Where's the captain?" said another. Cupping his hand over his eyes, he strained to see.

"Is the plot still afoot?" a different man asked.

"When can we go aboard?" said a woman. "I want to go home."

"Captain Carter is unharmed," Hattie said. "There was a plot against the *Michigan* and the Johnson's Island prison, but it has been thwarted. The captain will make sure you're soon safely on your way."

As the onlookers murmured their reactions, Hattie pushed through the crowd to Edith. Drawing close, she drew her into an awkward hug, the little bundle pressed between them.

"Motherhood would suit you," Hattie said, drawing back.

Edith harumphed. "I highly doubt it." But as she glanced at the child, a smile teased her lips. "I've only taken charge so the mother can get some rest."

A pair of familiar faces came up behind her, plastered with sheepish grins.

"Nick! Delos!" Hattie threw her arms around the boys, not minding that they smelled of sweat and hay. "I was hoping you'd gotten back safely."

"I knew Ma wouldn't sleep a wink till we got home," Delos said. "So we headed back at first light."

"And guess what we saw on our way here?" Nick said. "The *Parsons*, steaming toward Malden."

Canada. Of course that's where Beall and his men would go once they knew their plot had been foiled. Claiming neutrality, the British colony gave safe harbor to Rebels.

"Where you spent the night—I don't suppose you saw a stranger lurking about?" she asked.

The boys shook their heads. "Weren't no one but us around when we left," Delos said.

"One of them rascals got away?" Nick said.

"I'm afraid so," Hattie said.

Edith raised an eyebrow. "Cole?"

"Cole's in prison. But he had a man with him." Hattie turned to face Edith. "The man I was protecting. I shouldn't have. I see that now. He'd have killed me if I'd given him the chance."

"I'm glad you didn't," Edith said.

At the dock, another dinghy arrived from the *Michigan*. Ferry passengers jockeyed for position, eager to board.

"I'd best fetch my patient," Edith said, depositing the bundle of newborn in Hattie's arms. "She's desperate to leave."

"What am I do with the child?" Hattie called out as Edith trotted briskly toward the village.

"Keep her from fussing," the doctor called over her shoulder. "If it helps, her name is Edith."

Edith. How fitting, Hattie thought, looking down at the babe.

The child didn't feel entirely awkward in her arms. Having helped Anne through her delivery, Hattie had held Jo shortly after she was born. Still, as Hattie stood watching the ferry passengers board the dinghies, the child began to fuss.

Pressing the babe closer to her chest, Hattie bounced her lightly. For a moment, little Edith quieted, her gray eyes searching Hattie's face. Then she screwed up her face and let out a wail.

Hoping to calm her, Hattie paced the shore. Whenever this had happened with little Jo, she'd always been able to hand her back to Anne.

Over the sound of the crying child, Hattie heard a man clear his throat. She looked up to see Murray Wilson, his left arm in a sling and his right arm lugging a satchel.

"All that and you're a mother too?" he said.

"Not at all," she said. "I'm just the stand-in till the mother gets here."

"Try setting her at your shoulder and patting her back," Wilson suggested. "Might be she's got a bubble that wants to come up."

"Worth a try." Hattie shifted the child to her shoulder. Three pats to the back, and the baby let out a belch.

"I'm the eldest of ten," Murray said. "I've done my share of bouncing babies."

Relieved of her gas, the baby nestled against Hattie's shoulder. "And learned a great deal from it, it seems," Hattie said. "What are you doing ashore?"

"When the man that brought you over returned to the ship, he said he'd overheard someone say the *Parsons* had made for Malden. I begged Captain Carter to let me go after the pirates. It took some convincing, but with the surgeon saying I should recover in a few days, the captain could offer little objection. He's no more eager than I to see those men get off scot-free. "

"Be careful," Hattie said. "Beall seems determined to harm the Union in whatever way he can."

"I've got an advantage," Wilson said. "Born and raised in Canada. Once I catch up with him and his men, they'll be hard-pressed to give me the slip."

Canada. How often Hattie had dreamed of making her way there in hopes of meeting up with her brother. Now might be her chance. She could go with Wilson, help him track down the renegades.

"Where will you look?" she asked.

"Windsor. Niagara. Montreal. All hotbeds of Rebel activity."

"My brother, George, may be working in Canada, quite possibly in one of those towns. We've been separated since the start of the war, but I'm told he's doing the work of a spy."

"A spy, eh? Well, if he's half as good as you, he's worth his weight in gold."

She felt color rise in her face. "You're too kind."

Wilson shifted side to side. "You could come along with me. Wouldn't hurt to have another set of eyes and ears."

The offer was tempting. "I'd like to," she said. "But I've some loose ends to wrap up." She paused. "Still, if you happen to run into him, I'd be much obliged if you'd let him know you've spoken with me."

"Of course." Wilson took a stubby pencil from his pants pocket, then pulled a scrap of paper from his shirt pocket. Handing the pencil and paper to her, he said, "Write down the particulars. You never know."

She transferred the sleeping child to Wilson's good arm, then jotted her true name:

Hattie Logan

Underneath, she started to write Anne's address, where she'd been receiving her mail. But after learning what had happened with Franklin, she wasn't sure Anne would want anything more to do with her. She hesitated, then wrote:

c/o Lieutenant John Elliott, Army Police, Nashville, Tennessee

She handed Wilson the paper and pencil, then eased the child back onto her shoulder. Miraculously, the sleeping babe didn't wake.

Wilson glanced at what she'd written. "So it's Hattie, not Helen," he said. "I was confused on that point."

She smiled. "A necessary deception," she said. "All toward a good end."

Chapter Twenty-Five

SEPTEMBER 23. 1864

B efore leaving Sandusky, Hattie and Edith had to give their statements to the Union officials who were piecing together their case against Charles Cole.

Fortunately, the *Parsons'* crew, along with the crew from the *Island Queen*, had survived to tell their tales. With no signal from the *Michigan*—no Greek fire—Beall had ordered the *Parsons* to sail for Malden with the *Queen* in tow. At full steam, they'd proceeded at daybreak up the British channel.

A few miles above Malden, the pirates had offloaded plunder from the ferries—mirrors, chairs, trunks, bedding, even the piano from the *Parsons'* cabin—damaging both vessels in the process. They'd talked of burning the ferries but in the end, they'd abandoned them. A steamer had rescued the crews, towing both ferries to Detroit for repairs.

Safely ashore in Canada, Beall and his men had apparently dispersed. Cole claimed not to know where they'd gone. Murray Wilson would have his work cut out for him, Hattie thought.

Once she and Edith had completed their interviews, they'd taken a substitute ferry from Sandusky to Detroit. After a blissfully uneventful ride, they said their goodbyes. Edith was headed back to Washington. There she would make a full report to General Sharpe, citing what they'd accomplished in Indianapolis, Chicago, and Sandusky.

"I don't doubt he'll be pleased," Edith said in her usual understated way. "And while he's left off recruiting women to spy for him, I expect I could convince him to make an exception in your case. So, if you make your way back to Washington—"

"That's kind of you," Hattie interrupted. "But I need to take some time to decide what I'll do next. In the meantime, I've got some business to take care of."

Edith raised an eyebrow. "Business that involves your handsome lieutenant in Nashville?"

Hattie blushed. "He's not my lieutenant. But yes, I owe him a visit. He must be wondering what's become of me."

Promising to stay in touch, they boarded separate trains, Edith bound for Washington City and Hattie for Indianapolis to tell Anne what had happened. For the first time, Hattie dreaded seeing her friend. But she owed her an explanation.

The train seemed to chug along at a snail's pace, giving Hattie ample opportunity to stew in her thoughts. At each town the train stopped in, she watched passengers get on and off. Such strange times these were, with people trying as best they could to go on about their lives while the war raged on. In one town, the train's crew offloaded coffins from a boxcar while onlookers wiped tears from their eyes.

The train pulled into Indianapolis on Friday in the late afternoon. Leaving the station, Hattie found the air delightfully cool. Along the street, the town's stately maples and oaks wore the bright colors of fall. On the street corner, a paper boy was shouting out headlines. "Forrest raids Nashville rail line," he yelled. "Federals in pursuit." More evidence, Hattie thought, that as the war ground on, Rebel tactics were becoming increasingly desperate.

She hired a cabriolet, which dropped her in front of the Stones' white clapboard house. Without Franklin, would Anne keep it, Hattie wondered, or would she move back with her ever-gracious parents so she'd have help raising little Jo?

One thing at a time, Hattie told herself as she made her way up the flagstone walk. Aside from a few orange chrysanthemums, the flowers Anne had lovingly tended throughout the summer had all died back. Before long, they'd be covered in snow.

Satchel in hand, Hattie rapped on the door. She waited a moment, and when no one answered, she knocked again. This time, the door opened, revealing Anne. Looking harried, she wiped her forehead with the edge of her apron. Then a look of recognition brightened her face.

"Hattie!" Anne flung her arms around her, then ushered her inside.

Smelling of fresh-baked bread, the air inside was warm. "Jo's in the kitchen," Anne said. "Can't leave her for more than a minute. She's into everything these days."

Hattie set her satchel by the door and followed Anne to the kitchen. Propped in a highchair, Jo was banging a spoon on the chair's tray and babbling loudly. Seeing Hattie, she broke into a grin and dropped the spoon, which clattered to the floor. Then she lifted her chubby arms, wanting Hattie to pick her up.

"Look how she's grown in just a few weeks." Hattie went to the child, and after some wrestling with the tray, extracted her from the chair. "Heavy, too," she said, hoisting Jo to her hip. "Keep it up, and we'll have to tote you around in a wheelbarrow."

Anne laughed. "She'll be walking soon. Took two steps yesterday." Her expression sobered. "I wish Franklin had been here to see."

A sinking feeling spread across Hattie's midsection. There was no sense putting off the inevitable. She pulled a chair out from the table and sat, bouncing Jo on her knee. "Where is he now?" she asked.

"Ohio." Grabbing a hot pad from the table, Anne turned to the oven. "On business."

Hattie drew a deep breath. "I just came from Ohio."

Turning, Anne gave her a sharp look. "I thought you were in Nashville."

"Bah, bah, bah," Jo cooed, her wide blue eyes studying Hattie's face.

"I was," Hattie said. "But you remember Dr. Greenfield?"

Bending, Anne opened the oven door. A blast of hot air filled the room as she extracted two golden loaves of bread and set them on cooling racks. "Of course I remember her. If not for her sound advice, Henry would have lost his arm." Wounded at Antietam, Anne's brother Henry had ended up in a Washington hospital, which was where Hattie and Anne had first met Edith Greenfield.

"She's also a spy," Hattie said.

"You never told me that," Anne said, a hint of accusation in her voice. "You only said she'd been running a hospital in Nashville."

"I didn't want to compromise her work," Hattie said. "Or put you in the awkward position of knowing, in case someone asked."

"I should think you'd know by now you can trust me."

There was no getting past the edge in Anne's voice. But there was also nothing to do but have out with it. "I trust you," Hattie said. "It's just that at times I've had to make some..." She searched for the right words. "...Uncomfortable decisions."

Her gaze fixed on Hattie, Anne set down her hot pads, then pulled out the chair across the table and sat down. "So what does Dr. Greenfield have to do with you being in Ohio?"

"She came from Washington charged with stopping the Sons of Liberty from carrying out their plans to establish a Northwest Confederacy," Hattie said. "A man who had infiltrated the group was exposed, and Federal officials thought a woman might have more luck. But Edith was concerned that her unusual manner of dress would limit what she could do openly, and so she recruited me to investigate the rumors coming out of Indianapolis."

"Because you have friends here. How convenient that you were able to stay in my home and gather information about my husband."

Hattie shifted uncomfortably in her chair. "If I hadn't intervened on Franklin's behalf, he'd be in jail now." Which might have been for the best, as it turned out.

Abruptly, Jo quit her babbling. She grabbed a butter knife and began to clang it against the table.

Anne's expression softened. "I appreciate that."

Hattie took another deep breath. "From here, I went to Chicago, where I met up with Edith. The Sons of Liberty had plans to incite riots at the convention there. Their members were bringing wagons filled with weapons. But after the Indianapolis raid, they were skittish. After the police ignored our pleas, I spread rumors among the conspirators that their plot had been exposed."

Anne lifted an eyebrow. "From what I read in the papers, the convention went off without a hitch."

"It did," Hattie said. "By the last day, the drivers and their wagons were nowhere in sight. But then I came upon Franklin."

"He was a delegate," Anne said. "Nothing more. After the print shop raid, he promised he'd sever ties with the Sons of Liberty."

"He didn't," Hattie said. "I saw him passing a good deal of cash to a stranger."

"I'm sure there was a logical explanation."

"Damaging is how I'd describe it," Hattie said. "I overheard them talking about a plot set to unfold in Ohio, based out of a town called Sandusky. Edith and I went there to stop it. Posing as an invalid, with Edith as my doctor, I befriended the stranger Franklin gave the money to, Charles Cole. He and another man, a renegade officer in the Rebel navy, attempted a scheme to free over two thousand men from an island prison and go on a rampage around the Great Lakes. With help from Edith and a gunner on the Union ship that guards the prison, I managed to intervene."

Anne was silent a moment, taking this in. "You stopped the Rebels from taking control of Lake Erie."

"And possibly going from there down the Eastern Seaboard, freeing Rebel prisoners all along the way."

Anne looked thoughtful. "Grant might have been forced to divert troops from the Shenandoah to fight them. What little ground he's gained there could've been lost." She shook her head. "But I can't believe Franklin was involved. The money you saw him passing in Chicago could have been for anything."

"But where would Franklin have gotten that kind of money?" Hattie said. "Unless it was from a Rebel commissioner stationed in Canada and known to be funneling Confederate money to the Sons of Liberty to fund acts of sabotage."

Doubt clouded Anne's eyes. But then she straightened. "Circumstantial," she said, the lawyer's daughter through and through. "A court would never convict him on such flimsy evidence."

In Hattie's lap, Jo squirmed. "Ma-ma-ma," she said, still banging away at the table.

There was no easy way to say it except in a rush of words. "Franklin was on the gunship the night the Rebels seized the ferries," she said. "Charles Cole drugged the crew, incapacitating all but the captain and the gunner I mentioned."

Anne's face tensed. "Did any harm come to them?"

"No one was mortally wounded," Hattie said. "But it wasn't for lack of trying. When I disrupted their plans, Franklin came after me with a dagger."

Anne lowered her head to her hands, pressing her fingers to her temples. "There must have been some misunderstanding. Franklin would never harm you."

"There was no misunderstanding. Franklin stabbed the gunner, and he'd have stabbed me, too, if I hadn't gotten hold of a revolver."

Anne looked up, her face pale. "You...you shot him?"

Hattie shook her head. "When he saw he was cornered, he jumped from the ship into Lake Erie."

Anne slumped in her chair. "What became of him?"

"I wish I knew. The other conspirators escaped to Canada, all except Cole, who's imprisoned on Johnson's Island, awaiting trial."

Perhaps sensing her mother's dismay, Jo quit her babbling and banging. She reached across the table, flexing her tiny hands. A tear streaking her cheek, Anne took her from Hattie. As if trying to comfort her, Jo nestled against Anne's breast.

"I'm sorry, Anne," Hattie said. "I hope you know I'd never intentionally do anything to hurt you and Jo if there was any way around it. But in the end, I had to do what I had to do."

Anne looked down at Jo, absently stroking the child's fine, wispy hair. The house felt as silent as a tomb, the only sounds being the crackling of the fire that was dying in the cookstove and the ticking of the clock in the parlor, adjacent to the kitchen.

Her heart heavy, Hattie pushed back her chair. She knew what she'd done was right, but that didn't make it easy. "I understand if you don't want me here," she said. "I'm sure I can get a room at the Ladies' Home."

"No." Anne looked up at her. "Stay. Please. I'd rather not be alone right now. I just need some...some time."

~ ~ ~

Drained but relieved of a substantial burden, Hattie retired early to the narrow bed in the back bedroom. With the tension between her and Anne, she would have been more comfortable elsewhere, but after some tossing and turning, she finally fell asleep.

Over hotcakes the next morning, Anne thanked her for staying. "You must think me a feeble person," she said. "But it eased my mind knowing you were here."

"I'd never think you feeble," Hattie said.

Her expression wistful, Anne glanced toward the kitchen window, raised to let out heat from the cookstove. Then she looked back at Hattie, her eyes brimming with tears. "It's just..." She seemed to choke on the words. "It's just that I loved him so much. So smart and handsome. I couldn't believe that of all the women he could've had, he'd chosen me. I suppose that made me blind to his true nature." She paused. "Foolish, I know."

"Understandable," Hattie said. "And you soon had this tyke to consider too." Reaching over to the highchair, she brushed her hand over Jo's silky hair. Her face sticky with syrup, Jo grinned, showing two stubby teeth on her bottom gum.

"I don't suppose she'll remember him," Anne said.

"If he...survived...he may come home still," Hattie said.

Anne shook her head. "Even if he does, I don't see how we could mend things between us. Not after all the secrets he kept. Not after him trying to harm you."

Hattie set her hand over Anne's. "Either way, I'm glad you've seen fit to forgive me."

"There's nothing to forgive." Anne offered a weak smile. "What I asked of you was wrong. I'm glad you paid attention to what Franklin and those men were up to. I'd hate to think what could've happened if you'd listened to me."

When breakfast was over and they'd washed and put away the dishes, Anne asked Hattie to go with her to break the news about Franklin to her parents. Though she knew the situation would be awkward, Hattie was only too happy to do what she could to ease things for Anne.

In the morning light streaming into the sunroom of the Duncans' elegant home, Hattie repeated the story of how she'd come to be the last among them to see their son-in-law alive. Anne's parents were understandably incredulous, interrupting her at several junctures and asking her to repeat what she'd said.

When Hattie reached the end of her tale, there was a long silence. Mr. Duncan cleared his throat. "We didn't want to question your judgment, Anne." He shook his head. "But honestly, it's hard to feel bad about him being gone. Especially after all Hattie has told us."

Mrs. Duncan reached for her daughter's hand. "He wasn't good enough for you, dear."

"But he's Jo's father," Anne said. "I hate to think of her—"

Her father waved his hand through the air, cutting her off. "There's more than enough love in this house for Jo and you both."

"You'll move back with us," Mrs. Duncan said firmly. "Your bedroom's just as you left it. And with Henry in Washington, we'll have his room made into a nursery."

"And I'll file papers right away with the court," Anne's father said. "Your husband has abandoned you, and you mustn't be responsible for any debts he's incurred."

"Or anything else he's done," her mother said.

Anne looked from one to the other. "That's kind of you both. But I need to take some time to decide what's best for Jo and me.

Feeling as if she'd intruded on an intimate moment, Hattie glanced over at Jo, who was intent on cornering the Duncans' cat.

"Don't look now." Hattie pointed at the child. "But someone appears to be walking."

All heads turned toward Jo, who was toddling unsteadily, her hand stretched toward the cat's tail, twitching back and forth from beneath the chaise.

Mrs. Duncan gasped. "And only ten months old."

Her husband shook his head. "A determined little sprite."

And just like that, the tension in the room was diffused. Fitting, thought Hattie, that a child taking one step at a time could have such effect.

~ ~ ~

Not wanting to overstay her welcome, Hattie packed her satchel that night. When she told Anne she intended to leave on a morning train, her friend smiled knowingly.

"Eager to see a certain someone?" she said.

In spite of herself, Hattie blushed. Now that her life had settled back to something resembling normal, her thoughts drifted to John Elliott more often than she cared to admit. "I suppose I do miss him," she said. "A bit, anyhow."

"Then you should tell him so," Anne said.

"I don't know," Hattie said. "He's so...guarded."

"And you're not?"

"Perhaps a little," she said.

"Thom would understand, you know. He'd want you to be happy."

Hattie felt a rush of guilt at the secret she was still keeping from Anne. But until she knew for certain it was true, it didn't feel right to share it.

~ ~ ~

Eager as she was to see John Elliott, Hattie went first to St. Louis. It seemed as if ages had passed since she'd last been there, but in fact it had only been last spring, and she found the city little changed.

From the train station, she made her way to the provost marshal's office. When she explained why she'd come, a clerk directed her to Colonel Sanderson. Rising from his desk to greet her, he looked more haggard than she remembered. His blue eyes, once so intense, seemed to have paled, and his shoulders slumped. So many ways the war took its toll, she thought.

"I don't know if you remember me," she said. "Hattie Thomas. I brought—"

"Mollie Pitman," he said, completing her sentence. "You did us a great service." He gestured toward a chair. "Please. Have a seat."

She clasped her hands at her waist. "Thank you, but I can't stay. I was only hoping you could direct me to Mollie."

"You're lucky you came when you did. In the morning, Miss Pitman returns to the Alton Prison."

"Has she betrayed your trust?"

Sanderson shook his head. "On the contrary. She has done such a fine job of exposing Rebel spies and smugglers here that we fear for her safety. At Alton, she'll have more protection."

He called for his clerk to escort Hattie to the St. Charles Street Women's Prison. She assured him she could find her way, but the colonel insisted the streets weren't entirely safe for a lady, even on a well-lit afternoon, and so Hattie had relented.

Dropping her at the prison door, the clerk asked if he should wait with his cart. She thanked him but said she'd be fine getting to the hotel on her own. In case he was so inclined, she didn't want him reporting back to Colonel Sanderson how long she'd stayed.

Far smaller than the men's prison across the street, the women's prison had been converted from a Union-confiscated townhouse. Hattie rapped on the door and, when the matron answered, explained her purpose. Reluctant at first to admit Hattie, she relented when Hattie pointed to the departing clerk's cart, explaining that Colonel Sanderson had authorized her visit.

Hattie followed the matron down a long hallway with doors on either side. Though austere, with barred windows and hastily erected walls to partition the rooms, the facility looked decidedly more comfortable than the Richmond prisons where Hattie had been confined. Likely Mollie wasn't doing battle with rats as she had.

At the last door on the right, the matron took a large ring of keys from her apron pocket and unlocked the door. "Visitor," she announced.

The room was small and spare, with two narrow cots and a washstand. Pen in hand, Mollie looked up from where she sat, at a table that appeared to have been slabbed together from scrap lumber.

Seeing Hattie, she tipped her chin, offering a crooked smile. "Look who came to visit," she said. "I hope you aren't expecting tea and crumpets."

Hattie shook her head. "I only came for a word with you."

As if to assert her authority, the matron rattled her keys. "I'll be right outside in the hall," she said. "Don't dally."

She left the room, closing the door firmly behind her. Hearing the key turn in the lock, Hattie felt a sort of primal fear spread from her belly to her fingertips. *Only a few moments,* she told herself. *Then you're free to leave.*

Suspecting the matron would be listening through the door, Hattie stepped close to where Mollie sat.

"Have a seat." Gazing expectantly at Hattie, Mollie gestured at a straight-backed chair scooted close to the table.

Hattie remained standing. "I'll only be a minute." Her eyes flitted to the paper on which Mollie had written in neat, slanted script.

"I'm penning an account of my interactions with the woman who shared this room," Mollie said. "A Rebel spy, actually. Claimed she was paid seventy-five dollars a month for her service, though I'm disinclined to believe that detail. It's twice what Uncle Bedford paid me."

"It does seem generous," Hattie said.

Mollie shrugged. "Then again, maybe they're desperate for information."

"And where is she now?" Hattie asked. "Your roommate, I mean."

"Broke free from here last night. She didn't shoot her way out as she'd planned though. Last week, I got hold of her pistol and handed it over to the matron. Since then, her daddy's been trying to discredit me. Says he's got forty people lined up to sully my reputation." Mollie sighed. "Whatever reputation I've got left, that is. Anyhow, Colonel Sanderson asked me to put what I know in writing."

"He told me he's transferring you to Alton," Hattie said. "Has the father threatened you?"

Mollie nodded. "Him and others. Word's beginning to circulate that I'm no longer guarding their secrets."

"I suppose you know I've doubted your loyalties," Hattie said. "I was certain you were misleading Colonel Sanderson while passing Union secrets to the Rebels. Then I went to Lake Erie."

"Met John Beall, did you?"

Even knowing Mollie as she did, her directness could still startle Hattie. "Yes. The navy man you warned about. He and a band of renegades took control of a ferry. They intended to use it to seize a gunship and free thousands of Confederate prisons."

Mollie gave a low whistle. "I knew there was a plot, but I didn't realize the scope of it. I hope he was stopped."

"He was."

She tipped her chin. "You had some part in it?"

"Yes."

From the hallway, the matron pounded on the door. "Time's up."

"You'd best get going," Mollie said. "She gets testy, there's no telling what she'll say about me when the Alton guards come."

"If you'd like, I can put in a good word for you."

Mollie's eyes widened. "You'd vouch for me?"

"If you'll allow me the use of your pen and a clean sheet of paper."

Mollie set the pen and paper before her. Bending over the table, Hattie wrote:

To Whom It May Concern,

I am well-acquainted with Miss Mollie Pitman. Though at one time I might have testified against her, I now recognize the mistake that would have been. I believe her trustworthy, with great potential to aid the Union cause.

She signed her name, then returned the paper to Mollie.

Reading it, Mollie offered the truest smile Hattie had ever seen from her. It looked as though she was blinking back tears. "Thank you," she said. "You have no idea what this means to me."

"No more than it means to me," Hattie said.

Chapter Twenty-Six

SEPTEMBER 24, 1864

The town of Ellingsburg, Illinois, was only a short jog off the main rail line that ran between St. Louis and Nashville. Like the Indiana town where Hattie had grown up, it was a tidy little community surrounded by cornfields on lands cleared by long-ago pioneers.

Leaving her satchel with the stationmaster, Hattie set out on foot under a blue sky dotted with the sort of puffy white clouds that could set a child's imagination spinning. New in town, the stationmaster hadn't been much help with directions, affirming only that the community was small enough that she could easily walk its length and breadth and still get back in time to make the late train to Carbondale and then on to Nashville.

Heading east, she passed a mercantile and a white clapboard church, then came upon an elderly woman cutting back a hedge of sprawling rosebushes. The woman seemed happy to pause what looked like tedious work to point Hattie toward the Welton house, another two blocks east and three south.

"On the edge of town," the old woman said. "Blue shutters, white picket fence. The missus keeps it real nice." She shook her head. "Pity, what happened to Mr. Welton."

A lump rose in Hattie's throat. "It is," she said. "Thank you."

As she set out again in the direction the woman had indicated, Hattie's stride slowed. *The missus.* There was no need to go farther. She could go back to the station, wait there for her train.

But Hattie kept going, the autumn breeze on her face, the clouds racing across the sky, covering and uncovering the sun. One block, two blocks. Turn. One block, two blocks, three.

As the old woman had said, the house was easy to spot with its bright blue shutters and white picket fence. Along the far side of the fence was a row of orange chrysanthemums like the ones Anne kept in her yard.

Nearing the house, Hattie slowed her pace. A dark-haired woman, tall and slender, was in the backyard, hanging clothes on a line. Beside her, a little girl, perhaps four years old, reached into a cloth bag and handed two clothespins to the dark-haired woman.

At the washtub on the back porch, a boy who looked to be a year or two older than the girl was wringing out a shirt. Catching Hattie's eye, he smiled and waved.

Her heart skipped a beat. He was the spitting image of Thom.

The woman glanced over her shoulder, her face pretty but careworn. Holding out another pair of clothespins, the girl stared unabashedly at Hattie.

Tentatively, Hattie lifted her hand, returning the boy's wave.

"A good day to you," he called out. In this, too, the boy was like Thom, friendly and polite.

Hattie nodded, acknowledging his greeting. She wanted to linger, to take in the scene, to memorize its every detail. But she didn't want to draw undue attention, so she quickened her pace.

Thom could have had a sister, she thought as she circled around to the next street, then started back the way she'd come. *A niece and a nephew, who looks just like him.*

But she knew better. The secret she'd buried, the one she hadn't wanted to believe—it was true. Thom had called Hattie his wife, but he'd had another.

At her back, the wind seemed to push her along. Overcome by a jumble of emotions, Hattie focused on the ground, solid beneath her feet.

When she looked up, she saw that she was coming up again on the old woman, who was still wrestling with the tangled rosebushes.

"That was a quick visit," the woman said.

"They were busy," Hattie said.

The woman shook her head. "After all the trouble she went to, getting him back, I don't doubt she's got work a-plenty to catch up on."

Hattie shook her head, confused. "Getting him back?"

"Mr. Welton," the woman said. "His body, I mean. Just last week, the missus got him a proper burial here. Pert near the whole town turned out, and not a dry eye all around. Heard she's been going there every day since, freshening up the flowers."

"Oh," Hattie said. "I didn't realize." She swallowed back the lump forming in her throat. "After all he did, it's good he found his way home."

"It surely is," the woman said, and she went back to her clipping.

Hattie proceeded down the path. At the mercantile, she went in and asked for directions to the cemetery. Four blocks north and then out a pace, the clerk said. Nice grove of sycamores. No mistaking it.

~ ~ ~

Out a pace was a good deal farther than Hattie expected. Though her feet grew tired, the walk did her good, giving her time to clear her head.

The gravesite was easy to find, the cemetery being small and it being the only one where the earth was freshly turned. At the head of the mound was a simple wooden marker. *Thomas Welton, 1838 – 1862.* To one side sat a jelly jar holding three orange chrysanthemums.

Standing before Thom's grave, Hattie pictured the man she'd loved—his handsome features, his dark eyes, his broad shoulders, his kind smile, his jovial laugh. She thought of how he'd held her, how he'd kissed her, and the future they'd imagined together.

Tears streamed down her face, her grief welling up inside along with anger and confusion.

With the back of her hand, she wiped her cheeks dry. "I'm glad you're home," she said, gazing at the wooden marker. "Ellingsburg is just like you told me. Quaint. Quiet."

Breathing in, her breath caught. Then she went on. "I went by your house. Your...your wife and children are well." She shook her head. "Miss Warne told me, Thom. I didn't want to believe it."

She paused, looking up into the branches of a nearby sycamore tree, where an oriole sang. "I don't know what to think. It's a lot to take in." She drew a deep, uncluttered breath. "I only know that what I felt for you was real."

Lowering her head, she wiped a stray tear from her eye. Then she crouched next to the jar of flowers, reached in her pocket, and took out the gold watch Thom had given her. After having been so long put away, it needed winding. She gave the knob a few twists, and the familiar sound of its ticking resumed.

She set it on the ground, then wrapped the chain around the jar. "Rest in peace, Thom Welton," she whispered.

Then she stood. Without looking back, she left the cemetery, headed for town.

~ ~ ~

As the train's locomotive chugged into Nashville, Hattie reveled in the calm of her train car, the handful of passengers each seemingly wrapped in their own thoughts.

She'd wired ahead from St. Louis to let John Elliott know her plans. A courtesy, she'd told herself, so as not to surprise him as she had in the past. Now she was thinking this might have been a mistake. His position at the Army Police kept him busy, too busy to concern himself with a single spy who'd gone off on a mission that was beyond the scope of his office.

Maybe he wasn't even in town. The last time they'd spoken—more than six weeks ago, when he'd dropped her at the hospital where Edith was staying—he'd mentioned that he might soon be called upon for tasks outside of Nashville.

Even if he was in the city, he might be seeing someone. Walking beside him along Nashville's streets, she'd seen how women's heads turned. Even those who detested the Union army uniform seemed unable to stop themselves from admiring the tall, broad-shouldered lieutenant with the handsome face and gentle manner.

Hattie shook her head. She'd thought of John Elliott far too often these past few days. They had a professional relationship, nothing that warranted the fluttering in her chest that she couldn't seem to quell. Nothing that warranted going straight to Elliott's office. She'd secure a hotel room, get a good night's rest, and see him in the morning—if he was in.

The wheels screeched as the train slowed, entering the railroad yard where locomotives sat waiting to carry supplies to Union troops far afield. Then, with a jerk, the train car shuddered to a stop.

Hattie stood and, retrieving her satchel, joined the line of passengers waiting to exit the car—white-haired ladies in stiff hoops, smartly uniformed soldiers, a harried mother with a gaggle of children who'd slept most of the ride but were now complaining of hunger.

She gripped the satchel's handle with both hands as she approached the exit, the last of the passengers to get off. The conductor took her bag from her and swung it to the ground. Mindful of the steps, Hattie held onto the rail, watching her feet as she descended the steps.

Reaching the ground, she looked up. There was John Elliott, not three feet away. He strode toward her, beaming.

"Hattie," he said. "I thought you'd never get here."

Confused, she started to point out that the train was on time. But before she could get a word out, he took her into his arms. Wrapping her in an embrace, he kissed her lips, a display of affection that would have been scandalous had the war not made emotional reunions an everyday occurrence.

Pressed to his chest, she reveled in the warmth of his embrace. Pulling away at last, he looked her up and down. "I've waited far too long for that," he said.

"Far too long," she agreed.

He took up her satchel. With a smile she couldn't suppress, she linked arms with him. "You must tell me everything," he said.

"I shall," she said as they started away from the train. "But it might take a while."

"Fair enough," he said.

She gazed up at him, and he met her eyes, and she felt the longing that passed between them, a longing that might in fact be love.

THE END

Thank you for reading *Gray Waters*,
Book Three in the Secrets of the Blue and Gray series.
If you enjoyed this book,
please take a moment to share your thoughts with a review.
MORE BOOKS IN THE SERIES
Prequel *Lady in Disguise (exclusive to newsletter subscribers)*
Book One *The Courier's Wife*
Book Two *Enemy Lines*
Book Three *Gray Waters*
Book Four *A Fond Hope*
Be the first to know about new books and giveaways—
sign up for Vanessa Lind's newsletter and get a free copy
of *Lady in Disguise*, the prequel to *The Courier's Wife*

Author's Note

This is a work of fiction, but real women who spied during the Civil War inspired the story. Hattie Logan (Thomas) is based on Hattie Lawton (Lewis), a Pinkerton operative who posed as the wife of courier Timothy Webster, who inspired the character Thom Welton.

Pretending to be married, Lawton and Webster spied for the Union, posing as Confederate sympathizers in Baltimore and Richmond. When Webster fell ill with rheumatoid arthritis and was confined to bed in their Richmond hotel, Lawton took care of him. There they were arrested and imprisoned. When Webster was sentenced to death, Lawton did all she could to save him, including an appeal to the wife of Confederate president Jefferson Davis. But the Confederates wanted an example made of him, and he was killed.

The scant accounts of Hattie Lawton's life end with her release in a prisoner exchange. Timothy Webster did have a wife and children in Illinois though whether Hattie ever knew this is uncertain. After the war, his body was exhumed from Richmond and reburied in a family plot in Illinois.

The inspiration for Edith Greenfield comes from Mary Walker, a Union doctor who was also a spy. Convinced that the fashions of the era constrained women, she dressed in bloomers, raising eyebrows everywhere she went. After the war, she received a Medal of Honor for her service.

Pauline Carlton's character is inspired by actress Pauline Cushman, who spied for the Army of the Cumberland. In Cushman's biography, *Spy of the Cumberland*, her adventures are likely exaggerated, but Rebels did in fact capture and threaten to hang her. She became a popular figure in the North, touring with P.T. Barnum.

Mollie Pitman, better known as MaryAnn Pickett, was a spy for the Confederates who switched sides shortly before the Fort Pillow massacre. Claiming to be a niece of General Bedford Forrest, she supplied Colonel Sanderson with facts about the Sons of Liberty, although she refused to name names. I have altered a few minor details of her story to fit the narrative. Belle Edmondson, who makes a cameo appearance in this book, was also a Confederate spy.

In Nashville, Belle Monte (now called Belmont) is an expansive property once owned by Adelicia Acklen. In a rare achievement for anyone, much less a woman, she managed to sell close to a million dollars in cotton from her Louisiana plantations at a time when both sides prohibited such sales.

Financed in part by the Confederate government, the Sons of Liberty (also known as the Order of American Knights and, earlier, as the Knights of the Golden Circle) did attempt various plots to establish a Northwest Confederacy, including attacks planned for the 1864 Democratic Convention in Chicago and a nearly successful raid on the Johnson's Island prison. In Indiana, Harrison Dodd and William Bowles were among the group's leaders, and they did conduct a demonstration there using Greek fire.

There are all sorts of versions of how the Johnson's Island plot was foiled. In one, a high school girl overhears the conspirators talking and alerts Union officials. In another, a prisoner drops a note containing details of the plan. In yet another, a conspirator has a change of heart and informs the provost marshal in Detroit. In his memoir, the *Michigan*'s gunner Wilson Murray (the basis for my character Murray Wilson) also claims credit for thwarting the attempt.

For the integrity of my narrative, I have slightly altered the dates of certain real-life events, including Pauline's stint with Barnum, the Confederate attack on Bolivar, and Governor Morton's occupancy of the Indianapolis mansion (he moved his family out in 1863 due to sickness).

Where fitting, I've also paraphrased from firsthand accounts, including a letter from black Union soldier Morgan Carter, MaryAnn Pickett's testimony to Colonel Sanderson, Dr. Mary Walker's letter to her mother from prison, and portions of the Order of the American Knights/Sons of Liberty ritual.

Part of my delight in telling this story is to show the profound impact women had on the war and how it was waged. For more adventures of women spies in the Civil War, check out all the books in my series SECRETS OF THE BLUE AND GRAY. A sneak peek at Book Four follows here.

Excerpt from A Fond Hope

Book Four of the SECRETS OF THE BLUE AND GRAY series
featuring women spies in the American Civil War

by Vanessa Lind

S trolling under a starry sky with Lieutenant John Elliott at her
side, Union spy Hattie Logan could almost forget the country
was at war. For October, the air felt close to balmy, and the easy
rhythm of their steps on the boardwalk added to the comfort of
having enjoyed a fine meal—fine for wartime, at any rate—with
the man Hattie believed she was coming to love.

"When do you think you'll recover your taste for port?" John
asked. Illuminated by the gaslights along the street, his gentle smile
added to her contentment.

"Maybe when the war ends," Hattie said. After a harrowing escape from a Rebel who'd tried to take over a Union gunship by serving the crew drugged alcohol, she'd lost her taste for wine.

John pressed his hand over hers. "So much will be different then," he said.

"So much will be better."

"Provided the outcome is as we hope."

"But General Sherman has taken Atlanta, and we've got control of the Shenandoah."

"For the moment."

She smiled up at him. "You do know how to ruin a lady's good mood, Lieutenant Elliott."

"Sorry. It's just that when everything seems to be going well, there's always a chance that disaster lies right around the corner."

"That's quite enough talk of disaster," she said. "I for one am thinking of the future."

"And what, pray tell, will that entail?"

You, she almost said, but she checked the impulse. She'd known John Elliott for nearly two years. He'd supervised her work as a spy in Nashville, and together they'd survived an attack by the Rebel guerilla who'd killed John's wife. But until recently, she'd kept him at arm's length as she struggled with her feelings for her first love, a fellow spy who'd been captured and executed.

Now she felt as close as she might ever come to making peace with her memories, and she was glad to be here in Nashville, strolling beside the handsome and kind lieutenant. But John Elliott was a prudent man, steady in ways she was not, and he had his own memories to contend with. They would take things one step at a time.

"My future?" she said. "I suppose what I want most is a fresh start. A new beginning."

"No more spying? Somehow I can't imagine you not snooping around in things."

She swatted his arm. "You of all people should know it's not snooping. And I like to think my work will hasten our victory, even if only in some small way."

"I wouldn't call thwarting a Rebel plot to take over Lake Erie a small accomplishment."

"I had help, you know." But even as she said this, Hattie couldn't suppress the swell of pride she felt at having achieved something meaningful for the Union cause. Not that she intended to crow about it as some did. That would mean giving up spying, and she intended to do her part to make sure the war came to an end sooner rather than later.

"Having help diminishes nothing of what you did. Working with others is the nature of our enterprise. Which is why I'm glad you're staying on in Nashville to help with our Army Police work."

"Staying on for a while," she said. "If I'm needed elsewhere—"

"You are a restless one," he interjected.

"Not always. At the moment, I'm feeling quite content. Only..." Her voice trailed off.

"Only passing along rumors gleaned from Nashville's Rebel sympathizers isn't the sort of spying you signed up for," he said.

"I know it's important," she said. "Or at least it can be, every now and then, when something a woman whispers about at the market or in a shop or hotel lobby turns out to have merit. It's just that I'm...impatient."

"You want more."

She squeezed his arm. "No more than what I've got right now."

Rounding the corner, they fell silent. Ahead, the street was ablaze with light. Hundreds of men—and some women and children too—came marching past them, a sea of black faces. Each marcher wore an oil-cloth cape, protection from the open flames of the torches they carried.

Hattie slowed her steps, taking in the spectacle. Beside her, John slowed, too. Side by side, they stood among a group of spectators, listening as a song erupted from the marchers.

We'll join in the struggle with hearts firm and true
We'll stand by our chief and the red, white, and blue

"They be turning out in support of President Lincoln in the election next month," Hattie said, recognizing the words to one of Lincoln's campaign songs.

"That, plus I'm told Negro leaders here have been organizing to petition Governor Johnson to proclaim their emancipation here in Tennessee just as President Lincoln did for Negroes in the Rebel states." John pointed into the night. "See how they're turning toward the Capitol?"

Indeed, the marchers toward the front of the parade were veering off toward Capitol Hill, the highest point in the city. "I hope the governor grants their request," Hattie said. "Slavery is an abomination no matter where it's practiced. And we Northerners owe a debt to the Negro soldiers who've joined the Union cause."

A lump formed in her throat as she thought of Samuel, the black soldier who'd given his life to save hers during the Rebel attack on Fort Pillow last spring. After all he'd done, she'd never even learned his last name. He'd had a wife and baby girl, he'd told Hattie. She felt horrible knowing they'd never see him again.

The end of the parade neared, the marchers singing the final lines of the song:

We never will falter, our watchword will be

The Union, the hope of the brave and the free

As the last word reverberated, a dark object flew through the air in front of Hattie. One of the marchers ducked, narrowly missing being hit by it, but his steps never faltered.

Another missile flew. Hattie whirled around to see one of the bystanders, a bearded man wearing dungarees and a straw hat, with a large rock clutched in his raised hand.

She stepped toward him. "Drop that right now."

Visit vanessalind.com to order *A Fond Hope*, Book Four

in the historical fiction series Secrets of the Blue and Gray.

Want to be the first to know about Vanessa Lind's latest books and receive a free copy of *Lady in Disguise*, which tells how Hattie became a spy?

Sign up for her Passion for the Past newsletter.

Made in the USA
Monee, IL
01 February 2024

52676313R00184